FRANKLIN HORTON

ALSO BY FRANKLIN HORTON

The Borrowed World Series

The Borrowed World

Ashes of the Unspeakable

Legion of Despair

No Time For Mourning

Valley of Vengeance

Switched On

The Ungovernable

Blood And Banjos

The Locker Nine Series

Locker Nine

Grace Under Fire

Compound Fracture

Blood Bought

The Mad Mick Series

The Mad Mick

Masters of Mayhem

Brutal Business

Northern Sun

Punching Tickets

Ultraviolent

ALSO BY FRANKLIN HORTON

The Ty Stone Series

Hard Trauma

Child With No Name

The Way of Dan Series

Burning Down Boise

The Path Of Water

Stand-Alone Novels

Random Acts

RESURGENT

PROLOGUE

It had been a little more than a year since coordinated terror attacks knocked much of the United States off the rails. Without power, fuel, and communications, more than half of the people in the country had died in the interim. Starvation, disease, and violence thinned the herd with a sometimes arbitrary indifference. The healthy died alongside the sick. The prepared died alongside the unprepared. Those with weapons died just as frequently as those who defended themselves with golf clubs.

Those who survived could see that there was no quick fix to their predicament. Restoring power would not instantly restore civility. Restoring fuel would not restore law and order. Simply having a working cell phone and an internet connection would not give Americans the life they once had. That life was perhaps gone forever, the Golden Age of a nation that had seen its best days come and gone.

Jim Powell faced a different struggle than many of his countrymen. He was among those who had spent their lives preparing for such a disaster. He felt comfortable that he had the food, knowledge, and gear to get his family through tough times. Those tangible items, food and gear, were the easy part, though.

What he hadn't been prepared for was the emotional toll taken by the experience. He'd killed men and lost friends. Survival came at a price, and that price was often very traumatic. It gouged at the soul and left deep scars. The things he'd seen and done could never be forgotten and would always be part of him.

With helping his friends and neighbors survive came a responsibility Jim hadn't counted on. They began to look to him for answers. Without any discussion or planning, they bonded into some sort of tribe or clan. When their community faced threats, it often fell to Jim to come up with a plan to address them. It was not a role he was entirely comfortable with.

Although his friends hadn't intentionally dumped this responsibility on him, someone had to do something and no one else seemed ready to step up. Jim understood all too well why no one wanted to take that responsibility. Some of the decisions that had to be made would haunt people forever. There was no avoiding that. To save *his* people often meant condemning others to death. It was a simple equation with profound repercussions on the psychic, emotional, and moral levels.

Despite knowing there was no escaping this predicament—that such moral quandaries were an inevitable aspect of being a survivor —Jim's internal struggle never let up. It felt like every time he made a bold move toward keeping his people safe, there was an equally powerful backlash that made him regret his actions.

It was easy to make a decision for one person, though much harder to decide things for a family. Jim had learned that early in his marriage. But to make a decision that impacted an entire community and multiple families was more responsibility than Jim wanted. He constantly complained to his wife about the way his friends looked to him for answers, but who else had those answers? Jim was all they had and his discomfort with that never subsided.

The final straw came after Jim arrived at a radical plan to flood a local power plant in protest of the government's plan to tie power restoration to citizens surrendering their weapons. It angered him that local power wouldn't be available to his community unless residents surrendered their rights. While his mission to destroy the power plant was successful, it turned half the community against him and led to someone putting a price on his head. Flyers were dropped from the air offering a bounty for the capture of local insurgent Jim Powell.

It was a perfect example of the kind of backlash that came after Jim took decisive action. The threat his family and friends faced from amateur bounty hunters eventually led to him faking his death and going into hiding. The risk to his family was too high. For a while, he even thought they might be better off without him.

Under the impression that his absence would make his family safer, Jim took a trip with his friend Lloyd to help clear his head. They went into the mountains on horseback and spent a few weeks camping, telling stories, and exploring. Jim felt extremely guilty about leaving his family. For him, there was no peace at home and no peace away from home. With the realization that he could not escape his problems by exiling himself from his community, he chose to return to them and find a new approach. His old friend Lloyd did not return to the valley, however, choosing instead to stay at a music camp they visited on their journey.

Shortly after returning to the valley, Jim received a visit from a man who went by the name of the Mad Mick. While on his trip with Lloyd, Jim had heard of this man, who was practically a legend in the surrounding communities. As a government contractor, he'd been hired to kill Jim Powell for his role in destroying the power plant.

However, the Mad Mick chose to warn Jim instead of killing him and they formed an alliance. Included in that warning was the revelation that much of the intelligence the Mad Mick had received on Jim, his family, and friends had come from sources within their own community. Though the news that there were spies within the town was not surprising to Jim, it hardened his resolve that he had to do something about it.

Jim's pact with the Mad Mick nearly blew apart at the seams when Charlie took a shot at the Mad Mick's daughter for hitting his friend Pete. Had she not been wearing body armor, things would have ended very differently. Charlie's inability to follow orders had been par for the course as of late, but Jim and Hugh were becoming increasingly frustrated with him. Neither could trust the young man if he wouldn't follow orders. In the face of their rebuke, Charlie fled the valley and no one knew where he'd gone.

With all of these experiences under his belt, Jim Powell was now a different man than he had been only a few short months before. He'd come to accept that there was only one way forward for him. He understood now that the aspects of his personality that helped him and his clan survive were not passivity, compromise, and a willingness to accept the hand dealt to him. Instead, it was his ruthlessness, his hardness, and his unflinching willingness to kill that got them this far.

There was no other way. There was no compromise. Jim must return to being that angry, hard man who'd walked home from Richmond with only a handgun, a get home bag, and a heart full of determination.

He understood now that the only way for his clan to remain safe was to get ahead of anyone who meant them harm, and it wasn't a short list. There were the amateur bounty hunters hoping there might still be a price on Jim's head; the people who felt Jim harmed them in some way by destroying the local power plant, who blamed him for their powerless homes, the lack of government aid, and their relatives who died; and those who would gladly have moved into comfort camps had their construction not been canceled due to Jim Powell and his insurgent activity.

According to the Mad Mick, the biggest threat to Jim's group might be the informal intelligence network in the community, rumored to be collecting information on people they didn't agree with. Somehow they were funneling that information up the chain to the acting government. Jim had no doubt that his name was at the top of that list. His work was cut out for him, but he knew what he was going to do. He must find his enemies and strike at them before they could strike at him.

May God have mercy on their souls.

1

———

Jim Powell built the storage building his family called The Daddy Shack when his kids were toddlers. It was where they kept the fun stuff—bikes, kayaks, fishing gear, camping gear, and outdoor toys. In the year since the collapse, the building had taken on a more somber purpose. In those early powerless months, as violence became more commonplace, it became clear that the family would need a place to store those items Jim referred to as "battlefield pickups." In short, it was useful gear stripped from the dead or defeated.

As that gear began to accumulate in the basement and the barn, Jim decided he needed a better place to store it. He knew from his years as a prepper that such items might have barter value over time so he didn't want to get rid of them. Since he didn't envision they'd be doing any recreational kayaking anytime soon, he emptied the kayak rack built against one wall of the Daddy Shack and moved the colorful kayaks to the barn. It was a bittersweet decision. There were a lot of good family memories attached to those boats and they'd always been in the same spot.

In the vacant space left by the kayaks Jim installed some shelves and hooks. He filled them with the assortment of items they'd accumulated in their various skirmishes and conflicts. While collecting gear from bodies was grim work, there was no need to bury the dead with things that Jim's people might need later. Likewise, if they'd been forced to kill everyone in a particular house, there was no use leaving gear behind for others to take later. Houses were stripped just as thoroughly as the bodies of the dead. Survival didn't favor the squeamish.

Over the past year, they'd fought everyone from murderous criminals to drug-addled hillbillies to bad cops. Sometimes it was people who'd come to their valley looking to move in and run them out. Other times it was people who'd crossed them in some manner that Jim or his people just couldn't overlook. At its worst, it was agents of the acting government trying to open a power plant while refusing to provide power to local citizens.

Violence was the common language of this post-collapse world. It was the default greeting, replacing the friendly wave or casual nod. A stranger was as likely to mean you harm as to pass through peacefully. Without fail, every group that had ever shown up in force had come with war in their hearts. While killing had never become casual, it was easier for each of them than it had been that first time. All but the youngest children among them had taken lives.

The gear stacked on those shelves and hanging from those hooks told the story of the violent months that had passed. There were sets of body armor and bump helmets, some of them having been stripped from United Nations troops killed in the attack on the power plant. There was a bucket filled with pocket knives, fixed-blade knives, and multi-tools. A shelf held backpacks of all sizes and colors. There were holsters, belts, and pieces of web gear. There were brass knuckles and pepper spray in a clear plastic bin the size of a shoe box.

While no one cared to strip the dead of the clothes they were wearing, spare clothing was picked up when they came across it. Anything contained in packs, vehicles, or homes was fair game. There was an array of shirts, boots, pants, and belts in all colors and sizes. There were military fatigues and camouflage battle dress in various patterns. Hunting clothing was well-represented and offered some of the best camouflage available for their region of the country.

The more useful weapons were in the basement of Jim's house. Those included anything capable of full-auto, precision rifles, anything high-end, or weapons that matched something they used frequently. The less desirable long guns were kept in a blue plastic drum in The Daddy Shack, much like the way one would store rakes, shovels, and gardening tools.

The barrel held the decades-old shotguns that came from the backs of closets and the old hunting rifles in obscure calibers. It held the Mausers, the Enfields, the pump-action Stevens .22 rifles, and the single-shot Savage shotguns in 16-gauge. It also held the damaged AR-15s and AK-47s that could be used for spare parts.

A couple of five-gallon buckets that once contained drywall mud now served as the storage receptacles for the less desirable handguns. They'd accumulated a lot of those over the past year. Jim had distributed handguns to anyone in his group responsible enough to carry one so they all had decent sidearms and a serviceable backup. Everything else ended up in the buckets.

There was an Astra Cub in .22 short and a variety of pocket-sized .25s by Raven Arms and several defunct manufacturers. There were century-old break-tops in .32 and single-action Western-style revolvers. There were even modern law-enforcement semi-automatics in 9mm from Smith & Wesson and Ruger. Some of the UN soldiers they'd been forced to deal with had carried 9mm Berettas like Jim and he'd taken all those for his personal stash. It was always good to have spares.

Cardboard boxes, totes, and milk crates held the other items that the dead had carried. Methods of starting fires and cooking were in one box. Another held canteens, water bottles, and filters. Several held first aid kits, blowout kits, and trauma kits. A smaller box held medications and eyeglasses. Clear plastic baggies contained batteries, watches, and GPS units. A couple of olive drab duffel bags stacked in the corner were packed with even more clothing they hadn't sorted through yet.

The feeling this cache of supplies provoked in Jim was complicated. In the years before the collapse, staring at his piles of preparations gave him a sense of comfort and pride. It made him feel as if he'd done something very important and very tangible for the safety of his family. Ice storms, blizzards, power outages, tornadoes, and hurricanes didn't really worry him a lot. If one of those events took place, his family would be fine. His preparations gave him peace of mind.

He didn't feel the same about the contents of this building. This wall of gear had been paid for with blood, fear, and personal risk. It was a bounty that came from the death of others. There was a complex emotion attached to such things. While Jim was appreciative of the gear, it was hard to feel pride at what they'd amassed. Collecting it was grim work that left no one with a sense of satisfaction. Indeed, it was more likely to leave one with nightmares.

Jim dug out one of the oddball pocket pistols in .22 Short caliber and set it aside. From a shoebox of ammo, he found two tattered boxes of .22 Short rounds. The boxes were faded, perhaps fifty or sixty years old, and the paper worn soft as a flower petal. Jim dumped the rounds into a sandwich baggie and wrote the caliber on the bag with a permanent marker.

He dug through the bucket of knives and selected a dozen that he deemed were junk. They were the shabby knives sold by the cash register at convenience stores for a couple of dollars, with cheap steel and wobbly blades. Some of the fixed-blades he selected had come from flea markets judging by the poor-quality sheaths and loose handles. These were not knives that Jim would ever use or give to anyone he cared about. Still, they might be of use to someone who had no knife at all.

Jim spread a tarp on the ground outside the door and tossed out some other items of gear that he didn't expect to ever issue to his people. There were some off-brand backpacks and sleeping bags that were stained or beginning to fall apart. He included a set of boots with a floppy sole that could be repaired if someone found the right adhesive. After another hour of picking through gear he had a decent-sized pile on the tarp.

The impact of those removed items wasn't too apparent inside the building. The shelves were still overflowing. Sadly, he expected his people would continue to add to the inventory. There seemed to be no end in sight to the violence. Even when order was someday restored, he didn't expect people would immediately stop shooting at each other, especially there in the mountains.

People in that region had resorted to the same manner of resolving conflicts they'd used for centuries. Shooting at people they didn't like was the hillbilly way. They'd tried to act civilized for the last few decades, letting the courts and police solve their problems, but it wasn't who they were at the core.

As unpleasant as the collapse was, it had in some way restored them to who they were as a people. Hillbillies had found their way back home. It was only government intervention and overreaching social programs that had turned so many of them into unemployed drug addicts dependent on handouts. In their truest form, they were clannish hermits to whom independence and freedom were supreme over all things. It was why they'd chosen these mountains as home in the first place.

"Having a yard sale?" came a voice from the yard.

Jim wandered to the shed door, blinking as he stared out into the bright sun. He found Hugh on horseback, regarding the pile on the tarp. "Hugh, when did you get back?"

"Just now," Hugh replied. "On my way home for some beauty sleep. Been riding all night."

"Wasn't sure if we'd get you back or not. You were awful comfortable over there at the Mad Mick's place." There was a sparkle in Jim's eye as he made the teasing accusation. There'd been some odd spark between Hugh and the Mad Mick's daughter, Barb. Despite the age gap, Jim was certain that she'd been part of the reason Hugh had lingered at the Mad Mick's place.

Hugh frowned at the implication. "I was helping the man erect his antenna."

Jim bit his tongue against all the jokes that were begging to be made. "If you say so, Hugh. Did you get the antenna up and functioning?"

"I did. He obviously won't have the range he used to have since we couldn't raise all the tower sections. Some of them were just too damaged. We rigged up a hoist, and that allowed us to get about half the sections in place. He did some test transmissions while I was there and he was able to touch base with people farther away than we are. I'm going to do a test as soon as I get home and see if he receives it."

"I hope it works. He could be an asset. He seems to have some powerful connections."

"You've got no idea, Jim. It's not just connections. He also builds some sophisticated explosives and detonators from scratch. The kinds of things you see used in political assassinations on the news. I've never met anyone in his league."

Jim frowned at the odd image. "He seems like kind of a knuckle-dragger. That's hard to imagine."

"Looks are deceiving. He and I had a lot of time to talk while we were working, Jim. I've got stories to tell, lots of them, but it'll have to wait for another time. I need to get some sleep before I fall off this horse."

Jim flung his arm toward the mountain where Hugh's mobile home sat hidden in the woods. "Then get on home. We'll talk later."

Hugh started to ride off but hesitated. "Charlie ever show back up?"

Jim gave a somber shake of his head. "Nope. Haven't seen hide nor hair of him."

"How's Randi holding up?"

"She's not her old self. She's worried about him. I don't think she's cussed or insulted me in days."

"She's not blaming you, is she?"

"I don't think so. She understands that he's a problem, but she doesn't want to give up on him. She's been riding around the woods calling for him, but if he's out there he's not responding."

"It's the mother in her. She took him in to raise when Alice died. He's like a son to her now."

Jim shrugged. "She's welcome to bring him back, but that boy has a long way to go before he earns my trust back. That stunt he pulled with shooting the Mad Mick's daughter could have turned into a war."

"I know," said Hugh. "As much as I like him, the boy has to learn to follow orders if he's going to stay here. We have to act as a unit. If he wants to be an outlaw, he's going to have to do it out there on his own. Maybe that's what he needs? Pulling some time out there on the road might straighten him out. He'll realize how good he had it here."

"Maybe." Jim wasn't sure what it would take to fix Charlie.

Hugh gestured at the tarp. "You never did tell me what this pile was about."

"The market in town. It's time to get our network in place. We've been talking about it for weeks and we need to get it going. With people harvesting crops, attendance at the market is at a peak. This is the time to establish a presence."

They'd discussed the idea of building their intelligence network ever since Jim returned from his "exile" in the mountains.

"So, this is stuff to sell," said Hugh.

"It is. We're having a meeting after dinner this evening to get the ball rolling. I thought I'd donate some items. The building is getting a little crowded."

Hugh understood the full implication of the comment. A building crowded with battlefield pick-ups and "salvage" was a sign of just how many people they'd been forced to kill. "I might try to come down for that if I wake up in time."

"Please do," Jim said. "I'm keeping it low-key for now. It's not particularly a secret but we don't need everyone involved in the planning meeting."

"Sounds like you're trying to keep someone out of the loop. You might as well tell me who so I don't accidentally mention it to them."

Jim looked sheepish. "I'm not inviting Pops. He's a bit too friendly with folks and I'm afraid he'll give away too much about our group if he spends any time at the market. He's not the best at maintaining operational security."

Hugh held up a hand to stop Jim's explanation. "Hey, that's between you and your dad. You don't need to justify yourself to me."

"Thanks."

"But you might have to justify yourself to him," Hugh said with a laugh. He spun his horse and trotted off.

Jim sat down in the door of the storage building and mopped at his forehead with the tail of his shirt. Hugh was right. When Pops got wind of this, he was going to want to go and that was not a debate Jim was looking forward to.

2

———————

This time of year, Jim's house was uninhabitable by early evening. Even in the mountains, with all the windows open, an oppressive heat made the house feel like a car shut up in the hot sun. Nearly everyone found something outside to occupy them at this time of day. Nana and Ellen were canning. Pops was entertaining Ariel since the child had resisted all efforts to interest her in preserving food.

She'd selected several books from the family library and led Pops to a bench beneath a broad maple tree behind the house. She opened the book she wanted him to read, showed him where he was to begin, then took a seat beside him. He only made it through a couple of paragraphs before she stopped him.

"You have to do the voices, Pops."

"What voices?"

"The character voices. They're all supposed to be different. You're reading them all the same and using your normal old voice. That's boring."

Pops frowned. "My voice is boring?"

"Yes, Pops. I'm sorry if no one ever told you that. I mean, it's okay for you, but it's not good for a *Magic Treehouse* story. They're supposed to be exciting."

Pops began again, throwing a wide variety of different voices into his reading. Ariel sank her face into her palms and slowly shook her head.

"What now?" Pops demanded.

Ariel rolled her eyes. "You're making it sound like *The Three Bears* or something. These are children speaking, not bears."

Pops looked around the yard, trying to find some way to escape. As much as he liked spending time with Ariel, this particular activity was not playing to his strengths. He spotted Gary and his wife, Debra, disappearing into the barn. "What are they doing here, Ariel?"

"They're going into the barn," she replied, a playful lilt in her voice. "Isn't that obvious?"

Pops scowled at Ariel. "Yes, it's obvious, Miss Smarty Pants, but I was wondering *why* they were here together like that. They don't usually show up like that unless something is going on."

Ariel didn't answer and Pops closed the book, studying the barn. About that time, Gary's daughter Sara and her husband Will wandered into the barn, too. Pops turned his attention back to Ariel, more convinced than ever that something was going on.

"Are you sure you don't know what's going on in there? You always seem to know everything."

Ariel looked away, but couldn't restrain the sneaky grin that spread across her face. "I might have sneaked and heard something."

Pops raised an eyebrow. "Sneaked?"

"I was accidentally hiding behind the couch," Ariel said. "I was looking for something I lost there. Then when Mommy and Daddy started talking, I didn't want to climb out of there all of a sudden because I was afraid I might scare them." Her hesitant delivery made it clear that she was making up the story as she went.

Pops wasn't fooled. "Is that right?"

Ariel frowned, nodding seriously. She forced her cheeks to sag and her lip to quiver. The child was a master of heartbroken faces. "Don't you believe me, Pops?"

"Yes, Ariel. I believe you. Now, what did you hear?"

As quickly as it had come, the sad face was gone and Ariel was beaming with a conspiratorial grin. "Well, Daddy is trying to figure out who the people are in town that don't like him, so he's sending in spies. People from the valley are going to sell at the farmer's market to learn who we can't trust. Then Daddy says he's going to *deal* with them, and you know what that means."

The look of glee on Ariel's face as she relayed this information was slightly disturbing. Ariel apparently understood what Jim meant by "dealing" with them.

Pops turned back to the barn, thinking out loud. "I can't believe your father would hold a meeting of such importance without me. No one in this valley knows that town the way I do. I was principal at the high school years ago. I was in local politics. I probably know at least one person from every family in town."

Ariel gave Pops an awkward look. "That might be the problem, Pops."

He snapped back to Ariel. "What's that supposed to mean?"

"Uh, I'm not supposed to know."

"But you sneaked?"

She shrugged. "They talked about it while I was still scrunched down behind the couch. You know, when I didn't want to scare them?"

"Then I suggest you tell me what you heard before I go tell your mother that you were snooping on her."

Ariel looked appalled at the idea her own grandfather would rat her out, but she was astute enough to know he was serious. She heaved a dramatic sigh. "Daddy said one time the police in town asked about where you were living and you told them."

Pops recalled the situation. Once he and Nana realized they'd be staying with Jim for a while, he'd gone across town with Jim, Pete, and Buddy to haul back some stuff from their home. They'd brought back his side-by-side utility vehicle and more of their belongings. A pair of cops had pulled them over in town to make sure they weren't stealing. Jim wouldn't answer their questions but Pops, questioned separately, had seen no reason to withhold that information. He gladly told them he was staying in the valley with Jim. He'd also revealed they had an entire tanker of diesel fuel, which was why they were out driving when most people were on foot.

Jim wasn't happy about the situation. He complained that it exposed them to danger because more people would know where they lived and that they had enough fuel to operate vehicles. Once Jim had explained it, Pops had understood. It wasn't his fault that he didn't have the natural level of paranoia his son had. He was a trusting person by nature, not a distrustful one.

He wasn't an idiot, though. If someone told him to be quiet and explained the rationale, he was able to keep a secret. Jim should know that. If he was invited to participate in that meeting in the barn and Jim told him there were certain matters he couldn't talk about in town, then he wouldn't do it. It was simple. He couldn't believe Jim would leave him out of such an important plan.

Pops shot to his feet and placed Ariel's books on the bench. "I need to speak with your mother."

Ariel watched him go with uncertainty. She figured this would probably end up getting her in trouble somehow. Pops would rat her out. Like her father said, he wasn't always the best at keeping his mouth shut.

Pops stalked to the back porch and climbed the stairs where Nana and Ellen were canning beans on a Coleman stove.

"What're you doing, Pops?" Ellen asked, arranging jars in the canner. When he didn't respond immediately, she turned toward him and could tell by his body language that he wasn't happy about something. "What's the matter?"

"I was just informed by my granddaughter that your husband thinks I'm a tottering old boob who can't be trusted in public."

Ellen almost smiled at his pronouncement until she saw he was serious.

Nana looked confused. "What on Earth are you talking about?"

Ellen didn't have to ask, fairly certain she knew what he was talking about. "The meeting?"

Pops gave a curt nod. "Yes, the meeting to which I wasn't invited since I can't be trusted with anything of a sensitive nature."

Nana looked at Ellen. "Do you know what he's going on about?"

Ellen heaved a reluctant sigh. "You're going to have to take this up with your son. This is not my baby."

"But you acknowledge that there is indeed a meeting going on in the barn at this very moment?"

Ellen had no choice but to admit it. "Yes."

"Then that's where I'm headed." Pops headed back down the steps. "If you hear the sound of weeping, that's me giving Jim the spanking that he well deserves."

As Pops stomped off, Ellen had no choice but to tell Nana what was going on.

When she was done, Nana threw her hands up. "Well, he *does* have a big mouth. Once you get him talking, he won't shut up. I've told him that for years."

Ellen didn't respond to the comment, instead choosing to wipe down the canning utensils that she'd already wiped down moments earlier. In the days of cell phones she'd have sent Jim a warning text. These days he was on his own.

3

The interior of Jim's barn was slightly cooler than the outside. It was airy, with a high ceiling, and stood in the shade of several poplar and sassafras trees. If his farm was the headquarters of his clan, the barn was their conference room. The group he'd called together sat on an assortment of buckets, milk crates, and odd chairs. Jim stood and paced, too amped-up to sit still. He was excited about the actions they were preparing to take, his mind whirling through the possibilities.

Gary and his wife were there, as well as his daughter, Sara, and her husband, Will. Pete was sitting beside Hugh. Randi was also present, at least bodily. Normally she'd have been smoking a hand-rolled cigarette and wisecracking. Now, with Charlie's whereabouts unknown, she just looked serious and demoralized.

"Thanks for coming," Jim said, rubbing his hands together. "I'm excited about this new project. I've been open with you guys about my struggle to balance privacy against security. Remaining isolated hasn't done us any favors. We've missed out on intelligence that might have spared us some headaches. By not having ears in town, we've allowed people to openly plot against us while having no idea what was going on. That ends now."

Jim was preaching to the choir here. They'd all lived through the same things he'd experienced. After the year they'd gone through, they all knew the risks of operating in a vacuum. While Jim had prepared for a lot of things over the years, this was one area of prepping he'd neglected. He understood in hindsight that he should have immediately begun building an intelligence network after he returned from Richmond.

He hadn't, because he'd thought the best strategy was to fly under the radar. He had a fantasy that his family could live in an isolated bubble, a vacuum, and stay safe while the rest of the world disintegrated around them. Certainly, he'd anticipated conflict and knew there would be times they had to defend themselves, but his entire survival strategy was built around laying low.

That had proven impossible. It was inevitable that people would notice them and talk about what they saw. Word got around, sometimes traveling much farther than anyone might imagine. Often, people investigated the stories they heard out of sheer curiosity. Even gossip, which could be exaggerated and off-base, usually contained a grain of truth. By isolating themselves, Jim's people had cut themselves off from even that most basic form of intelligence gathering. They were operating blind and that needed to change immediately.

"I see this as a multi-pronged approach," Jim continued. "I think we have two vendor booths, or stalls, whatever they call them. Gary's family can run one and Randi and Pete run the other. Originally, I'd intended to stick Charlie with Randi and Pete, but that's obviously not an option at this point."

Jim looked at Randi but she didn't meet his eye, staring instead at her fingers laced together in her lap. She was all too aware of Charlie's absence already.

"What about Hugh?" Pete asked. "Can he help out at our booth?"

Jim shook his head. "The idea of having two booths is that I want you guys to cultivate different sources. Two booths doubles our information gathering capabilities. Hugh, on the other hand, is going to be mobile. He's already established a connection with the guy who makes and sells weapons."

"Ian," Hugh said.

"Hugh can build more of those connections over time," Jim went on. "You guys working booths are free to speak to each other, but it's probably best that you don't look like you're part of the same group. You can acknowledge that you all know each other, but I'm concerned that people might grow suspicious if we seem too organized. We want to appear like we're just regular survivors out there trying to trade for things we need. Does that make sense? Any questions?"

"I've got a question!" someone snapped.

Jim looked to find Pops standing in the door, an offended expression on his face. Jim's smile was defeated. "Hey, Pops."

"You asked for questions and I've got a question for you. I want to know why I wasn't invited to this meeting."

Jim didn't want to get into that right now. He didn't want to have that discussion in front of his friends and make them uncomfortable. That left only one option. He had to roll with it. Jim grabbed a folding chair leaning against a wall, opened it, and placed it beside his dad. He gestured at the open chair. "Have a seat."

"That still doesn't answer my question," Pops said, remaining standing.

"You can stay or go," Jim offered. "I'm not going to beg."

Pops turned his nose up but took the seat.

Jim continued. "We want to build as complete a picture as we can of what's going on in town and the surrounding communities. I'll need you guys to take notes of certain types of things. We can't rely on memory. What are people gossiping about? Who are the people that are being talked about? Are there people claiming to be in charge of particular things? Are there people making or enforcing rules? Are there people who are instilling fear in other people? Are there groups that are known to be trouble? Are there people who have traveled to other communities? What have they learned? All of those are things we should be making notes about."

"That's just one more reason I should be involved here," Pops said.

"Why is that?" Jim asked patiently. He didn't want their conflict to dominate the meeting but he couldn't be rude about it.

Pops swept an arm around the room. "Aside from Pete, there ain't a soul in this room who's familiar with the town. They don't know the faces. They don't know the significance of any names they might hear. Someone like me, someone who knows the town, is familiar with the historical perspective. I know which families had money or power. I know which families have close social ties or intermarriages. Sure, your people can take their notes, but you need someone with my insight to put that information into perspective. You can't even do it yourself. You may live close to town but you rarely go there. You don't know the town like I do. I lived there over fifty years."

Jim's immediate reaction was that he wanted to shut down this argument. He'd already decided he didn't want to debate Pops in front of these people. That would be uncomfortable for everyone. He was trying to come up with a diplomatic response when Hugh spoke up.

"Your dad's comments are valid. He *does* know the people. He recognizes the faces. Your dad might even notice things that the rest of us wouldn't, like alliances between people who never got along before. You should consider letting your dad participate in a similar role to mine."

Jim cocked an eyebrow. This was unexpected but he respected Hugh's insight. "How so?"

Hugh held up an apologetic hand. "No offense, Pops, but there are certain things that older people can get by with that the rest of us can't. They can be nosy about who people are and who they're related to because that's common in rural areas. Old people are always asking who people are, who their family was, and where they live."

"What's wrong with that?" Pops asked.

"Not a thing," said Hugh. "I'm only saying that we could play that to our advantage. I'm suggesting you might be able to get away with things the rest of us couldn't. You can ask to take a seat at a stranger's booth to get out of the sun and strike up a conversation with them. You can butt into conversations that I can't. In this community, people will treat you with a politeness and acceptance that I won't get. People tend to be suspicious of me."

"Can't imagine why," Pete cracked.

Hugh gave Pete a playful shove.

"Hugh is right," Debra stated. "My dad was the same way when he got around people. He wanted to see everyone and talk to everyone. He had to know who they were because he was certain he knew every family in the community."

"I do," Pops said, as if that were common knowledge. "I worked in the school system, then at the local community college. When I ran for political office, I spent a year visiting every single home in this county. There are a lot of names, faces, and history in this noggin." Pops tapped his head, still thick with mostly white hair.

Jim let out a long sigh. "I see the point you're all trying to make and I agree that there's merit. But if we're going to go down this road, we need to address the obvious. Pops, you know my concern, right?"

Pops looked off and tightened his mouth. "You think I'm an old man who can't keep his fool mouth shut."

Jim stood there a moment gathering himself before he replied. He'd just opened his mouth to speak when Gary jumped in to rescue him.

"Pops, I don't think that's what Jim thinks at all. We've all been through this on one level or another. I would never have understood the risk of talking about my level of preparation if I hadn't read all the post-apocalyptic books Jim introduced me to. If I got one thing out of those books, it was an understanding of just how dangerous it was to say too much to anyone outside of your own group. Probably everyone in this room except for you, Randi, and Pete has read those kinds of books."

"I like history," Pops said. "Local history. Not interested in that gloom and doom stuff."

Hugh turned in his chair. "Gary is right. The thing that Jim is over-looking here is that a lot of us already know what *not* to say. You don't, Pops, but it's something we can coach you on. The basics are that you never talk about what you have. Always make it sound like you're just barely scraping by. In fact, I'd probably just tell people that I was living with friends outside of town. If anyone asks for more information, tell them that your friends don't want you to talk about it because they're paranoid. You don't have to lie, you just leave out anything that might make people want to come pay you a visit. No bragging about how well you're doing. Make it sound like you're miserable."

"I can do that," Pops said. "That's pretty simple. If someone had taken the time to explain this to me in the beginning," he cut Jim an accusing look, "I might have known to keep my big trap shut."

Jim didn't take the bait. "Are we good here?"

"I guess we are since someone finally took the time to explain it to me," Pops huffed.

Anxious to get the meeting back on track, Jim let the comment slide. "So, anyway, I'm ready to get started tomorrow. You don't have any obligation to be there every day, but I know there are things that all of us need even beyond information. I know diapers, hygiene products, and children's clothing are in demand. It might even be helpful for each of you to post a sign at your booth listing things you're interested in. I'd also recommend that you don't display everything at your booth at one time. You don't want to look too prosperous and possibly tempt a thief. If you discover someone is wanting to trade something you have back here in the valley, you can always offer to bring it back the next day."

"So, who's going tomorrow?" Debra asked.

"All of you should go tomorrow," Jim said. "Work together to get a feel for the place and try to figure out your strategy. Then figure out who you'll need the next day. If you all want to go each day, that's fine. If you don't need a full crew, that's fine, too."

"I'm not partial to horses," Pops announced. "Haven't ridden one in years. I might need a little assistance."

"I'll ride with you," Hugh said. "We can find you a camping chair to take along with you. An umbrella might be handy too with this heat."

Pops smiled. "Excellent idea. Glad to hear that someone thinks about an old man's comfort."

"Any questions?" Jim asked.

Randi held up a finger. "What time should we plan on leaving?"

Jim shrugged. "I'd plan on leaving at first light. Have your stuff ready to go so you can saddle up and ride. Based on my experience with flea markets, the good stuff goes early. If you want the high-demand items, you need to be there before the crowd shows up."

They broke up soon after that with Randi being the first to go. She was already grumpy because Lloyd hadn't returned from the road trip he took with Jim. Charlie running off had been the last straw. Now, she was consumed with worry and had little time for socializing. Jim had hoped that participating in the market operation would be a distraction for her, but she'd immediately latched onto it as an opportunity to expand her search for Charlie.

"You going with us?" Hugh asked when it was just him and Jim left.

Jim shook his head. "I don't think so. Not yet anyway."

"I'm headed home. I'm supposed to do another test connection with the Mad Mick. We'll see how it goes." He waved and headed off.

"Good luck," Jim told him, then headed toward the house. They had a watermelon cooling in the creek and he was anxious to slice into it.

4

———————

The group setting up at the market left the valley together the next morning. They weren't very talkative at the early hour but grew more so as they rode toward town. It was a beautiful morning with birds chirping and sunlight reflecting off damp grass. The peaceful beauty eventually lifted even the most tired spirits.

"You know, this is the first time I've ridden toward town without feeling a sense of dread," Debra said. "I'm hoping that's a good sign."

They'd just crossed the bridge they'd installed to replace the one Charlie burned down. It was made of a flatbed trailer hoisted across the gap with an impressive array of ropes, pulleys, and levers. They hadn't put up safety rails, so everyone stuck to the middle of the flatbed-bridge, crossing single file.

"I think it's because we have a plan this time," Gary said. "We know what we're going to do and it's a long-term plan, not just a reaction to something bad that's happened to us. I'm kind of excited, too."

There was a murmur of agreement, everyone interested in what the day would bring. Once they left the valley and got on the main road, even the town itself felt different. Things seemed less ominous, less menacing. While people weren't overly friendly, some nodded. It was much different than things had been a few months earlier.

"I wonder if it's the summer day that's making everyone feel so good," Pete ventured.

Hugh shrugged. "I wonder if it's something about reaching the one-year point. People realize this disaster isn't just a bad memory that's going to go away one morning. Those who've survived must have realized by now that they need to get on with their lives to whatever extent they can. They can't hide from the collapse."

"They need to be growing food," Pops said. "There better be some gardens behind these houses or they're going to be hurting in a few months."

About a half-mile from the market, Hugh waved everyone to a stop near the old primary school. "We don't need to ride in together. We're going to draw enough attention as it is, having all these horses and being new vendors. We shouldn't look like we're part of a single group."

Randi gestured toward Gary and his family. "You guys go on first if you want."

"What should we do with our horses?" Will asked.

"I'd expect someone is running a corral," Hugh said. "If there's no corral, just tie them out close enough that you can keep an eye on them."

They said their goodbyes and Gary rode on toward the farmer's market with Debra, Will, and Sara.

"You guys can go next," Hugh told Randi and Pete. "Pops and I will ride in last."

Without a word exchanged between them, Randi and Pete nudged their horses and rode off down the street. Just past the fire station, they cut through a field that shaved a little distance off the trip to the farmer's market. In a world without cars, shortcuts had faced a resurgence in popularity. The high grass of town was now bisected with hundreds of worn paths that hadn't been used since cars became commonplace.

At this early hour, the market was bustling but not yet crowded. Pete saw Gary's family unloading their horses at one of the designated stalls in the old parking lot. Above the parking lot, the county had built an enormous pavilion that had served as the farmer's market before the collapse. The market had grown in popularity this summer and had quickly overflowed the available space.

The last time Pete had been here, those covered stalls beneath the pavilion had filled up early. Not only did they have a roof to block the sun and rain, they had vendor tables built into place. Vendors who arrived after those desirable covered spaces were filled had to set up in the parking lot. Some vendors, such as Hugh's friend Ian, actually preferred the open parking lot.

"You want to be under the pavilion or in the parking lot?" Pete asked.

Randi considered it, then replied, "We should spread out. Since Gary's in the parking lot, we should go to the pavilion."

It made no difference to Pete. They rode their horses up to the pavilion and grabbed one of the last remaining spaces.

"This looks good." Pete slid off his horse.

Randi pulled alongside him, dismounted, and began untying the load from her horse. As Pete was unrolling a tarp over their table, he noticed a woman sitting in a camping chair a few spaces away. She was wearing shorts, a burgundy hoody, and had a crew-cut that looked as if it had been done with hedge trimmers. She was glaring at Pete in a hostile manner and he began to get nervous when she didn't avert her stare.

"Randi," Pete hissed.

"What?"

"That woman is staring at us."

Randi turned toward the woman Pete was discreetly gesturing toward and glared back at her. "You got a problem?"

The oddly-shaped woman looked like a gargoyle, as if she'd perched in that very chair for eons without moving. When she spoke, her voice was a croak almost as deep as that of a Tibetan throat singer. "Melinda usually sets up at that booth. She sells quilts and whatnots."

Randi put her hands on her hips. "Bitch, I don't care if the pope hands out blessings and little crackers in this spot. I don't see a name on it."

The gargoyle shrugged as if she'd said all she had to say on the matter.

Randi flashed her a wicked smile. "Yeah, that's what I thought you'd say."

Pete rolled his eyes. "Way to make friends on the first day, Randi."

She frowned at him. "What would you have suggested? You think we should move so Melinda can sell her stupid whatnots in this spot?"

"No, but it's like the first day of school. You have to be nice to people."

Randi shook her head. "Forget that, I approach it like it's the first day of prison. One, you don't let anyone push you around. Two, you find the biggest, meanest person around and beat the hell out of them."

Pete looked alarmed. "So, that's what I have to look forward to today? You're going to get in a fight?"

Randi tossed the last of their packs down onto the tarp. "If I have to."

"I don't think that's what Dad had in mind. I thought we were supposed to be listening for gossip, not becoming the thing that people gossiped about."

Randi let out a long sigh. "I guess you're right, Pete, but I'm going to keep my eye on that bitch." She threw another nasty look at the burgundy gargoyle.

"You do that," Pete said. "Look but don't touch." He opened a pack and dumped the contents on the tarp, then tossed the pack aside. They had several backpacks of items for this first visit, as well as a few things stuffed into saddlebags.

"I can set all this up, Pete. You want to see about the horses?"

Pete looked for the spot where the old corral had been set up and was pleased to see it was still there. He was more pleased to see that it wasn't being operated by the previous proprietors. That had been a boy Pete knew from school, his brother, and their dad. They'd been jerks to Pete, forcing him to pull a gun on them when they'd refused to return his horses one day.

Charlie had dealt with the matter in his typical heavy-handed approach. He'd gone to the man's home one night and killed him. As with most of Charlie's actions, although his heart had been in the right place, his approach was a little over the top. Recalling Randi's interaction with the burgundy gargoyle, Pete wondered if that tendency toward impulsive action was why Randi and Charlie got along so well.

Pete gathered the reins of their horses and led them across the large parking lot to the corral. It was made of prefabricated corral panels assembled in the grass beyond the lot. Patches of low grass and horse manure showed that the corral was being shifted whenever the grass was eaten down too far.

The new corral tender was a man in bibbed overalls with no shirt. He wore a straw hat and carried a hand-carved toothpick in his mouth. The loose fabric around the middle of his overalls showed that he was probably a much bigger man before the world changed. Like everyone else, he was eating less and working harder these days.

He grinned when Pete walked up. "What can I do you for, pardner?"

"I've got a booth here all day. How much to keep my horses?"

The tender regarded the horses, then studied Pete. "What you got to trade? The last feller to have the corral preferred ammo as currency. I take a little of everything."

"How about a .22 shell for each horse for the day?"

The tender gave Pete a wary look. "You're quite the trader, aren't you? Two shells for two horses? How about five shells and I'll keep the two all day."

Pete shook his head. "I'll give you two per horse. Four shells total for the day. We'll be setting up nearly every day so you'll get that same amount regularly if you do me right."

The corral tender did some quick calculations in his head and decided he could work with that. "Four shells. I'll take it."

Pete handed over the reins. "And I'll just go ahead and warn you that the woman I'm set up with is downright *mean*. So, don't play games with us. Don't even joke about losing those horses. I'm serious. She's the kind that will kill you for looking at her wrong."

The man's smile faded. "Gotcha, kid. No jokes. You can pay when you pick them up."

"Good enough," Pete said, heading back to rejoin Randi.

Despite the lack of an organized timetable, people were steadily rolling in, as if driven by some biological imperative. The pavilion was full now and the vendor space in the parking lot wasn't far behind.

When Pete reached their stall, he found that Randi had finished setting up their wares. It didn't look like much in old-world terms, but there was enough there to hopefully lure prospective customers to their booth. They had some plastic baggies of loose ammo, most of it fitting weapons they didn't own. They had some oddball knives and multi-tools, some camping gear, some packs, a few odd pots and pans, and baby clothing that was too small to fit any of the children of their clan.

Randi had some baggies of tobacco from the stash that she and Hugh had found hanging in one of the barns. She'd rolled some into cigarettes using rolling papers they'd found in a looted convenience store. She also had a few pipes to sell with it. Hugh put them together in his spare time from brass plumbing parts he'd found in the valley. Anyone missing nicotine as badly as Randi had might not be too picky about their method of administration. Cigarette, pipe, or chewing would all work.

Scanning the crowd, Pete spotted Hugh and Pops riding into the parking lot. "The gang's all here now," he said to Randi.

She shook her head. "Not all the gang, Pete. Not until Charlie comes home."

Pete hadn't forgotten Charlie. He couldn't forget his best friend, despite struggling to understand why Charlie had done the things he had. It put Pete in a tough spot sometimes. He wanted to defend Charlie, but there was no way to defend the violent actions he took. Wherever Charlie was, Pete hoped he was getting his head together. He hoped he found his way back to the valley too because nothing was as fun without a good friend to share it with.

5

Hugh searched the growing crowd with a wary eye as he and Pops descended into the farmer's market. With so many folks beginning to pour in, they drew little attention, even on horseback. Smoke from cooking fires hung in the air as food vendors prepared for the day.

"Where do we start?" Pops asked.

"Let's get these horses dealt with and we can take a look around. We should probably split up and cover more ground. I'm sure you can keep yourself entertained and out of trouble."

Pops laughed. "I'm going to surprise Jim. Just wait and see. I might be the master spy that brings him more information than he knows what to do with."

They worked out a deal with the corral tender for their two horses. Hugh was able to leave both horses for the full day for a single hand-rolled cigarette. Just as it had been with the Native Americans centuries earlier, tobacco was proving to be a valuable commodity.

"Could a man get more of those?" the corral tender asked, gesturing toward the cigarette.

Hugh nodded. "I might have more to trade off."

The one thing Hugh hadn't told anyone was that the stash of cured tobacco he and Randi had found in a barn wasn't the extent of his supply. He'd also found seeds and had a nice little tobacco patch growing up on the mountain. He'd spent much of his childhood working tobacco and was well versed in every step of the process.

"I got ammunition. What's your flavor of choice?"

Hugh studied the corral tender, aware that trading was only the secondary goal of this mission. The primary goal was cultivating information assets. "What's your name?"

The corral tender stuck out a hand. "Hatfield."

Hugh shook his hand. "Good to meet you, Hatfield. My name is Hugh."

Pops, not to be outdone in the arena of shaking hands and kissing babies, stuck out his own hand. "Everyone just calls me Pops."

While Hatfield and Pops were shaking hands, Hugh made a show of looking inside the backpack he carried. "Hatfield, I don't need any ammunition right now. I'm set in that department. I might be able to bring you some more tomorrow, though. We'll work something out."

"You have a regular source of tobacco?" Hatfield asked.

Hugh shrugged. "Not an unlimited source, but I do have access to a quantity of cured tobacco."

Hatfield couldn't hide his eagerness. "A man with tobacco could probably set his own price. People are hurting for it. I could probably sell as much as you could get me and you wouldn't have to bother dealing with folks directly."

Hugh smiled. "Now that does have some appeal to me, friend. There are things I need to trade for, but all the wheeling and dealing does wear me down. I ain't much of a people person."

Hatfield laughed. "I'm your man, Hugh. I can move it for you, for a small fee. Say a cut of the tobacco?"

"How about we talk about it more when I come back for the horses?" Hugh offered.

"I'll be here," Hatfield replied.

Pops was shaking his head. "I'm a bit surprised people would be trading for tobacco. You'd think that would be the least of their needs."

Hatfield gestured at the growing crowd. "You got people out there who spent the better part of a year desperate for the basics. They're trying to figure out what normal life is like now. For some of them, that means going beyond the basics and experiencing some of the things that people considered luxuries back in simpler times, like tobacco and a sip of liquor. You spend enough time here at the market, you'll see that it ain't just about the basics anymore."

Hugh cocked an eyebrow. "What do you mean?"

"Hell, you've got people here selling wacky tobacky. You can buy a bag or a single bud. They've even got pipes so you can smoke it there at the booth. You've got people selling homebrew beer and liquor. There's a man running a tattoo machine off a battery and a solar charger. There's even a whorehouse in town. How long you reckon it's been since anyone ran a whorehouse on Main Street in this town?"

Pops and Hugh both stared at Hatfield slack-jawed.

"I-I'd say it's been a few years," Pops stammered.

"I'm serious!" Hatfield added. "An honest-to-God whorehouse."

Hugh lowered his voice, though no one was even close to them. "Look, I know there are women around who find themselves in a tough spot. I'm sure they've faced some difficulty finding the things they needed for their family. Is that what you're talking about?"

Hatfield grinned and shook his head. "Nope, I ain't talking about a woman trading her goods for someone else's goods. I'm talking about a genuine whorehouse. They took over a big old empty Victorian there in town. These women live there full-time and take visitors all day, every day. Besides the obvious, they also sell weed and shots of liquor."

"I'm pretty sure that's not legal," Pops said.

Hatfield busted out laughing. "I'm not sure what legal has to do with anything. There ain't no law anymore. Keep your eyes open today. You may be surprised at what you see."

"Who's running this whorehouse?" Hugh asked.

Hatfield squirmed uncomfortably. "I hear things, but I ain't sure it's the kind of thing I want to be talking about. It ain't no secret though. You spend enough time here you'll figure it out."

Hugh held up a hand. "No worries, man. I was just being nosy." He didn't want to get pushy about it. Better to brush it off and get back around to it later, when the two had established a rapport.

Hugh and Pops said their goodbyes and wandered off. Pops was wound up, barely able to contain himself until they were beyond Hatfield's earshot.

"I'm having trouble processing what he said. I can't believe there's a...*house of ill repute*...on Main Street."

"He's right. With no law, things go backward. There's always a market for vice."

"I get that. I'm old, though, and this goes back even beyond the Russell County of my childhood. This is more like the 1920s, except the citizenry is less adept at the basic skills of survival. The real people of the 1920s knew how to farm and hunt."

Hugh paused for a second and studied the market. "I'm going to mill around in the parking lot and see if I can find Ian, the weapon maker."

"I'm going to head for the covered section," Pops said. "I'll set up my chair somewhere and loaf. They might need a greeter."

Hugh smiled. "I'm sure they do. Stay safe. If you need anything, just let me know."

They parted ways and Hugh watched Pops wander off with his chair hung over his shoulder. There were more vendors than the last time Hugh had been here. The place seemed to be growing each day. Some sellers were pulling wagons that allowed them to haul more gear. They had pop-up awnings, flags, and banners made from old bedding.

The smell of cooking meat permeated the air, tormenting those who, like Hugh, might have skipped breakfast. Hugh decided that looking for the weapon vendor could wait until he had a bunny kebab in his belly.

As he walked toward the smoky section of the market, he noticed the market had a particular smell, much like the county fairs he'd gone to as a child. They'd smelled of horse manure, sawdust, and grilling food. This smell was nothing like that.

There was the tang of marijuana smoke in the air, which was a much more common commodity than tobacco. The odor of wood smoke and charring meat filled the air. There was a lingering scent of body odor that was so prevalent it wasn't assignable to a particular person. It was everyone. And without restrooms, the smell of human waste mixed with all of it. Hugh wondered if this was how medieval fairs had smelled centuries ago.

6

Hugh crouched on a concrete parking block and gnawed at his breakfast. The barbecue rabbit kebab was especially delicious, though Hugh couldn't push away the thought that the meat looked uncomfortably similar to cat. He tried to focus on the taste and not the critter of origin. After all, if it tasted good what did it matter? When he was done, he tossed the wire skewer into the weeds and got back to his feet.

The market was in full swing now, the rows of stalls filled with all manner of patrons. There were surly folks in ragged, dirty clothing who barely appeared to be scraping by. There were fragrant families dressed in camouflage hunting clothes who looked like this was just another weekend at the local flea market. There were sunken-eyed women who clutched at themselves as they made their way from booth to booth, exchanging fleeting glances with the vendors. Every person was a story and some of them ended better than others.

Hugh could tell some of these people would survive this collapse and life would go on for them. It was apparent in their attitude, their demeanor, and their condition. After all, they'd made it through that critical first year. One day it would be nothing more than a story they told their grandchildren. Others seemed on the cusp of utter disaster, ready to topple over the edge into starvation, disease, or total madness.

It made one think. If this motley and tattered lot were the survivors, the seeds of the future generations to come, how different would the America of their children and grandchildren be? This experience would be formative for them. Gunfire, screams, hunger, and horrific sights would be scrawled into their living memory.

They would most certainly be harder people, distrustful and independent. They would never again be as trustful of comfort, technology, and convenience. They would see it for what it was—a fleeting illusion that could be gone in a second, without warning or apology. They would never have the faith in those luxuries that previous generations so blindly placed there.

A few minutes of wandering the armed and wary crowd brought Hugh to the vendor space he was looking for. The hulking Ian was sitting at his booth, smoking a curled pipe. The aroma of that smoke told Hugh it wasn't the same plant he was carrying in his pocket. Ian used a bicycle to transport his wares, towing a trailer that had originally been designed for hauling children. With his assortment of rings, leather wrist bands, and piercings, he looked like a man who'd been preparing for the apocalypse most of his adult life. If not in skills, certainly in his personal appearance.

"Ian," Hugh said, throwing up a hand as he approached the booth.

"Hugh! How's it going, my brother? Haven't laid eyes on you in a while."

"Wouldn't even know where to start," Hugh replied. "Crazy times. Lots happening."

Ian bobbed his head through the cloud of smoke. "That's a fact. Crazy times indeed."

Hugh stepped around the blanket of wares and sat down cross-legged on the ground near Ian. He'd only spoken to him a couple of times, but they'd instantly hit it off. Ian was someone Hugh would have been friends with in the old world if they'd crossed paths.

Ian held the pipe aloft. "Toke of the devil's weed?"

Hugh shook his head. "No thanks. I've already elevated paranoia to an art form. Don't need to throw gas on the fire."

Ian chuckled. "A healthy paranoia keeps one alive these days. It's a useful state of mind."

"Truth," Hugh agreed. "How have things been around here? I've been busy for a few weeks and haven't made it into town."

"The market keeps growing. I swear there are more folks every day. I don't know where the hell they're all coming from because I didn't know there were this many townspeople still alive."

"I guess word is spreading and they're rolling in from the outlying communities."

Ian took a hit of his pipe, held the smoke, then blew it out his nostrils. "Must be. Some of them even camp here overnight."

"Who are the newcomers? Buyers or sellers?"

"Both," Ian replied. "This place has become the hub of the community. There's even a guy doing tattoos now and he's not half bad. I talked to him the other day and he has a shop over in Wallace County but attends markets and festivals to bring in new customers."

"Is he doing any business?"

Ian gave a hearty nod. "Folks are becoming more tribal than they used to be. They're forming into clans and choosing to mark themselves to show their affiliation. People used to distinguish themselves with their clothing, their cars, and the technology they owned. None of those things matter anymore. People are going back to body modification as a way of making a statement."

"That makes sense, but it's nothing I would have predicted."

"It probably wouldn't have come to this if the event hadn't persisted so long. You leave people to their own devices for a year and society changes. New cultures are forming and I'm not sure they'll all go away just because the lights come back on. Some of this may be permanent."

Hugh knew he was correct. It all went back to what he'd been thinking about earlier. This wasn't just a life-changing event, it was an event that could change American culture forever. Then something Ian had said a moment earlier came back to Hugh. "You mentioned the tattoo guy was going to markets and festivals. What kind of festivals?"

Ian tried to take another hit from his pipe but found that it was empty. He tapped the bowl on the palm of his hand, let the ash fall to the pavement, then pocketed the pipe. "There's a few of them starting up now that it's harvest season. By God, it's like ancient times. People feel like they have something to celebrate now because they have a little food to put away. They're exuberant that they had a good growing season."

"That's crazy."

Ian shrugged. "Maybe, but wait and see if there's not an outgrowth of weird religions coming from this experience. Pagans and druids and shit."

Hugh raised an eyebrow. "You really think so?"

Ian pulled a pair of sunglasses from his pocket. They had round pink lenses and hooked earpieces. He planted them on his face and grinned at the pleasant change in the appearance of the world. "Yeah, this event has the potential to rewrite religion for some groups. Think about it. The notion of sacrificing a member of the village to assure a good harvest seemed ludicrous to people a few years ago. Now I'd bet there are folks out there who'd see that as a small price to pay for the guarantee of enough food to get them through the winter."

Hugh turned over the implications of Ian's words for a moment. It made sense. He had to believe there were probably cults and pagan groups being formed around the country at this very moment. Desperation had a way of changing a person's spiritual beliefs. He'd seen it before on a much smaller scale, the way the loss of a loved one could affect a person's feelings about spirituality. Sometimes they lost their faith. In other cases, they suddenly found themselves believing in mediums who could reconnect them with their deceased loved one.

"I haven't heard about any festivals around here," he said, "but I assume they can't be too far away if vendors are traveling to them."

"They're around. Floyd County is having one. Grayson, too. That's what I hear. Damascus, Virginia is probably the closest. They stagger the schedule so the vendors and musicians can attend one and have enough time to travel to the next one."

Hugh chuckled. "Festivals aren't something I expected to be hearing about. Feuds, battles, and wars, but not festivals."

"Hell, I never expected there would be weed vendors selling their crop at the local farmer's market, but here we are." Ian patted the pocket containing his pipe to emphasize the point.

"It appears you did some bartering with them, my friend."

"We did some trading." Ian grinned. "By the way, you see that box truck over there?"

Hugh looked around but didn't see any truck. "Where?"

Ian tipped his head, gesturing toward an abandoned furniture delivery truck parked in a field near a dentist's office. "There."

"Oh, I see it now."

"The weed vendors aren't the craziest part. There's been a fellow here for a couple of days who has two girls working in there. He only takes silver coins, liquor, and ammunition."

Hugh thought he understood, but he wasn't certain. "Working?"

"As in turning tricks," Ian confirmed.

"I'd heard there was a brothel in town, in one of the old houses." Hugh gestured toward the downtown area. " Is it the same people?"

"No. Different people."

Hugh had lost track of just how many times he'd been shocked that morning by information he'd heard. "Wouldn't have figured this for a two whorehouse town."

Ian cracked up. "Me neither, mate. I haven't talked to the guy at the truck, but one of the other vendors did. He said they don't live here. They travel a circuit of small towns on foot and stay until they get run off. They have little two-wheeled garden carts that they carry their belongings in."

"I'm surprised they get run off. With the state of things, who's offended by a little prostitution?"

"It's not the good and proper people of the towns running them off. It's the competition. Know what I'm saying?"

"Ah, I get it now."

"And it'll happen here any day now. Rumor is, the brothel in town has connections."

"Connections? To whom?"

"I'm not one hundred percent certain," Ian admitted. "I was fairly new to the town when the lights went out, so I don't know all the players. Some say it's one of the county politicians."

Even though Ian had offered most of this information up on his own in the course of casual conversation, Hugh didn't want to give the impression that he was being too inquisitive. He was burning up with curiosity but decided to wait with the rest of his questions. There would be other opportunities.

Hugh was pleased that he'd not only learned a few things about the community in this brief conversation, but he'd learned a few things about Ian, too. More accurately, he'd confirmed some things he'd suspected about Ian based on previous conversations. He understood now that Ian was an astute, intelligent observer of what went on around him. Perhaps more importantly, it was clear that Ian trusted him to a degree, perhaps sensing a kindred spirit of sorts. That was how Hugh felt about Ian, too. They were similar personalities who'd arrived at this place and time through completely different paths.

In his long and varied career history, Hugh had never been an interrogator, but he possessed a natural ability to cultivate sources. He was able to befriend people and get them to share information when he needed them to. He knew this was a skill one either had or they didn't. He'd been born with it and had gotten even better at it over the years.

One of the things he'd learned was that he sometimes had to give up a little about himself to cement the relationship. It had to be a two-way exchange. He had to give to get. That showed trust and demonstrated that he valued the bond. It was time for Hugh to share a little. Keeping his voice fairly low, Hugh posed a question.

"So, just between us, how do you feel about the current government most days?"

Ian chuckled. "Greedy bastards who are only out for themselves. They'll tell any lie that will keep them in power."

"That's about the size of it. Have you been hearing any scuttlebutt about how things are going at the national level?"

"Everything I hear has passed through so many hands I wouldn't take a word of it for gospel."

Hugh understood. Were he in Ian's shoes, his resources would probably be just as questionable. However, that wasn't the case with Jim's people. Hugh's resources were much more considerable. They had radios and had been in contact with actual human assets such as the Mad Mick and the energy restoration group who'd passed through the valley.

"I get a lot of information, Ian. Can I trust you with a few things?"

Ian extended a meaty paw in Hugh's direction. "You have my word."

Hugh shook his hand. "I'm an amateur radio operator and I have a setup in the community where I live. I hear a lot of information from all over the country and there's a certain consensus to what I'm hearing. If you hear a story from one man, it might be bullshit. If you hear the same story from a hundred men with no connection between them, then you start to take it a bit more seriously."

"I'm nearly afraid to ask, my friend. Sometimes ignorance is bliss. But what are you hearing?"

Hugh went on to explain the highlights of the comfort camp system, which Ian had heard of, and the presence of UN troops, which he hadn't. Several times they had to pause for Ian to deal with customers or because someone lingered within earshot. Without disclosing the experience they'd recently had with the Mad Mick paying a visit to their valley, Hugh went on to talk about the larger struggle taking place within the government. This was information they'd first received from the men with the energy recovery group that had wandered into the valley, and it had been verified by the Mad Mick.

Ian absorbed it all with a stoic acceptance, keeping his eyes on the crowd for most of the time. Occasionally he'd raise a bushy eyebrow or frown. When Hugh was finally done with his abridged version of the state of the nation, Ian shook his head.

"All I can say is that I'm glad that mess is far removed from our little hamlet. Those things don't seem to affect us as directly as they once did."

"But they do," Hugh countered. "I have a friend who is directly impacted by all this craziness. Perhaps you heard about the attack on the power plant?"

Ian smiled faintly. "Of course. Don't tell me you're friends with the man they put the bounty on? That's been the talk of the town all summer."

"I *do* know the guy," Hugh replied. "We go way back."

"Well, for what it's worth, I support his actions. It's vile what the government was trying to do, though he kind of opened up a big can of worms for himself. At least from what I've heard."

"Then what you've heard is accurate. He's had a rough go of it. Then we learned something even crazier about two weeks ago."

Ian gave Hugh a wary look. "It would have to be pretty crazy to top everything you've already told me."

Their conversation was halted again as a kid approached. He removed a bottle of Xanax from a fanny pack and held it out for Ian to see. He was careful to not let anyone else see the bottle, not wanting anyone to try to take it from him.

"What you wanting?" Ian asked.

"I'll give you one pill for one of those spikes," the kid said, pointing to one of the icepick-style weapons that Ian fabricated.

Ian shook his head. "Two pills."

The kid frowned, considered it, then shook two pills out into his hand. He handed them over to Ian, who dropped them into a tin he kept in his pocket. He showed the kid how to carry and use the weapon, then the kid wandered off with it tucked into his belt.

Ian tossed his head toward the kid's back as he left. "There's a lot of them out there like that. Kids with no parents now, getting by the best they can. Lots of predators taking advantage of them. People assume they can steal from them because they're kids. They need to be armed or they don't have a chance."

"That kid would be a lot better off if he'd been raised around guns," Hugh said. "I'm not insulting your merchandise, but I'd take a gun over a stabby thing most days."

"Oh, I agree with you a hundred percent, Hugh. A lot of people have come to that conclusion too late, though. They come to me as a last resort because they can't find guns. But back to your story."

"Again, I'm trusting this to stay between us, Ian. This is sensitive and it's part of why I'm going to be hanging out at the market a lot more."

"You have my word."

"The government sent a man to kill my friend. They've built a network of security contractors, rats, and spies to help them keep up with what they label as 'insurgent' activity. The government plans to weed out these threats so they can get on with their plan of establishing comfort camps."

Ian twisted in his seat and stared at Hugh, his eyes barely visible through the dark pink lenses. "Surely you're not implying that such a network exists here in *this* community."

"Oh, I certainly am. I know it does because we got verification of it straight from the assassin's mouth. There are local people feeding information into this spy network and I'd like to know who they are. No one in this community is safe when people are being paid for information. Hell, someone could make up anything just to gain favor with the people in power."

"So, you're here to flush out rats?"

Hugh smiled. "I am."

Ian studied the crowd moving through the market with a new eye. "Alright then. Game on."

7

———

After leaving Ian, Hugh found Pops. The two visited several booths together, touching base with Randi and Pete, then Gary's group. It was agreed they would leave as individual groups and meet up just outside of town. The market activity began to taper off in the early afternoon and most of the vendors started packing up around that time.

Hugh picked up their horses, promising Hatfield he'd bring him more tobacco the next day, then he and Pops left the market. Neither had purchased anything of consequence, other than to barter with the food vendors. Pops had sampled more than Hugh, bartering off over a dozen rounds of .22 shells for a variety of treats. He'd had grilled jalapeno poppers stuffed with homemade cheese, then some homemade pork rinds, known as "cracklins" to country folk. He'd also tried the rabbit kebabs and some sticky popcorn balls made with honey and cinnamon.

Pops was quiet on the ride from town and Hugh assumed he was beat. Between his age, the heat of the day, and the ride on horseback, this was a higher level of activity than he was used to. Even though most of Pops' day had been spent socializing, that could be tiring when one was out of practice.

They'd agreed to meet up with the others at the river crossing into the valley. Although they didn't need to cross there any longer since the bridge had been rebuilt, it was still a good spot to meet. Hugh suggested they climb off their horses and sit along the cool river bank while they waited. After a day of walking on hot asphalt, they took their shoes off and soaked their baked feet in the cool creek water.

Hugh dipped a bandana in the river and handed it over to Pops. "Put this on the back of your neck. You look like you're a little overheated."

Pops took the bandana, wiped his face with it, then plastered it to the back of his neck. "Ah, that feels good."

"You have to be careful in this heat and stay hydrated. We all do."

"It's not just the heat that's bothering me," Pops said, staring at the creek. "It's everything I found out back there at the market."

"What did you learn? Anything useful?"

Pops shook his head. "Nothing specific to what we were looking for. Just bad news and more bad news. Sad stories that I wish I'd never heard. It was utterly depressing."

"You don't have to go back tomorrow if you don't want to. If it's too much..."

"Nah, I need to go. All of the things I told Jim in the barn were true. I know this town and these people. I saw a constant stream of people I knew today. People I've known since they were kids. The stories they told were a little overwhelming. They made me realize how good we have it. Despite all we've been through, we're doing better than most."

Hugh tossed a rock into the creek, aiming for a fat water snake curled up on a distant rock. He missed but it was close enough to make the snake ooze into the water and swim off. "I could have told you that, Pops."

"Jim told me that all the time, but I didn't want to listen. I guess I wanted to believe that most people were living in a situation similar to ours. Clearly, they weren't."

"This isn't camping—it's long-term survival. Other people

couldn't be living like you guys unless they'd put in the level of advance preparation that Jim did. Most people didn't do that."

Pops bobbed his head, staring at the water. "I get that now."

"What kind of things did you hear?"

"Nana and I have lost a lot of friends. Perhaps all of them. People our age haven't fared all that well unless they had family they could move in with. A lot of the people we went to church with, the people we worked with over the years, they're gone. They passed away over the winter or just plain disappeared." Even the tone of his voice revealed that he was still trying to process this information. It was beyond anything he'd expected to hear.

"I'm sure you've heard us talking about this before, but all of the official studies put the death rates as being pretty high after an event like this. A winter without power, medical care, and food is devastating to a population. The elderly and sick are especially vulnerable."

"Everyone I ran into today was friendly and excited at first. It was like old times. Then, without fail, every conversation turned dark. There was nothing good to talk about. Everyone was struggling. They all had news of some mutual friend who'd passed away. After a while, I didn't want to talk to anyone else because I knew what was coming. They'd just be carrying more stories about more dead friends that I didn't want to hear."

Hugh understood. "That is a lot to deal with if you weren't expecting it."

"Is that what you expect now when you see someone you know? Stories of death and loss and suffering?"

Hugh nodded.

Pops shook his head in disgust. "When people asked how I was doing, I had to make something up. I knew I was supposed to keep quiet about the valley, but it didn't really matter. I'd have felt guilty telling them the truth anyway. Who wants to admit you're doing well when everyone else is suffering? It's safer to claim you're miserable like everyone else."

This was probably the most Hugh and Pops had ever talked. They were friendly but not close. Hugh was Jim's friend and he listened when Jim complained about his dad, but he tried to stay out of it. Everyone had conflicts with their parents and it was best to steer clear of them.

Yet it was hard not to be sympathetic to Pops in this situation. It was obvious that his time at the market had been life-altering. He'd seen firsthand a lot of the things that Jim had tried in vain to explain to him over the winter. While Pops had been able to shut out his son's words, he could not shut out all of the stories he'd heard this morning.

"Listen, Pops, I'm not a father so take this for what it's worth. I can see how it might be hard to accept that your son has insights that you don't have. You probably still see him as a kid. Besides, Jim is opinionated and can be kind of abrasive sometimes."

Pops frowned at the water. "That's an understatement."

Hugh laughed. "Yeah, it might be, but he does know what he's talking about. He's tried to insulate you all from the struggles going on outside of the valley. You can see what he's talking about now, can't you? The risk of letting desperate people know you're doing well is that they'll want to come share in your bounty. Then it's not a bounty anymore. Suddenly there's not enough to go around and all the preparations you made—all that you sacrificed to prepare for your family's safety—is gone in the blink of an eye. That's how fast it can happen if word leaks out."

"I get it now. I probably owe him an apology."

"Are you sure you want to do that?" Hugh teased. "It might go to his head."

Pops waved him off. "Let it go to his head. I still need to say it. It'll make me feel better."

The plodding of distant hooves on the road caught their attention. Soon Pete and Randi joined them, cooling off in the water. Gary's group wasn't far behind. Despite their weariness, Pops encouraged everyone to splash some cool water on themselves before they rode on toward the valley.

Watching from the river bank, Hugh noticed that everyone looked much as Pops had. They were tired, drained, and overloaded from the experience of spending so much time around so many suffering people. He was certain they'd all heard stories today that they'd have preferred not to hear.

He hoped they'd garnered some useful information, too. He wanted to start peppering them with questions but restrained himself. There was no use making them tell their stories twice. They'd reach home soon enough and Jim would start his interrogation.

Hugh didn't feel as drained as the rest of the group. While he wasn't exactly energized by the experience of going into town, it felt no worse than any other day. Perhaps he'd spent so much of his life in third-world countries that he was a little more immune to suffering than the rest of these people. He'd seen ugliness enough that it no longer shocked him. He had his own ways of shutting it out and dealing with it, which was a skill people had to develop to keep their sanity sometimes. If this group kept going to the market, they'd eventually develop those same coping skills.

Hugh climbed back onto his horse and the rest of the group took that as a signal that it was time to go. He waited until they were all mounted, then led the group back onto the road and toward the bridge. They were a bit more talkative now, the cold water and familiar territory having had a restorative effect on them.

After they'd gone two more miles, Hugh fished his radio from a cargo pocket and contacted Jim.

"Hey, guys, good to hear from you. Can everyone come by first thing to give me an update?"

Hugh turned around to check out the faces of the other riders. Debra was scowling. She nudged her horse forward and reached out her hand for Hugh's radio. He handed it over.

"Jim, this is Debra. That's not just a no, that's a *hell* no. I need to get home, cool off, eat something, and change into cooler clothes. It's been a long day. We'll head over to your place after dinner. Is that clear?" She released the mic button and waited on his response.

Hugh grinned, seeing Debra's expression out of the corner of his eye. Like the tone of her voice, it left no room for argument. She was too hot and tired to be grilled by Jim right now.

"Uh, okay Debra. Sounds...fine. I'll see you whenever you guys make it over."

She handed the radio back to Hugh with a satisfied expression on her face. Hugh caught Gary grinning, too.

Debra saw them looking at each other and threw her hands up in the air. "Am I wrong?"

"No ma'am," Hugh replied.

Debra looked around the group. "Anyone else?"

Pops elbowed Pete. "Not sure that gets us off the hook. We have to live with him."

"You're probably right."

They all split up at Jim's gate, heading toward home and family, with plans to get together at Jim's barn after dinner that night. Randi returned home by the road instead of taking the shortcut behind Jim's house. She too must have been afraid that she wouldn't get away from Jim if he started badgering her about the market. As far as she was concerned, her day there had been a loss. She hadn't learned a single thing about Charlie.

Hugh, Pete, and Pops opened the gate and rode down the long driveway toward home. In the distance, they could see Jim waiting on them in front of the barn.

"Reckon he stood there all day?" Pete asked.

Hugh chuckled. "Maybe. You know it killed him to think he might be missing something."

8

Despite his eagerness to hear how the day at the market had gone, Jim attempted to show restraint. Perhaps Debra's remarks over the radio had reminded him of how tired everyone might be after the long, hot day. It was a reminder to be patient. This was a marathon and not a sprint. It was a long-term intelligence strategy and this was only day one.

Bearing this in mind, Jim focused on the needs of those returning from town and put his questions aside for later. He helped Hugh, Pops, and Pete unload their gear and care for their horses. He retrieved a gallon jar from the spring box and led them onto the front porch. Sliced peaches bobbed in the dark tea as Jim poured them each a glass. Everyone kept looking at Jim expectantly, waiting for the barrage of questions, but he held his tongue.

"Can I fix you all anything to eat?" Ellen asked.

"Pops needs a nap," Nana interjected. "He looks tired."

Pops drained his glass and got up from the table. "I think you're right." He patted Jim on the shoulder and headed back through the stuffy house.

"I'll take something," Pete said. "I'm starving."

"Didn't you get to try any of the food they were selling at the market?" Jim asked.

Pete crinkled his nose. "No way. It was all weird stuff. Goat burgers with goat cheese on them. Some kind of cookies with marijuana in them. Cat on a coat-hanger."

"Those were rabbit kebabs," Hugh corrected.

"I saw you eating one," Pete said. "You keep telling yourself it was rabbit. Looked like cat to me."

"Mommy!" Ariel shrieked. "Cat?"

Ellen gave Pete a stern look. "It wasn't cat, Ariel. It was rabbit."

"Rabbits are cute, too. How is that any better?" Ariel's eyes were wide.

Ellen had her hands on her hips, looking from Pete to Hugh. "I'm more concerned about the marijuana cookies. They really sold those?"

Hugh nodded. "It wasn't just cookies. You could get weed by the bag or by the bowl. There's no law, so people are selling all kinds of things. Weed is only the tip of the iceberg." His look warned Ellen and Jim that he'd explain that later, in front of a smaller audience.

Ellen turned her attention back to Pete. "You better not be trying any marijuana at the market, in a cookie or otherwise. You got it?"

Pete threw his hands up. "I didn't, Mom. But that wasn't even the worst of it. They got a cathouse in town."

Hugh sank his face into his hands. This was exactly the story he was hoping to save for later. Ellen's eyes went wide. Jim looked aghast. Only Ariel was excited by this revelation.

"Can I visit?" Ariel pleaded. "I love cats. Is it like a rescue or something?"

Ellen took a deep breath and let it out through her nose, glaring at Pete. "No, Ariel, you can't see the cathouse."

Ariel stomped off in tears. "I don't know why Pete gets to see the cathouse and I don't."

"Where on earth did you hear about cathouses?" Ellen hissed.

"Randi told me," Pete explained. "A man was handing out these little pieces of paper at the market." He fished one from his pocket and placed it on the table.

Jim got up from his seat and stood beside Ellen so they could read it together. It was a crinkled sticky note with the details handwritten. There was a street address on Main Street. Below it, the words:

Sexy girls
24-7
Reasonable rates.
Barter only

"I RECOGNIZE THAT ADDRESS," Jim said. "That house used to be a coffee shop before the collapse."

"This guy was going around with a notepad," Pete said. "He was tearing pages off and handing them out to people. One man threw his away after he read it, so I picked it up. I thought you might want to see it since we were supposed to be collecting information."

Ellen started to reach for the piece of paper, but Jim snatched it up.

"Oh, you think you need to hang onto that?" Ellen asked. Her voice was more teasing than accusatory.

Jim waved the piece of paper in front of him. "Knowing who runs this place might be an important piece of our intelligence picture. Someone is running a successful enterprise. They're building power. They could be an ally or an enemy. We need to know which they are."

"A criminal enterprise," Ellen said.

"The lines as to what's *criminal* are a little blurry right now with no law enforcement in place," Hugh said. "It's closer to a black market. In a warzone, the people running the black market always had better networks in place than the occupying armies. Sometimes the military has to turn to those black markets to fill in gaps when they can't get the supplies they need. Sometimes unconventional forces also use those black markets when they need something smuggled across a border."

"Makes me wonder if this is the only enterprise they've got going. It could just be the tip of the iceberg." Jim winked at his son. "Good going, Pete."

Pete beamed. "Thanks, Dad."

Ellen wagged her finger at Pete. "If your sister asks you anything about this 'cathouse' you mentioned, you better tell her it was a joke."

Pete frowned. "Geez, I have better sense than that, Mom." Just then, his stomach emitted a serious, prolonged rumble. He bestowed his mom with a pitiful look.

"Sorry, I'll get you something to eat. Anyone else want something?"

Hugh got to his feet. "I appreciate the offer, but I have a few things to do before we meet up tonight. The Mad Mick and I were able to connect by radio last night, but there are some changes I can make to my end to pick him up better. I need to do some tests."

"I meant to ask about that but totally forgot in the excitement this morning," Jim said.

"It worked, but it can work better. I'll head back down here later."

"Say hello to the Mad Mick for me," Jim said.

"No greeting for Barb?" Hugh teased.

Jim shrugged. "We were getting along better by the end of the visit, but I don't know if we'll be exchanging Christmas cards this year."

9

Jim was chomping at the bit by the time his market vendors gathered in the barn that night. Will and Sara stayed home since they figured Jim didn't need four members of Gary's family in attendance. Everyone else straggled in after dinner. Well aware of how overbearing he could be in these situations, Jim intended to make a serious effort to not be too aggressive in questioning his people.

If he wanted them to keep doing this, he couldn't make it some unpleasant chore. They might be tempted to quit if they knew they were going to face some painful interrogation at the end of each day. He decided the best way to start might be to let everyone tell their own story, then he could ask for elaboration where needed.

"Let's start by going around the room," he suggested when everyone was seated. "Just give me an overview of what you saw or noticed today. You can read from your notes if you have any. Share anything that stuck out to you."

Debra and Gary went first. As vendors, they had a good day of trading. They found several of the things on their want list and had also fetched good prices for some of the items they sold. Discussions they had with customers gave them an idea of other popular goods they intended to take when they went back tomorrow.

"Any indications if there are people out there with the buying power to purchase guns?" Jim asked. "We have a few that we don't need, but I don't want to send any with you unless it's worthwhile. Even if it's a crappy gun, I don't want to trade it off for travel-size toothpaste or old hotel soap."

"There was a man there selling livestock," Gary said. "He didn't have much with him, but he had a sign saying he had chickens, goats, hogs, and cows for sale. The sign said he'd take guns, gold, silver, or horses in trade."

"I'd trade some of the older guns for hogs," said Jim. "There's still plenty of loose cattle wandering around this valley but no hogs. Having an ongoing supply of pork would be nice."

Gary held up a notepad to Jim. "Make me a list of what you've got and I'll talk to him tomorrow."

Jim took the notepad and wrote down a few guns off the top of his head. There were some junk pistols and a few older hunting rifles with uncommon ammo that he didn't have in quantity. "Randi, what about you?"

She hadn't had a lot to say since she arrived at the barn. Pete said she'd been that way most of the day, distracted by Charlie's absence. She took his departure as a personal failure and no one would be able to convince her otherwise.

Jim, on the other hand, was almost relieved the boy was gone. Charlie had become so erratic in his behavior that no one knew what he'd do next. Jim wasn't so much concerned that Charlie would harm one of them, but he'd become increasingly willing to do violence against those he perceived as a threat to their group. Jim appreciated the sentiment but couldn't have Charlie going rogue.

Randi absently swatted a fly from her knee as she looked off into space, recalling her day. "I traded a few things. Pete traded a few things. Like Gary said, we all got a better idea of what people were looking for. I noticed that the weed vendors were making out pretty damn well. They always had people lined up at their booths. I'm not sure how you guys feel about this, but I'm determined to get some good seeds this summer and start some seedlings in the house. Next year, I want to be selling weed, too."

"I got no problem with that," Jim said. "That's a sound business decision. But if you decide to open a brothel, you might have to deal with Ellen. She wasn't very excited to hear that prostitution was being conducted in the open."

Randi frowned at Jim. "Just what are you trying to say, Jim Powell?"

"Uh, nothing."

"That some kind of comment on my character?" she snarled.

Jim flushed and tried to backpedal. "Now, Randi, you know me better than that. I was just messing with you."

She broke into a weak smile. "Sorry, just messing with you. I know what you meant."

Debra and Pete laughed at Jim's discomfort.

"You got me there for a second," Jim admitted, glad to see a faint glimpse of the old, snarky Randi showing through.

"That brothel wasn't the only prostitution going on. It was there at the market, too," Hugh added. When his comment was met with shock, he went on to explain what Ian had told him about the group working out of the abandoned box truck at the market.

"Wait a minute," Jim said. "You say those people are going around to festivals? There are actually festivals taking place?"

"I asked the very same thing," Hugh said. "I couldn't believe it either. But, according to what Ian told me, there are some harvest festivals already taking place."

Jim's brow furrowed as he considered this. "Listen, if you ever catch that vendor...the *pimp* or whatever...off to himself, ask him about those festivals. Not that I want to attend, but that's kind of an interesting phenomenon."

"Ian and I talked about that," said Hugh. "We could both imagine people getting desperate enough that they'd probably be willing to make a sacrifice if it would ensure a good crop next year. People living out of their gardens would do just about anything to guarantee their success."

Debra shuddered. "You guys are creeping me out. That's like some weird movie or something."

Gary nodded in agreement.

Jim pointed at Randi. "Before we get too sidetracked, was there anything else you wanted to mention?"

"There was one thing," Randi said. "There was a guy with a pop-up tent and it had a sign on the front that said 'Apothecary.' Being a nurse, I had a basic idea of what an apothecary was so I went up and talked to him. He told me that he sold medicines. He had a *Physician's Desk Reference* on his table and a big list of the medicines that he had in stock. He said he used to display them on the table, but they kept getting stolen. Now he carries them in a pack that stays on his back all day long. He also had a list of medicines he was looking for, based on things people had asked about. If we come across any meds we don't need, we might be able to trade with him for medicines that we could use."

"That's a good point," Jim said. "I'll check through our supplies. You guys should do the same. It might also be a good idea to make a list of any medications anyone in your family might need."

"One more thing," Randi continued. "He said there was a rumor going around that they were going to start charging people to sell at the market. He was kind of pissed off about it and I guess he just wanted to vent."

Jim frowned. "Who did he say was going to start charging?"

Randi shrugged. "He didn't say, but said a lot of people had heard the same rumor."

"You guys might bring that up in your conversations with other vendors," Jim said. "Tell them you heard the rumor and wondered if it was true. If someone intends to start taxing vendors, it would be interesting to know who they are and why they think they're in a position to do it. I'd like to know if it's someone who worked for the town or county government, or if it's just someone who thinks they have enough muscle to strong-arm people into paying."

"Like the mafia," Pete said. "It could be a shakedown."

"The county government did build that facility," Pops put in. "It's entirely possible that someone with the county is behind it."

"Where there's a vacuum, people will rise to fill it," Hugh said.

"Or where there's a dollar being made, someone will rise up to try and snatch it," Jim corrected.

They kept going around the room and Pete talked about the cathouse card he'd picked up. Hugh talked more about his conversation with Ian, including how he'd disclosed a little about himself to see if that would encourage the other man to talk.

"If this Ian character thinks like we do, it might be nice to invite him to move into the valley," Pops offered.

Jim held up a finger. "Or, it might be nice to leave him where he is so he can collect information for us. If we bring every good source here to live with us, we lose a data collection point. We need more eyes and ears out there in the community, not in the valley."

"Good point," Pops conceded. "Guess I'm not as naturally devious as you are." He grinned at his son to show he was joking.

Jim yielded the floor to his dad. "So what else did you learn, Pops?"

Pops' face clouded and he looked down at the ground. "Nothing good, really. I was pretty overwhelmed by most of what I saw and heard. It was depressing. The first thing I noticed today was that I was probably the oldest person there. What does that tell you?"

When no one took the bait, Pops answered his own question.

"It tells me that most of the people my age passed away this year. If they didn't have family to take them in, they probably didn't make it. Just like I told you I would, I saw a lot of faces I recognized, but nearly everyone I talked to had some story about people they'd lost. It was damn depressing. If Hardee's ever opens back up, they're going to be selling a lot less coffee in the morning. All their regulars are pushing up daisies."

Some smiled at Pops' weak attempt at humor, but no one knew

what to say to him. He was just coming to terms with something Jim had understood for years. Vulnerable populations faced a tougher challenge in surviving an event like this. They had to prepare differently, taking their individual needs into account.

"You want to go back tomorrow or do you need a break?" Jim asked.

Pops met Jim's eye. "I reckon I need to stay at it. I'll do better next time. Now that the initial shock is over, I can start poking around a little."

"Is there anything you think we should do differently tomorrow?" Gary asked Jim.

Jim grinned wickedly. "How about we play that by ear."

Hugh gave Jim a wary look. "That smile is a little concerning. What's that all about?"

"I think I'm going with you guys tomorrow," Jim announced. "Maybe my presence will stir the hornet's nest a little. If we give the gossip network something to talk about, it might be a little easier to trace the flow of information."

"I guess that works," Pete said, a worried look on his face.

Jim leaned forward and patted him on the back. "Don't you worry about a thing, Pete. You're not going to do anything different tomorrow than you did today. I'll ride into town last and make my way around the market. I'll be just another shopper, like Hugh or Pops."

"You're hardly just another shopper," Debra said. "Hugh and Pops never had a bounty on their head."

"There's still time!" Pops said, raising a fist in the air. "I could break bad any day."

"Are you sure that's necessary?" Gary asked. "Give us enough time and we'll learn more about what's going on in town. We've only been there one day."

Jim smiled sympathetically at his old friend's uneasiness. "I'm not saying I'll go to the market every day. I'll just go tomorrow and we'll see what happens. We'll watch how people react and how people talk about it. You might overhear things. You can ask your fellow vendors what all the hubbub is about and see what they have to say about me. My presence might shake things up a little bit."

"That's an understatement," Randi quipped. "Like calling an earthquake a little shake-up."

Jim threw his hands up and grinned at her. "What can I say?"

10

The ride into town the next day should have been more relaxed because the group had a rough idea of what lay ahead of them. They'd attended the market yesterday and survived. Now, Jim had chosen to throw something new at them by deciding to attend the market himself. As was often the case, he was the wild card. Trouble followed him like a buzzard circling a carcass. As a result, the group was even more unsettled than they'd been the previous day.

When they hit the outskirts of town, they began to stretch out along the road. Gary and his crew led the way, riding into town at a steady pace. Randi and Pete were behind them but allowed space to grow ahead of them. Jim insisted that it was better for them to appear to be several small groups rather than one large one. Any large contingent arriving at one time would draw more attention, while smaller groups would blend in.

Pops, Hugh, and Jim hung back on the empty road, letting the others get farther ahead of them. Their horses tugged at the high grass along the shoulder. The men talked about nothing in particular for several minutes—the weather, the low water level in the river, and who'd once lived in the houses that stood nearby.

Finally, Hugh gestured at Pops. "You ready?"

Pops gave Hugh a thumbs-up. As he rode off, Pops gave Jim some departing advice. "Be careful today. Don't start any trouble."

Jim threw his hands up in a "who, me?" gesture, as if he was constantly being characterized as a troublemaker when, in his own mind, his motivations were as pure as the driven snow. As far as he was concerned, it was never him that caused the trouble that came his way. It was usually because some asshole had to get pushy. If there was one thing Jim couldn't stand, it was a bully. Try to force him to do anything and things would get ugly.

As Hugh and Pops rode off, Jim gave them some space. He turned his horse and studied his surroundings. There was an older cemetery that began at the edge of the road and, beyond that, a public housing development. Despite all the craziness that had taken place in their town over the past year, Jim had heard nothing of the folks who used to live there. He wondered if they'd moved out in search of more survivable accommodations or if some of them still lingered in the recesses of those bland, generic apartments.

He glanced up the road and saw that Hugh and Pops were a good distance ahead of him now so he got moving. As often happened when he rode through this town, it was hard not to succumb to the memories that surrounded him. He'd spent most of his life here and there was personal history along every single mile of these streets. To the left was the bank that had financed his first house. To the right was the street that led to the pool where he'd swum with his friends when they were children.

Going back to the 1970s, there had been a market along this street where a shirtless man sat in a peeling red kitchen chair and watched the cars go by. He sold watermelons, cigarettes, candy, and bread. He'd let you sample the watermelon before you bought it so you didn't go home with a bad one.

A few minutes later, Jim passed the old neighborhood where he'd lived for several years when he was growing up. It was one of those archetypal childhood neighborhoods where the kids stayed out until dark, rode bikes in the street, and played baseball in backyards. Jim felt a surge of emotion and wondered if that sense of melancholy was for that neighborhood or for that sense of growing up at the peak of the American empire.

Though he hated to see it like that, he knew the truth of it. His kids would not know the country he'd known. The United States had become a micro-managed, intrusive nanny-state where freedom was a bad word. Jim didn't think it was repairable at this point. He couldn't imagine people actually being able to wrest their freedoms back from the government. He wanted to believe it was possible, but he couldn't imagine how it might happen. It was that very frustration that had made him long for a reset in the first place, for a great disaster that would purge the weak. Now that disaster was upon them and Jim had no idea of the state in which it would leave them. Maybe he should have thought that part out better.

He passed the house where Lloyd had lived when his parents first moved to town, then the coal company headquarters where Lloyd's mom had worked. On the left, he passed the lot that had once held the Tastee Freeze restaurant. When he was growing up in this slow country town on the border of coal country, you were as likely to see a horse, a dirt bike, a riding lawn mower, or a tractor in that parking lot as a car. Life was easy and people were simpler.

Memory could be such a powerful thing. Jim was constantly amazed by the recollections that rose from within him. Some memories clawed their way from the recesses of his mind that he never knew he'd stored, yet there they were. Flashes of people long dead and gone. Withered old men in suits walking the streets of the town on their canes, their wives at their sides in elegant hats and white gloves. A soldier home from Vietnam sitting on his duffel bag, eating sardines from a tin as he waited on someone to give him a ride home. A drugstore with a stamped tin ceiling and a soda fountain.

It had been a world peopled by the well-dressed and the well-mannered. They were civil, smiling folks who didn't discuss politics or religion except with their closest of friends. They understood the importance of voting and felt a profound sense of patriotism, even at their nation's darkest moments. It was a world that had come and gone.

The oldest of buildings in the town had changed hands many times or been torn down to make way for new ones. The grandest of homes had been allowed to fall into decline until they were unsalvageable. Fields once thick with cattle now held vacant industrial buildings. Woods had been dozed to make room for homes.

So many people and so many memories. Sometimes Jim felt like getting older was an affliction, like the weight of those memories was nearly disabling, a paralyzing cancer that tugged at him constantly as he tried to go about his day. He'd seen elderly people who were sometimes unable to distinguish if they were living in the real world or within their memories. They spoke to the living and the dead with equal fervor and both answered.

Jim wondered how long he had before the people he'd lost over the years came back to him, ready to pick up on the conversations they'd never finished. Perhaps they'd show up just to tell him what a dumbass he was and how he'd wasted his youth. Even at the risk of doubting his sanity, he'd gladly welcome a visit from his grandfather about now. He could use the advice of someone who'd lived in a harder world, where casual violence was the norm. A world where a man might kill someone on the way home from work, then still enjoy his dinner and an evening with his family.

He was grateful when he finally rode into sight of the market, anxious for something to pull him from the weird reflective state he'd fallen into. Sentimentality was an odd thing, a nearly useless, emotional form of memory. Jim saw no purpose for it, but neither did he know how to purge it from his system.

There were more people on the street and sidewalk now, all heading in the same direction he was going. Some carried wares to sell or trade. Others pulled wagons or pushed wheelbarrows. Though horses were not common, he was glad to see that his people were not the only riders. There were other folks on horseback, though he didn't recognize any of them offhand. In fact, he recognized very few of the people he saw.

He passed the fire department and followed the others across the grass toward the market. A well-worn path of dirt and dead weeds revealed that this was now the route most people took. It was still early and the vendor area was not nearly so crowded as it would be later in the day. People were still setting up and laying out their wares.

Jim passed a food vendor pushing a wheelbarrow onto which he'd mounted an open charcoal grill. Oak firewood was packed around the grill, split into lengths the size of road flares. The vendor had enlisted his children to tow the cages of live meat to the parking lot with rusty old wagons. Without refrigeration, he had to keep his inventory alive until the last possible minute. Rabbits and squirrels were crammed into pet carriers. After the discussion with Pete and Hugh the previous day, Jim was pleased to note that there were no cats in the cages. He could report to Ariel that the kebabs were definitely not cat meat.

A few heads swiveled in his direction as he rode across the parking lot toward the corral. He couldn't tell if anyone recognized him or if it was natural curiosity. He didn't care. Over the past year, there'd been times he'd ridden into unfamiliar situations with the nervousness of a man walking into the fight of his life. Jim didn't feel that today. He was strangely calm. Though he didn't understand why he felt that way, he preferred it over the anxiety.

At the corral, he dismounted and unhooked his backpack from behind the saddle. "How much?"

"What you got?" the corral tender, Hatfield, asked.

Jim hadn't brought a lot with him to trade. He looked down at the gear he carried, aware that his spare mags were probably packed with the preferred currency. "I got 9mm and 5.56."

"How long you staying?"

Jim shrugged. "Half a day, I expect."

"I'll take one round of either flavor, then."

Jim wasn't wearing a chest rig, both because of the heat and because he didn't want to attend the market looking like he'd come to wage war. Instead, he wore a battle belt setup that held his holster, spare mags, first aid kit, knife, and a few pouches. If he burned through all the ammo on his weapon and in his belt, he had a few more magazines in the backpack, but he hoped it didn't go in that direction. He removed a Beretta mag from a holder and thumbed a single round off the stack, then extended it to the tender.

Hatfield looked like a farmhand in his overalls and hat. He tipped his head toward Jim's rifle. "That thing looks like it has some miles on it."

Jim looked down and saw what Hatfield was referring to. This wasn't the original M4 he'd carried when he got home. It was a select-fire law enforcement model he'd ended up with after one of their conflicts. Still, nine months of daily carry had worn through much of the factory finish. The rifle now had that battle-worn finish that a lot of gun collectors tried hard to replicate in the days before the collapse.

He shrugged. "It's not a safe-queen."

"Mine neither," the tender replied, pointing to a crusty Remington 870 propped up nearby.

Jim shouldered his pack, then slung his rifle. "See you in a couple of hours, I guess."

Hatfield pocketed Jim's payment. "I'll be here."

The market was filling quickly. With this being the only activity in town, people flocked in. Despite the Old West vibe, the market was now the grocery store, the county fair, and the evening news all rolled into one. There was a musical act of some sort setting up at one corner of the parking lot. A rail-thin man with a long beard hung a guitar around his neck, while another approached with two plastic buckets. The drummer took a seat on one, then began playing the other with drumsticks. The guitar player left his instrument case open in front of them to encourage tips, then jumped in on a tune Jim didn't recognize.

Seeing a musician reminded Jim of his buddy Lloyd and he wondered what his friend was up to this morning. Lazy bastard probably wasn't even out of bed yet. Jim suspected he worried each night if Jim was drinking up his entire stash of homemade liquor.

Jim strolled up the first aisle he came to, deciding to shop the parking lot before heading into the pavilion. There was no theme to most of the vendor booths. The sellers simply threw out an assortment of cast-off goods on a ratty old blanket, hoping they could convert them to things they needed. It was the kind of roadside display often seen along the side of the road before the collapse, especially in poor areas like the Appalachian Mountains. Those hovering around the poverty line struggled to find some way to get by when the money ran out at the end of the month. They'd find any wide spot on a main road and drape their car with old clothes, toys, or whatever else they decided they could live without.

A terrified chittering drew Jim's attention and he turned to see a man in thick leather welding gloves extracting a single squirrel from a cage packed with them. The food vendor snapped the squirrel's neck with a wet pop and tossed it to his son for cleaning. He did the same with a second squirrel and tossed it to his daughter. The two children gleefully beheaded them with bloodstained butcher knives, using scraps of plywood as cutting boards. They raced with each other to see who could skin, gut, and skewer their carcass the fastest.

When Jim returned his attention to the row of vendor booths ahead of him, he caught someone meeting his eye. Jim stared back, wondering if the person simply recognized him or just didn't like his looks? He eventually figured out it was an old coworker when the guy smiled and waved.

Jim waved back, but didn't feel any need to chase him down and talk to him. They hadn't been close. Besides, it took a lot of effort to fake any level of friendliness when he didn't like people. It quickly became exhausting.

The encounter was just another example of how hard it was to recognize people these days, even if he'd once known them well. Everyone looked older, harder, and beat down. Most had lost weight. Even with the hard work required to survive, everyone had lost muscle mass. There were no more "soy boys" with their protein shakes, supplements, and gym muscles. People had the frames of 1930s coal miners or farmers—lank, lean, and sallow-cheeked. They were bodies shaped by endless labor and by walking everywhere they needed to go.

Most men had beards, which they either allowed to grow long or trimmed with scissors to an approximate length. Hairstyles were done the same way, cut and hacked to a poor semblance of the style they'd once preferred. Women had returned to their natural hair color. Overall, the tough year they'd all been through had given everyone more gray hair and left lines on their faces.

Some had given up entirely on grooming. There were knotted masses of tangled hair and dreadlocks. There were misshapen, clumped hair-dos that were flattened to the head on one side and projecting like mossy growth on the others. Some heads, shorn to the scalp, told the story of lice infestation, and it was common to see entire families in that state. If Jim mentioned that to Ellen, he knew she'd never attend the market.

As Jim became more accustomed to searching for familiar features below beards, long hair, and grime, he saw more people he thought he recognized. There were former teachers, coworkers, childhood acquaintances, and friends of his parents. Some looked at him with vague and indecipherable expressions, as if they couldn't figure out who he was beneath his layer of scruff. Others clearly knew who he was and regarded him with open contempt and blatant dislike, but none said anything.

Word must have reached them of how Jim dealt with his critics. That thought almost made him smile. He'd always been such a good, law-abiding citizen, flying under the radar and minding his manners. At least he had been, back in the day.

If people thought the stories they'd heard were the limits of what he was capable of, they were in for a rude awakening. They were in new territory now and he was a man without limits. The Jim Powell who struggled with the ferocity of his actions was gone. The new Jim Powell would stop at nothing to assure his family's peace and safety. There would be no mercy and no guilt.

When some whispered between themselves or pointed at him as he walked down the rows, he ignored them. No one seemed interested in confronting him, which was fine with him. He knew that moment would come eventually. When one pockmarked and grungy vendor gawped at Jim with open disdain, Jim tried to imagine that his notoriety was the result of being a celebrity instead of an outlaw.

He couldn't make that fantasy stick. He was not famous, but infamous. The smells of this market, of these unwashed people, the undercurrent of garbage and human waste in the air, all made it difficult to imagine this place as being anything other than it was. He could no more escape *where* he was any more than he could escape *who* he was.

11

Jim spent over an hour strolling through the open aisles of the parking lot. When he moved up the hill to the covered pavilion of the original farmer's market, he found that all the stalls were filled and there were even more shoppers there. It was a more orderly environment in some ways, with established booths and vendor tables. There was nothing orderly about the commerce taking place there, though. The sounds and smells brought to mind video footage he'd seen of bustling Arab street markets.

With no standard currency, every individual transaction was a piece of performance art and the sounds of barter filled the air. Loud negotiations were followed by mock offense, with each party pretending to be insulted. Customers acted as if they were going to walk off. Vendors folded their arms across their chest and declared each concession they made was the last. Everyone professed the items they offered might be the last of their kind and would be gone soon. Who knew *when* or even *if* there would be more available?

It was a lively and almost festive atmosphere until one voice rose above the rest and caught Jim's attention. Soon it had everyone's attention. It was the profanity-laden tirade of an angry woman and Jim recognized the voice as soon as he heard it.

It was Randi going off on someone. Jim knew that voice well because he'd been on the receiving end of that fury more times than he could count. The only thing that concerned him about Randi's fury was that she was with Pete, so he needed to get closer and see what was happening. He knew Randi could take care of herself, but whatever she was dealing with, Pete was dealing with as well. Jim needed to make sure his son was safe.

As he wove through the crowd, he experienced the same thing he had in the open parking lot. There was a swelling of awareness as some in the crowd figured out who he was. There was the same pointing and the same long stares. When Jim met those eyes, just as he'd experienced earlier, he recognized some of the faces, but not all. The whispering around him grew louder and several times he almost thought he heard his name being spoken.

Some whispered his name among themselves, clinging to their Southern manners even in this time of strife. Others spat it angrily, boldly, unable to contain their vitriol for the man they felt had compounded their suffering. For them, his name was an epithet. A curse.

Jim tried to catch the angrier of those faces and commit them to memory. He needed to know the people who so vehemently disliked him. As he locked onto each of them, he had to wonder if their dislike for him was strong enough to motivate them to conspire against him.

Were they informants or simply vocal critics? Had they dreamed of collecting the bounty on him, perhaps going so far as to make their own nighttime forays into the valley? Had they dreamed of attacking his farm? Had they laid in wait for him on the roads? Had they imagined watching him die a miserable death in front of his family and friends?

A crowd was forming around the heated disagreement, so Jim assumed it must have gone beyond the normal animated banter of commerce. People were laughing and smiling as they listened to Randi colorfully berate the target of her fury. Jim couldn't see who was on the receiving end yet. Most of the crowd probably couldn't either, but the lack of visibility did nothing to decrease the entertainment they got from it. Comic relief was a rare commodity these days and people had to take a smile anywhere they could find one.

Jim shouldered his way through the throngs of people. At six foot one, he wasn't the tallest man there, but big enough that most people stepped aside as he pushed his way forward. His insistence on getting through the crowd drew more attention. More looks, more whispers. When some people stood their ground and resisted his attempts to get through, Jim had to grit his teeth against the instinct to start throwing elbows.

He reminded himself to stay calm. No knives, no guns, no bodies. Not today.

When he finally reached the front of the encircled crowd, there were nearly as many people staring at him as at Randi. She frowned at Jim like he was a pile of cat vomit as the throng of people practically spit him out within feet of her. Pete was sitting on a bench behind their vendor table, staring wide-eyed at the confrontation. Jim caught his eye and gave him a reassuring nod.

The plan all along had been that Jim would maintain his distance from his people. While he might visit their booths, he wouldn't hang out and give away anything that told people they were part of the same group. What did he do now? All eyes were on him. He'd injected himself into the situation and now there was no backing up from it.

"What's going on?" he asked Randi, trying to sound as casual as he could under the circumstances.

She pursed her lips, bobbed her head, and jabbed an angry finger at the guy across from her. "This asshole says we have to start paying to be here today. He was looking through the stuff on my table and said he was going to help himself to a little *something* for the booth fee. I told him if he touched the first thing on that table, he'd be drawing back a nub."

There was scattered laughing among the crowd as she recounted her story for Jim.

Jim turned his attention to the man she'd been yelling at. He had the sagging cheeks of a hound dog which, along with his nose, had the blotchy red appearance that came from a life devoted to hard drink. He looked to be someone who'd once been overweight, but had shrunk within his skin once a good meal became harder to find. He had a cropped beard and greasy hair that had been slicked down on his head with some kind of oil.

Jim recognized him as one of the members of the Board of Supervisors, the governing body of Russell County. He wore a stained white polo shirt with the county's logo on it as if that logo in itself granted him some sort of authority. He raised his hands as he spoke, as if there were nothing he could do about the situation. He raised his voice so everyone in attendance could hear.

"Honey, we spoke to all the vendors about this last week. The county built this facility and maintained it. Without any system of tax collection at this time, it's only proper that the county find some way to bring in operating funds."

Randi set her jaw and narrowed her eyes. "Did you just call me *honey*?" She balled a fist and stepped closer to him.

Sensing imminent peril, he flashed a weak smile at Randi and took a step back.

As much as he wanted to see Randi deck the guy, Jim decided he should probably intervene for the sake of the larger mission. "So the Board of Supervisors is still meeting?"

The man turned on Jim and blinked with heavy, reptilian lids. Jim recognized the look. His questions weren't welcomed.

"Not formally, friend. The board members are scattered around the county and not everyone has the means to travel to town. This is my district, and I feel an obligation to uphold my duties to the people of this county. It would be a dereliction of my duties to allow people to use this facility for free. I gave ample warning that this was coming."

Everything about this man grated on Jim. He didn't like the way the guy looked at him or the way he answered his question. He came off as pompous and dismissive, the kind of petty tyrant that often showed in local politics.

"Seems to me the best way to help the citizens of the county would be to encourage commerce," Jim replied. "Let people do business and trade for the things they need. Why don't you let them get back on their feet before you start picking their pockets again?"

There was a general murmur of agreement and it irritated the county supervisor. He much preferred the official forum of the regular monthly meetings that the Board of Supervisors had before the collapse, where he had the advantage.

He glared at Jim. "To whom do I have the pleasure of speaking, friend? I'm not sure we've met before."

Jim sighed. "My name is Jim Powell."

The reaction that name provoked was interesting, to say the least. For some, it was as if Jim had dropped from the sky and introduced himself as some famous serial killer, there to ravage their community. From others, the mention of his name provoked grumbling and a barely-restrained hostility. The only encouragement Jim found in the moment was that there was a third group who did not react at all, as if they were undecided yet as to whether he was a man or monster. That was good. One day Jim's fate might depend on people like that.

The county supervisor smiled a wicked smile. "Well, Mr. Jim Powell, I am the honorable Hadley Wright of the Russell County Board of Supervisors. I would shake your hand, but I reserve that for decent folks and you don't qualify. I know your daddy and he's a good man—in fact, I spoke to him earlier—but the apple has fallen far from the tree, and perhaps gone a little rotten."

Jim grinned at the insult. He loved it when politicians had the nerve to call other people names. "How did you arrive at the conclusion that I don't qualify as 'decent folk'? What have you heard about this monster Jim Powell?"

Wright looked around the crowd, searching for supportive faces. It was a gesture designed to point out that the answer should be obvious to just about everyone. When his eyes returned to Jim, he pointed an accusing finger at him. "Oh, it's common knowledge in these parts that you're the very reason we didn't get any government aid. You flooded the power plant that would have restored power to the community. The government was already in the process of building a comfort camp to help us and that project got canceled because they couldn't power the darn thing. From what I hear, that all falls back on you."

A chorus of agreement empowered Wright and his grin broadened. He knew how to whip up a crowd. He was no novice to tugging at their sympathies.

Though fighting his way through the mob to Randi's side had made Jim a little anxious, he was cool and calm now. He was in the moment. This was the inevitable, unavoidable confrontation that he knew would have to occur at some point. He was almost glad that the time was upon him and they could get it out of the way.

"You're only telling part of the story," Jim began. "There was never any plan to restore power to our community. The government was going to use our local plant, with *our* local coal, to provide power to that comfort camp. All the rest of that power would be sent to Northern Virginia and the DC area. You're also leaving out that the comfort camps were not going to distribute food to people. They were going to feed the people who surrendered their weapons and chose to move into those camps to live. If you wanted to keep your guns so you could defend your family, you wouldn't be getting any power or any aid at all."

The smile never left Wright's face, but his eyes held a menace that his stature could never back up. He had the glassy stare of a pit viper preparing to strike. "I'm not sure where you came up with such an absurd conspiracy theory, Mr. Powell, but nothing could be farther from the truth. Why the fine folks of this community would probably have power in each and every home at this very moment had it not been for you. The United Nations might be in this very parking lot handing out food and bottled water for everyone to take home. Instead, the government has labeled our area as unstable and unsafe. We've been put on the back burner. That's on you."

Wright's statement not only provoked cries of support, but some folks even raised their voice in outrage. People had no idea if Wright was telling the truth or not, but the very idea that their personal struggles might have ended some time ago if not for Jim Powell made them angry. Jim knew Wright was lying, but he wasn't certain yet if Wright was simply ignorant of the government's true plan or if he had some ulterior motive for covering it up.

"You're a damn liar," Jim said. "Everything I told you has been verified to me by multiple sources. I know what the government had in store for us. They intended to turn neighbor against neighbor in an effort to disarm people. There was never going to be any local aid until everyone agreed to surrender their weapons."

Wright let his smile fade and shook his head as if he were disappointed by Jim's response. "That's all you've got, Mr. Powell? To call me a liar? If I recall, evidence of your crimes was distributed to this entire community in the form of a flyer airdropped from a United States government helicopter. That flyer, which I read *personally*, labeled you as a dangerous insurgent. You folks don't have to believe what I say about Mr. Powell, but you should believe the words of your own government."

Jim snorted dismissively. "Those weren't the words of the government, *Hadley*. That flyer was distributed by someone with a grudge against me who wanted to even the score. That bounty he offered for bringing me in was just a scam to make other people do his dirty work."

Wright looked doubtful. "Oh, is that right? You sound just like every other criminal making excuses to the judge. Perhaps I'll check into that bounty myself and see if it's still available for collection. That might be something important for the people of this community to know. And trust me, I have the connections to find out the truth."

From the corner of his eye, Jim spotted Pete squirming uncomfortably. At some point his son had pulled his rifle across his lap, ready to open fire in an instant. Pete was afraid this was going to turn into a fight and that was the last thing Jim wanted to happen. Hugh seemed to be leaning the same way. He stepped into the booth behind Pete, his rifle now swung around to the front of his body, thumb resting on the selector lever.

Jim didn't like the way this was going. There were too many people here for a firefight. Too many guns. He had to steer this in another direction. He turned his attention back to Hadley. "You know what happened to all the men who tried to collect that bounty?"

"No, what?" Wright asked.

Jim gave a cold smile. "I killed every damn one of them, including the bastard who threw out those flyers. If I get any more unwelcome guests in my neighborhood, they'll get the same. That includes you."

Wright flattened his palm across his chest in a dramatic gesture. "Is that a threat? You have the audacity to stand here in public and threaten a county official?"

"I don't make threats, Hadley. If you and I ever get to that point in our relationship, you'll be dead before the threat ever comes."

Wright laughed dramatically, a hand resting where his generous belly used to be. It was the shrill cackle of a man trying to fake bravado. "Apparently this crisis has gone to some people's heads. They start thinking they're Clint Eastwood and this is the Old West."

"We're getting off track here. This isn't about me. This is about the people who've come to this market trying to improve their odds of survival. I don't think you or the county have the right to charge them for being here. If I was selling here, I wouldn't pay you anything. I expect I'd be talking to you just like this sweet little lady right here." Jim grinned at Randi.

Hadley frowned at the two of them, obviously missing the sarcasm in Jim calling Randi sweet.

"Most of us are barely scraping by," Jim continued. "You've got a lot of damn nerve coming through here with your hand out. You're trying to take from people who have nothing. That just proves you're another greedy politician who's only concerned about yourself."

Of everything said in this exchange, this comment from Jim provoked a powerful reaction from the crowd. Despite how some of them might feel about Jim, they agreed when it came to being taxed for selling at the market. After all, most of them weren't there to make a profit, they were there in a desperate attempt to find things they needed.

Sensing a shift in the mood of the crowd, Wright waved his hands to silence them. "Okay, I'll let this go for today, but I can't put this off forever. This isn't the end of it. Local government will have to be restored at some point and taxation will be part of it. That's just how it is."

Before Jim could say anything else, Wright turned away from him and Randi, shoving his way out of the crowd. As Wright stomped from beneath the covered pavilion, Jim saw two men fall in behind him. They weren't men Jim knew, but he knew the type and he knew what they were there for. Armed with rifles and handguns, they were Hadley Wright's security detail.

Seeing that the man traveled with guards made Jim wonder if it was because he'd expected trouble today or if they went everywhere with him. He'd need to look into Wright. If he wasn't an enemy before, he was damn sure an enemy now.

The crowd began to break up when they saw the excitement was over. They almost seemed disappointed that the situation hadn't escalated. Hugh patted Pete on the shoulder and the two relaxed their rifles. Randi shot Jim a glance, then went back behind her table of wares. Jim stood his ground, not wanting to discuss the situation with his people while the crowd was still milling around.

Jim was startled when a hand touched him on the back. He spun, dropping a hand to his holstered pistol. He found himself looking at a very startled man with both hands raised in the air to demonstrate he wasn't a threat.

"Easy there, Jim. It's me, Spenser Brick. You may not remember me, but we went to high school together."

It took a moment for Jim to put the name, bearded face, and voice together. Then he superimposed that over a mental image he recalled from a yearbook photo. He remembered a much younger man who drove a red Volkswagen Beetle. When Spenser extended a hand, Jim took it and shook, trying to recall the last time he'd seen him.

"How long has it been?" Jim asked. "The twenty-year class reunion?"

Spenser bobbed his head. "I think that was it."

"I don't recall you living around here. I thought you lived further south."

"I didn't...don't...well I do now," Spenser said. "I was in town for my aunt's funeral and got stuck here because I couldn't get fuel to go home. I've been staying with my parents for a year now."

Jim knew all about being stranded away from home. Someone else approached and patted Jim on the shoulder, and Spenser waved and excused himself.

"I'll see you around, buddy. Just wanted to say hello."

The guy who had patted Jim on the shoulder was somehow clean-shaven and had neat, short hair. Jim wondered how he managed that because both of those things made him stand out in this crowd of shaggy, bearded men.

The man stuck out a hand. "I'm Luke Lindsey. I had you in school."

Jim's eyes widened in recognition. "Oh yeah, seventh-grade science. You were the guy always doing those crazy experiments."

Luke smiled. "Hard to get kids' attention at that age. It just got worse over the years. At least you guys were nice about it. Kids these days..." He shook his head.

"So, you're retired?"

"Retired and living here in town. I was traveling up until this disaster happened. I'm lucky I was at home. If it had happened a week later, I'd have been overseas."

"That might have sucked," Jim said.

"Or it might have not," Luke argued. "I'd have been in Europe and they weren't attacked. I'd probably have a job teaching somewhere and be living comfortably. I'd have electric lights, television, and cold wine."

"I've almost forgotten what that's like," Jim said.

Luke gave a sad smile. "Tell me about it. Now I live in squalor, like everyone else." Seeing more people were waiting to speak to Jim,

Luke patted him on the shoulder. "Just wanted to say hello and tell you I think you did the right thing in standing up to Hadley Wright. I grew up with the man and he was always a little sleazy. He probably intended to pocket whatever 'taxes' he collected and keep them for himself."

After Luke walked off, an older woman took his place in front of Jim. She wore glasses repaired with tape and had her hair pulled back into a tight bun. Jim extended a hand out of reflex, but the lady didn't take it.

"You may have been correct about Hadley Wright, but I don't agree with what you did at the power plant," she snapped.

Jim retracted his hand and glowered at the woman. "Excuse me, but who are you and why the hell do I care?" Despite the words he used, he delivered them in an utterly charming and friendly manner. He hoped his tone irritated her.

"I'm Cheryl Wilson. I was your guidance counselor in high school."

Jim shrugged. "Obviously you failed. Look how I turned out. A little more guidance might have been in order."

"My thoughts exactly!" She spun on her heel and stomped off.

Jim noticed more folks lingering on the fringes of the crowd, looking as if they had something to say too, but he'd had enough of people. He stepped up to Randi's booth and flashed a smile. "Okay, my work here is done. I'm going to head back to the valley while I still can. You guys be safe."

"Same goes for you," Hugh said. "Head on a swivel."

Jim strolled out of the pavilion. On the sidewalk, he ran into Pops making his way up from the parking lot.

"What did I miss?" Pops asked. "I heard there was some argument going on up here and figured you were in the middle of it."

Jim shrugged. "Nothing much. I exchanged a few pleasantries with Hadley Wright."

Pops crinkled his nose in disgust. "That man is a selfish little troll. I was on the Board of Supervisors with him for years and never did like him. He was only interested in what he could get for himself."

That was strong condemnation coming from Pops, who generally gave people the benefit of the doubt.

"Apparently he's not changed much. He wanted to charge folks for setting up here. He had Randi all riled up and I intervened. It went off the rails from there."

Pops' look of disgust turned to anger. "He should be ashamed. People need a little breathing room right now."

"I don't think he has any shame, Pops. Anyway, I'm headed back home. I've had enough excitement for the day."

"I don't blame you," Pops said. "You be careful. I'm going to go up here and hang out with Pete for a while."

As Jim walked to the corral, the occasional glances he'd gotten earlier had given way to being openly stared at by an increasing number of people. He was no longer a low-key presence slipping quietly through the market. The exchange with Hadley Wright had guaranteed that nearly everyone here now knew his name and face. He was fine with that. When he was done with this town, they'd have some new stories to hang alongside that name.

12

———

On his ride back through town, Jim was on alert. He wasn't particularly anxious, but the experience at the market had raised his internal threat level by a notch. More people knew him now. More people might potentially see him as the punching bag onto which they could vent their rage and frustration. He could almost imagine a contingent of pissed-off people sneaking out of the market to follow along behind him.

He stayed on Main Street, constantly watching his surroundings. With the rows of houses and buildings, it was prime territory for a sniper attack or an ambush. Across from the cemetery where he'd paused that morning, he spotted a man sitting on the concrete island of a long-abandoned gas station. He was reclined against a rusty gas pump, an old mountain bike sitting nearby on a kickstand. His shape and the dirty white polo shirt told Jim that it was Hadley Wright even before he saw his face.

Jim reined his horse to a stop and stood there in the road watching Hadley. Why would he be sitting there in the open like a passed-out wino? Was he unconscious? Was he waiting on Jim? If so, what would be the point?

Returning his attention to the cemetery across the street with its multitude of grave markers, Jim suddenly knew. It was a distraction.

He flattened himself against his horse and kicked it hard. "Go!" The horse lurched and Jim held on tight.

In the periphery of his vision, ahead and to the right, a man popped up from behind a gravestone and shouldered a rifle. Releasing one hand from the reins, Jim drew his handgun and sent two wild rounds in his direction. Jim had no hope of hitting him, but was determined to put the fear of God in him and hopefully throw off his aim. The shooter managed to get off a single, rushed shot before dropping back down and taking cover.

Catching movement on the other side of the road, Jim spotted Hadley running for cover, heading for the open bay of the old garage. Seeing how quickly he moved when bullets were flying further convinced Jim that this had been some kind of trap. Hadley had been hoping to delay Jim long enough that one of his henchmen could shoot him, perhaps hoping that reward was still available.

Jim yanked on the reins and dropped to the ground as his horse slowed. When he was off, he slapped it on the rump to send it clear of the gunfire, then took cover behind a tree at the entrance to the cemetery. He peeked around the corner of the broad old maple, looking toward the general area where the shooter had taken cover, but he saw nothing.

He snapped his head back at the sound of another shot, hearing the projectile whistle as the round passed within feet of him. Jim was afraid to stick his head out again, but a standoff like this could go on all day and he was at the disadvantage because of numbers. There had been two men with Hadley earlier, though Jim was reluctant to include Hadley among the number of combatants. Even if Jim only counted Hadley as half a shooter, the odds were still against him. He needed to push them and make them show themselves.

He extended his rifle from cover and fired off two rounds jihadi-style, then ducked from behind the tree and sprinted for a high marble monument, firing as he went. As he ran, he caught sight of a leg sticking out from behind a grave marker fifty feet ahead of him.

Jim ducked behind the base of the marble monument, then scrambled to the far side and peeked around the corner.

He could still see the leg in the distance. Grubby jeans and tattered cowboy boots. Jim put his red dot on the fattest part of that target, the calf, and squeezed the trigger. There was a spray of blood and a scream.

The man twisted and grabbed at his leg, no longer concerned about anything beyond the searing pain. He flopped from behind the cover of his grave marker, writhing on the ground. His eyes were crushed shut and his mouth contorted in pain. He cried out, cursing every member of Jim's family for the last two centuries. Jim sent two rounds into his chest, instantly silencing him. As his body fell still and his face relaxed, Jim confirmed that it was one of the armed men who'd been escorting Wright back at the market.

That was when the dead man's companion, someone Jim hadn't spotted up until this point, made a fatal tactical error. "Casey?" he called out to his friend. "You okay, old buddy?"

Jim kept his head low to the ground and watched for the gunman from behind the corner of the marble monument. Soon he was rewarded with the sight of a camouflage cap rising up above a distant tombstone. Jim threw the red dot of his optic onto the camo hat and sent a round, expecting a spray of blood. Instead, the hat went flying off his head, followed by a cry of terror.

"Dammit!" Jim growled.

Ready for this to be done, Jim decided he needed to move while the man was still recovering from his close call. He sucked in a couple of quick breaths, then broke cover. He charged forward, laying down rounds on all sides of the tombstone behind which the man took cover. Divots of grass flew into the air as Jim's rounds ate up dirt.

He was able to advance four rows before the gunman raised a heavy stainless revolver overtop his cover and began blindly pulling the trigger. The rounds weren't aimed, but Jim took no chances. He dropped behind the nearest marker and flattened himself to the ground. Partially concealed by the high grass, he proned out, took aim at his target's position, and waited.

After the concealed man fired five shots without taking any return fire, he apparently decided he had hit Jim out of some stroke of extraordinary luck. With a dumb grin on his face, he bobbed up over the stone marker to assess the situation.

Jim fired as soon as the grinning man's nose cleared cover. His round caught him between the eyebrows, punching a hole in his forehead and sending him spilling over backward.

He knew he'd taken out the two men he'd seen with Wright earlier, but there could be more. He wasn't going to take the time to search the cemetery, knowing that Wright was just across the street. Jim carefully retreated from the cemetery, trying to watch all directions at once. It was nerve-wracking. Sweat rolled into his eyes and he didn't dare try to wipe it away, afraid to take a finger off his weapon for even a second.

When he reached the cemetery entrance without taking fire, Jim turned toward the gas station and did a quick mag switch. That was when he spotted Wright pedaling away on his bicycle. The bike was wobbling all over the place as the out-of-shape man tried to make a hasty escape. Jim knew he could probably outrun him on foot. He threw up his rifle and put the red dot on Wright's back, then laid a finger on the trigger. The selector was still in the Fire position.

Jim screwed up his mouth, took a deep breath, then lowered the rifle. He hissed out a curse, then began cursing himself for his indecision.

The two men Jim had just killed minutes before had attacked him. It was clearly self-defense. While he had no doubt that the two only attacked him under orders from Wright, the public might feel different about Jim shooting a fleeing man in the back. People could be watching from the dozens of houses alongside the road. If they were, this story would make the rounds and people would know what happened here.

Why did he suddenly give a shit?

He'd never cared about the public's judgment or opinions before, but he hesitated because he was trying to make things better for his family, not worse. Something in his gut told him to let this go, but that didn't mean he was happy about it. The gut didn't always explain itself. It might try to steer you in a particular direction, but it was left up to you to figure out why.

He called to his horse and it ambled into sight at the far end of the cemetery. Jim headed for it, offering soothing words to try and calm it. When he had a hand on its reins, he walked it back to the cemetery where he relieved the dead of their guns, ammo, and knives. It wasn't like he needed them, but his folks could trade them off at the market. Even when he was in a hurry, some habits were hard to break, and he never liked leaving weapons behind.

His horse sniffed at the dead while Jim worked. Neither the man nor the horse felt much in the presence of dead bodies these days. A year ago, a corpse had been a mystery and had possessed a revolting fascination. Now they were little more than the annoying aftermath of a piece of dirty business.

Jim no longer cared to whom they belonged. They might be sons and fathers, but fate had put them in the wrong place. Whether they fell to bullet or blade, starvation or disease, didn't matter to him. In this particular case, he was simply glad the world was down two more assholes.

13

———————

Hadley Wright pedaled as hard as his legs would go. He only used the bike for short distances, so it wasn't like he was in peak riding condition. In fact, the cemetery had been the farthest he'd ever gone and now he was regretting it. He was certain the shots he'd heard meant his men were dead.

He'd only wanted to teach Jim Powell a lesson, to scare him a little and put the fear of God in him. He was going to threaten him against returning to town and interfering at the market, but things had gone south before he could even issue his warning. That one gunshot from his men, intended to stop Jim Powell in his tracks, had unleashed a gun battle he hadn't expected.

Why didn't Jim Powell just throw his hands up in the air and surrender? That was what he was supposed to do.

Hadley's legs were growing stiff, the muscles burning, but he was nearly to the hill that marked the end of this climb. Once he was beyond it, he could coast most of the way back into town. He wasn't going to the market and he wasn't going home either. He was going to what he referred to as his "office." It was a place where he could get his head together and recover from this inordinate amount of physical exertion. Once he'd calmed down, there were some people he needed to see. They needed to have a talk about Jim Powell.

Just as he began to think he was in the clear, Hadley heard the clatter of hooves behind him and to his left. He spun his head in a panic, catching only the briefest glimpse of a galloping horse bearing down on him. He screamed and flinched, the motion throwing him off balance. He got a sick feeling in his stomach as he started to wreck, the entire thing happening in what felt like slow motion. Even before he hit the pavement, warm urine ran down his leg. He'd pissed himself, certain his death was upon him.

He cried out as he tangled in his bike and hit the ground. Flesh abraded against pavement. There was a mélange of pain from his knee, his elbow, and hip. His spine jarred from the impact and the pain nearly took his breath away. He weakly kicked at the bike, trying to free himself from it.

When he couldn't disentangle himself, he threw his hands up and begged for mercy, surrendering to his fate. He opened his mouth, hoping with all his soul that he could talk the barbaric Jim Powell out of killing him. His desperate pleas died in his throat when he saw it was not Jim Powell who'd ridden him to ground, but a much younger man whom he didn't recognize. Perhaps not even a man at all, but a teenager. He sat atop his horse and stared down at Hadley with an amusement that infuriated the battered man.

"Who the hell are you, boy, and why did you come up on me like that? You could have killed me."

Charlie shrugged lazily. "I heard shots."

Hadley frowned. "You're damn right you did. That rogue Jim Powell ambushed us. He killed two of my companions and would have killed me too had I not outsmarted and outmaneuvered him."

The young man smiled wryly. "I *saw* what happened. I was watching when you all set up a trap for him. I also saw him turn the tables on you and drop those two fellers. Then you pissed yourself trying to run away."

Hadley got to his feet and dusted off in a puddle of his own urine.

Blood-tinged sweat ran down both arms. "What's this about, boy? I've got a mind to pull you off that horse and teach you some respect."

With a slight motion, the boy twisted his rifle around to level it on Hadley. "I've got a mighty short fuse, mister. I suggest you watch your mouth or I'll be the one teaching you about respect."

Hadley snarled. "You just chase me down to taunt me? What the hell do you want, boy?"

"After what I saw back there at the cemetery, I began to think we might want the same thing."

"And what's that?"

The boy tossed his head. "To see that son-of-a-bitch back there get what's coming to him."

Hadley looked doubtful. "What son-of-a-bitch might you be referring to?"

"Jim Powell."

The boy had Hadley's attention now. "And just what did Jim Powell ever do to you?"

"He got my mother killed. I reckon he felt bad about it cause he took me in to raise for a while. Then he got tired of taking care of me. Decided I was too much trouble. His people threw me out a couple of weeks back and I've been on my own since then."

Hadley raised an eyebrow. "You *lived* with Jim Powell?"

The boy nodded. "I did. I can tell you anything you might want to know about him. I know how many people he's got and how many guns. I know how to get into his valley without getting caught. The only catch is that I want to be in on it. I want to see his face when he finds out it was me who gave him up."

Hadley slowly raised a hand and approached the gun-wielding boy. "I'm Hadley Wright, county supervisor for this here district. What might your name be, son?"

The boy took the hand and grinned as he shook. "My name is Charlie."

"Charlie, I've got some people you need to meet, but we've got a few stops to make first. It's a good ways out of town, though. Think I might be able to climb on that horse and ride with you?"

Charlie regarded the bloody man in his piss-soaked pants. "Reckon you'll need to change your britches first. I ain't riding double with a man who wet himself."

Hadley frowned, then picked up his bike, and inspected it. "Follow me." He climbed on and began pedaling. The handlebars were bent, forcing him to hold them at an odd angle in order to go straight.

Charlie rode behind him, grinning and shaking his head at the sight of it.

14

Charlie followed Hadley to a stately Victorian house in one of the older residential neighborhoods in town. The street was a mix of every style of home from ranches to Victorians to post-war brick cottages. It had probably been a lovely street at one time, but now there were no nice streets in town. There were rows of dust-covered cars with empty fuel tanks. Some had flat tires or shattered windows. Garbage collected against the wheels, wind-blown from the heaps gathered outside of occupied homes. Lawns stood as high as they had been since the invention of the lawn mower, with paths beaten through them by feet, paws, and bicycle tires.

"I'm going to change pants," Hadley spat, dragging his bike up the steps. "You can wait out here."

Charlie didn't reply, watching as Hadley pulled a key from his pocket and opened a door of quarter-sawn oak with wrought-iron hardware. He disappeared inside and tugged the bike in after him. After he slammed the door, Charlie's eyes wandered around the rest of the neighborhood.

The large Victorian across the street was painted an ugly color of green and had a garbage pile higher than a man growing in the driveway. There was a high porch outside of the kitchen area and it must have made for a good place to step outside and dump trash. Charlie saw several rats tunneling in and out of the pile. He wanted to take a shot and see if he could hit one, but figured the gunfire would bring the whole neighborhood running.

He wondered how long it had been since this fancy neighborhood in the middle of town had experienced a rat problem. Seventy years? Eighty? A century or more? He'd seen on a television show once that rats spread disease. He didn't know how that worked, but suspected these people might find out at some point if they didn't do something about all this trash.

The front door to Hadley's house opened and Hadley's footsteps came across the porch.

"Can I ride with you?" Hadley asked. "It's a far piece."

Charlie steered his horse close to the porch to allow Hadley to climb on behind the saddle.

"Hold this," Hadley said, handing Charlie a backpack.

Hadley had several things working against him when it came to climbing onto a horse. He had short legs and had never been in very good shape. It took him a long moment to determine an approach and get on with it.

Charlie rolled his eyes as the older man jostled and tugged at him while trying to get aboard. It irritated Charlie and he was tempted to swing the horse hard to the side, dumping Hadley onto the ground. In a gesture of unusual restraint, he sucked it down and let his irritation pass. Nothing would be served by angering the man.

"There," Hadley said when he finally settled himself behind Charlie.

Charlie handed the backpack around to his passenger, then steered the horse toward the street. "Where to?"

"We're heading to Wallace County, but we need to make a little stop first." He held a scraped hand up for Charlie to see. "I need to get some bandages on this road rash. Can't afford an infection these days."

"Some kind of doctor?"

"You might say that. They're known to cure what ails a man."

Charlie had no idea what that meant. He hated when people talked in riddles. Why couldn't people just say what was on their minds in plain English? He never understood if people who talked like this were trying to appear funny or smart, but all it did was piss him off.

At Hadley's direction, they stayed on the back streets and rode for several blocks.

"There," Hadley said, pointing to the back of a house sitting on Main Street.

As they got closer, Charlie could see that it was a house that had been converted to a business, which was the case with many of the older homes on Main Street. They rode into a gravel parking lot in the back. A sign on an open screen door marked it as being the employee entrance.

Hadley rolled himself off the horse, nearly pulling Charlie from the saddle as he struggled to lower himself to the ground. Again, Charlie bit his tongue, ready to curse the man for his awkwardness. Once he was on the ground, Hadley wasted no time heading for the back steps.

"Am I supposed to wait on you?"

Hadley turned around and grinned. "Nah, son, I reckon you'll enjoy this. Come on in."

Charlie looked around, assessing the neighborhood. "What about my horse?"

Hadley pointed to a nearby garage with an apartment above it. "Park it in there." He yanked open the back door without knocking and went inside.

Charlie looked at the closed garage with uncertainty. He considered just staying on his horse and waiting on Hadley, but he had no idea how long he might have to wait. With a sigh, he climbed off his horse and led it toward the closed garage door. He bent over, twisted the handle, and tugged on the door.

The door didn't roll smoothly, binding on the track somehow. Charlie yanked hard, turning loose of his horse and using both hands. It wasn't until he got the door up to head height that he heard the splashing of water.

"Thank you!" came a female voice from inside the garage.

Charlie stepped back startled. When his eyes finally adjusted to reveal the dark interior of the garage, he found a woman sitting in a washtub taking a bath. The water only came up to her waist and Charlie couldn't pull his eyes off what he could see of her body.

She smiled as he stared at her wide-eyed. "What's the matter? Cat got your tongue?"

"Uh, I'm sorry. I was just...uh...my horse."

"This ain't a garage no more, hon. We bathe in here. It's easier since we heat the water in the yard. Ain't got to haul it so far."

"I can see that. I mean, that you bathe in here. I can see that part."

She raised an eyebrow at him. "Apparently you can."

He turned away in embarrassment. "Why were you thanking me?" He heard the water splashing as she went back to washing herself.

"Because it smells in here and we've been trying to get that door open for some time. It's been stuck. You must be really strong."

"I'm just going to tie my horse off to the porch rail," he said, heading toward the house.

"Don't rush off!"

But he did, tying his reins off in a hasty knot before scrambling up the back steps. He paused at the door, uncertain if he should just walk on in like Hadley did or if he should knock.

"You can go on in," the woman in the garage said. "Visitors are always welcome here."

Without thinking about what that might mean, Charlie mumbled a thanks without turning around, then yanked open the door. He paused inside, waiting for his eyes to adjust to the darkness. The place had the same musty smell as most houses had this summer. The lack of air conditioning left them humid and smelling of mildew. The people in this house were trying to counter that with lots of competing scents. There were perfumes, candles, and a variety of other smells hitting his nose all at the same time.

"That you, Charlie?" It was Hadley, somewhere deeper in the house.

Charlie followed the voice, weaving down a hallway where elaborate trim had been coated with so many layers of paint that its once-crisp lines now appeared melted and soft. He entered a living room and was shocked to find Hadley sitting on a couch in his boxer shorts while three women dabbed at his road rash with damp rags.

"This is my new friend, Charlie," Hadley told them.

The women were dressed in a manner that Charlie's mother would not have approved of. Their shorts were too tight and too short. Their t-shirts were missing enough fabric that they no longer looked like t-shirts. They seemed friendly enough, but they smiled at the boy in a way that made him uncomfortable. At their various greetings, he nodded and shifted from foot to foot.

"You like my nurses?" Hadley asked.

Charlie shrugged. "I like them just fine. Are they really nurses?"

Both Hadley and the women laughed at this comment, though Charlie didn't know why they found it so funny. Their behavior angered Charlie enough that it made him want to draw his pistol. He imagined that laughter would die off pretty quick when he started pulling the trigger.

Perhaps sensing Charlie's anger, Hadley raised a hand. "Easy there, boy. We were just funning with you. These ladies aren't nurses, but they are good for what ails you."

Charlie looked around, trying to look everywhere but at the women. "What is this place?"

Hadley winked. "Son, this is a whorehouse. *My* whorehouse. These fine ladies all work for me."

That revelation did nothing for Charlie's discomfort. He knew what whores were and what went on at a whorehouse. This was the last thing he expected to find in town, but he expected it made sense. Outside the valley where he'd lived with Jim and his group, people were having to work a little harder to feed themselves. It made sense that people would do about anything they needed to do to get by.

"People pay for that?" he asked.

Again with the laughter, all of them cackling as if Charlie's comment was the most absurd thing they'd ever heard. This time the rage flooded his body in a rising tide that he could not stem. Before he even knew what he was doing, Charlie drew his handgun and pointed it at Hadley. All laughing immediately ceased.

"Dammit!" Charlie barked. "Y'all best quit fucking with me. What I was trying to say is that money ain't no good and there's not much food to go around. What are people paying you with?"

Hadley raised a hand slowly. "Easy there, Charlie. Just put that gun up. Nobody here is making fun of you."

Charlie's jaw was set and his face flushed red. His aim didn't waver. Whatever unsteadiness rocked his emotions did not reach his hand. "I was just trying to ask a simple question."

One of the women answered him, turning away from Hadley to meet his eye. "They pay with ammunition, silver, gold, watches, whatever they have. Cigarettes or drugs. Whatever has value."

It was the first time Charlie felt like he'd gotten any respect since stepping foot in this house. He smiled with satisfaction. "Thank you." He holstered his pistol and headed toward the hall, stopping just before he left the room. "I'm leaving in five minutes, Hadley. If you're outside, we'll go wherever it is you're wanting to take me. If you're not, then I'm done with you."

He didn't wait for an answer, stalking down the hall and toward the back door. Just before he shoved his way back outside, he caught sight of another door standing partially open to his left. Something he saw through the crack of the door caught his attention. He pushed it the rest of the way open and stared at the familiar packets stacked around the room.

Charlie knew exactly what they were. They were MRE packets, Meals Ready to Eat. He wasn't a fan, but had eaten them occasionally because there were a lot of them stored in the valley. Not only had Jim put cases of them away in preparation for an event such as this, but they'd also obtained more in various skirmishes with different groups. Charlie had never seen this many before. There must have been hundreds of them stacked around the room.

Hearing movement deeper in the house, perhaps Hadley getting to his feet, Charlie went on outside. He took a seat on the steps, blinking against the harsh light of the day. When his eyes adjusted, he caught movement in the garage. The bathing woman was smiling and waving at him.

"Lord God," Charlie muttered, looking the other way.

15

———————

"So, when did you get into the pimp business?" Charlie asked when they were finally riding out of the neighborhood. Charlie had caught the smell of liquor in the man's breath and decided that Hadley must have gotten a dose of medication to go with his bandages.

"I've always been a businessman. I've owned several businesses here in the county over the years."

"Whorehouses?"

Hadley chuckled. "No, son, legitimate businesses. But obviously, most legitimate businesses are closed right now and a man has to do what he can to make ends meet."

"So, why not take advantage of the situation, right?"

"Don't be naive, Charlie. Fortunes are made in times like this. Generational wealth often emerges from times of war or political strife. While I might be running a business that would have been considered illegal in normal times, I'm not taking advantage of anyone. Those women are well-fed, protected, and they have a roof over their heads."

"Speaking of them being well-fed, where did they come up with all that food?" Charlie hadn't been certain he was going to mention what he'd seen to Hadley but there it was, the words out of his mouth before he even had the opportunity to think about it.

"You saw that, huh? Hopefully, you can keep a secret, since we're friends now."

"So, you ain't going to say?"

"It has to stay between us."

Charlie sighed. "Okay. Between us."

"I have connections. They get me the food. One of the guys you're going to meet tonight is one of those connections."

Charlie didn't ask for any more of an explanation. It already sounded kind of fishy. He might be young, but he wasn't dumb. He suspected that Hadley was taking advantage of his political position for personal gain. If he gave it enough time, he'd figure out what was going on. Besides, whatever Hadley told him was likely to be a lie.

They approached an intersection on Main Street. "Speaking of this guy we're going to meet, which way do I go?"

"Go like you're going to Wallace County. Head out of town, then get on the four-lane highway."

"Wallace County? How far are we going?" Charlie asked. "I ain't got nothing with me but my guns and a little spare ammo."

"You won't need anything. We're headed to a friend's house outside of town and he'll put us up there for the night. It'll be fine."

"If you say so."

Charlie fell silent as they rode down Main Street, heading out of town. A few months ago he'd have been scared of being robbed if he rode through town like this, but tensions had eased off some this summer. Whether it was the market or the gardens, food seemed to be slightly more available. Perhaps, too, there were fewer mouths to feed and that made the supply go farther.

"So, you lived out there with Jim Powell, you say?"

Charlie nodded but didn't elaborate.

"He got a good setup? That's what I've heard."

"He was a little more prepared for this than most folks. His house has running spring water that doesn't need power. He doesn't have a fancy solar system or anything, but he's got enough solar that he can run a few lights. He's got this black water tank that gives hot water when there's enough sunlight to heat it."

Hadley sighed. "Running water would be nice. Hot water would be nice too. Baths take a lot of work right now. I have to pay someone to haul it in for my girls back there at the house. They fetch more if they're clean."

"Whereabouts you get water in town?"

"There's a spring not far from the end of the house. Little area called Slabtown. You know where I'm talking about?"

"I know the place."

"There used to be a sawmill and a quarry in that neighborhood. That was decades ago. A lot of people worked there and they built their houses from the slabs of wood that got cut off the sides of logs. That's how the place got its name. Everyone who lived there got their water from the same source. In fact, they were still hauling from a spring long after the rest of the town already had running water, because they were outside the town limits."

"That right?" Charlie's tone was noncommittal. For him, talking just served to pass the time and he didn't really care much for the history of this place.

"Wasn't a problem until the 1940s, I guess. Then the spring started getting contaminated from the sewage coming out of all those houses. The town didn't want to spend the money running pipes out there. They were concerned the town water source wouldn't support adding that many homes to it."

"I guess they figured it out."

"They did eventually. It took a few years," Hadley said. "And a few rounds of disease. Once it was dysentery. It spread through all of Slabtown, then on through the rest of town. Nearly half the town got sick from it. Second time it was typhoid. In both cases, the state health department tracked it back to that spring in Slabtown. I reckon the townspeople got tired of getting sick so they finally ran water out there."

Charlie mulled this over. "And this is the water you're drinking now? Water that used to make people sick?"

"Yeah, but we've been trying to filter everything we drink. Not everyone is doing that. Some still drink it straight."

Charlie didn't say what he was thinking. Surely, Hadley was smart enough to figure it out for himself. If there were people who *weren't* filtering their water, they'd eventually get sick and start spreading disease throughout the community, just like those people had done back in the 1940s. Charlie began to realize that history might have some practical use after all. Maybe it was supposed to stop them from doing the same stupid things the people before them had already tried.

They rode for several hours, eventually passing through the Hansonville community and crossing the county line into Wallace County. It was early evening now and the sun was dropping in the sky. While Charlie was glad to see the sun disappear because it brought some relief from the heat, it brought other concerns. It would be dark in a few hours and they were in unfamiliar territory.

Then, for the first time, it began to occur to Charlie that perhaps this was just an elaborate way for Hadley to steal his horse. He felt stupid. He should have thought of that possibility earlier. He reined his horse to a stop. "I need to take a leak."

Charlie swung a leg forward, over the horse's neck, and slid off the saddle. Once he was on the ground, he spun and pointed his rifle at Hadley's face.

Hadley's eyes went wide and he raised his hands to his sides. "What are you doing, kid?"

Charlie glowered at the man still sitting on his horse. "I may be young, but I ain't no stranger to killing and I'm fixing to kill you here in a minute if you don't tell me what's going on. Is this some kind of trick? You going to have people ambush me like you did Jim Powell back there at the cemetery? You better tell me the truth." To emphasize his seriousness, Charlie flicked the selector on his rifle to the Fire position, the click audible in the silence of the road.

Hadley shook his head back and forth, wagging it like a dog's tail. "It's no trick. I swear. I have a friend who lives on the road up to Hidden Valley Lake. He's a radio guy."

Charlie knew a little bit about radio communication from his time in the valley with Hugh. It did make sense to him that a man interested in radios would want to live high on a mountain, just like Hugh did.

"How does he power his radios?" Charlie narrowed his eyes, intending this as a test question. He'd seen how Hugh powered his and Hadley's answer better be pretty damn close if he wanted to stay alive.

"He's got some solar panels and they charge a couple of batteries. There's all these wires and adapters but the power comes from solar. This guy is my connection to the outside world. It's how I get news and how I reach my contact over in Wallace County."

Charlie flicked his safety on and glared at Hadley. Perhaps he was telling the truth after all. "How much further?"

Hadley Wright pointed up the mountain to their left. "Up yonder."

Charlie shaded his eyes and looked in the direction Hadley pointed. "How far up?"

"All the way up."

Charlie mumbled a curse and climbed back on his horse.

16

"They ambushed me," Jim said when everyone reached the barn that evening. Pete, Pops, and Hugh had already heard the story, but it was news to the rest of them.

"I swear we didn't hear the shots," Gary said. "If we had, we'd have ridden out to check on you."

Debra was shaking her head. She hadn't heard anything either.

"I think it's the terrain," Hugh said. "The hill on that end of town must have blocked the sound."

"It's probably just as well you didn't hear it." Jim took a seat on a bucket. "If you all had heard it and come running, the rest of the market wouldn't have been far behind you."

Randi's brow was furrowed with concern. She'd been distracted since Charlie disappeared, but news of Jim being attacked had cut through her mood. "Where'd it happen?"

"Hadley was waiting at the gas station across from the cemetery. He was sitting on the old pump island like some kind of gargoyle. I wondered why he was sitting out there in plain sight, then it hit me that it had to be a diversion. He wanted me looking at him so I wouldn't be looking toward the cemetery. About the time I put that together, a round nearly took my head off. I got off my horse and went after them. Didn't have any choice but to take them out. They'd have shot me if I'd tried to ride off."

"We probably went right by their bodies on our way home," Pete said.

Jim shrugged. "I left them lying in the graveyard. It'll make easier work if someone cares to break a sweat planting them."

"You killed Hadley, too?" Pops asked.

Jim shook his head. "No, I didn't kill Hadley. He took off on his bike when the shooting started. I got a bead on him as he was riding away, but decided not to shoot him in the back. It wasn't easy, but I let him go."

Debra let out a groan. "That's too bad. That might have solved the whole issue with him wanting vendors to pay for selling at the market."

"It wouldn't have solved my issues," Jim said. "Not everyone understands the logic behind shooting a fleeing man. People would have raised hell about it."

"But since he escaped, we'll have to deal with him again." Hugh sighed.

Jim shrugged. "I knew that and still let him go."

"He never did come back to the market today," Gary said. "I'm surprised he didn't show up and try to organize a posse to go after you."

"He's not done yet," Randi said. "Little weasel like that doesn't give up easily. He's probably working on a plan right now."

Jim straightened up on his bucket and stretched his back. "So, putting the whole ambush thing aside for a moment, was there any good gossip at the market after I left? Did you learn anything new?"

"I don't know how good it was," Hugh said. "There was definitely a lot of discussion. though. When I was wandering around, I heard a lot of people arguing about you and the things you said. There's a variety of opinions. Standing up against Hadley Wright seemed to earn you some points, but most folks still blame the lack of power on you. I did hear several people say you couldn't be all that bad if you were trying to keep the market free. You might win them over."

Randi burst out laughing, perhaps for the first time in weeks. "Jim win people over!" The idea was too much for her.

Jim frowned at her. "Stranger things have happened, Randi."

"If you say so," she breathed, her laughter trailing off. "I'm not seeing it, though. Making you into a people person is going to take more than a coat of paint. You'd need rebuilt from the ground up."

"You need Hadley around," Pops said.

Everyone looked at him like he was crazy.

He raised a finger into the air. "Listen, I learned a thing or two in my day. I was in local politics for years. A man doesn't stand out if he's among a bunch of other nice men who all agree with him. Having a jerk alongside you, someone like Hadley Wright, allows you to say the things the people want to hear. It's like having a straight-man in comedy. Someone has to be there to set up the jokes, right?"

"I never thought of it that way," Jim said.

"Because you killed all your straight men," Randi cracked.

Jim cut her a look. "I'm sure there'll be another opportunity for folks to watch us argue in public. I doubt we've seen the last of Hadley Wright."

"People should refuse to pay his fees," Debra posed. "If everyone refuses to pay, what's he going to do? He can't make us."

"Some people might be willing to pay," said Hugh. "There are always those who don't want to rock the boat."

"Then should we try to organize people in advance so everyone presents a united front?" Gary said. "That way everyone knows they have support in refusing him."

Randi cut her eyes at Jim. "Or we just let nature take its course and Jim kills him."

Jim cocked his head as if he was considering the idea. "I'm not saying I won't, but I don't think it's time yet. However, there is some merit to the idea of trying to organize everyone."

"Like a union!" Pops said.

"It also opens the door to have other conversations," Jim said.

"How?" Pete asked. "I'm lost."

Jim smiled at his son. "If we go to people and start having the conversation about standing up to Hadley, it opens the door to talk about other things. People might start talking about their opinions on me and on the acting government. Those conversations might give us insight into the mood of the community."

Hugh looked at Pete. "If one of our goals is building a picture of the community—an area study—then we need to know how public sentiment goes. We know a lot of people dislike your dad."

Randi chuckled.

Hugh frowned at her before continuing. "We know a lot of people feel *strongly* about your dad, but there's a difference between feeling strongly about someone and wanting them dead. We're trying to find those people who feel strongly enough about Jim that they might provide information about him to an intelligence network. We know from the Mad Mick that such a network exists here locally and that they had information about us. It's important we understand how that information is moving around."

"So Jim can kill them," Randi added bluntly.

Teasing Jim about his heavy-handed idea of justice was one of her favorite pastimes. It seemed to bring her joy when nothing else did. Her laughter faded when she glanced at Jim and saw the look in his eyes. It told her all she needed to know. The idea that Jim might kill those working against him wasn't just a joke. It was the plan.

17

After a long ride up a steep and winding road, it was nearly dark when Charlie turned his horse into a driveway with several warning signs at the entrance. Two mixed-breed dogs charged from beneath a porch, snarling, hair standing on end. They were like furry projectiles fired from a double-barrel shotgun. Charlie's horse startled and skittered sideways, forcing Charlie to rein it in. Hadley grabbed tightly to Charlie's waist, afraid he was about to be dumped off the back.

"Who the hell is that?" barked a voice from the porch.

"It's Hadley Wright!" Hadley called, uncertain the occupant of the home could see him in the low light. Besides the late hour, the home sat in deep forest. The dense leaf canopy filtered out much of the light on even the brightest of summer days.

The snarling dogs were hunkered down only feet away. There was still enough light that Charlie could make out their snarling faces and bared teeth. "Can you call these dogs off, mister?"

"Who you got with you, Hadley?"

"Got a boy I want you to meet. His name is Charlie."

There was a shrill whistle and the man called his dogs. A figure on the covered porch stepped to the edge and waved a pale arm in their direction. In the low light, the arm appeared almost disembodied, a thick limb operating independently in mid-air. "Come on then. Show up this late you must be planning to stay the night."

"Reckon we might," Hadley replied. "Got a few things to talk about."

"Well, let's get that horse in the barn. Don't want the bears tearing into him."

Charlie swallowed. "Bears?"

Hadley grew serious and spoke in a low voice. "The place is thick with them, boy. Thicker than the valley where you lived."

They rode to the barn where Charlie dismounted and led the horse into the dim interior. He pulled a tiny flashlight from his pocket and scanned the ground for snakes before going too far. Snakes worried him even more than bears. When he didn't spot any, he held the flashlight in his mouth while he removed the saddle and the bridle, then led the horse into a stall.

When Charlie turned around, the owner of the place extended a hand. "My name is Garvey. You're Charlie?"

Charlie shook the hand. "Yessir."

"Well, Charlie, there's a crick running down the mountain behind the house. You best get that horse some water. I'm sure he's thirsty if you rode here from town. There are buckets stacked by the door. I don't have hay so you'll have to gather grass if he needs fed. There's a couple of places where it grows thick by the driveway."

"I'll do that," Charlie said.

He grabbed a bucket and took care of the water, then set off to find some grass. Garvey and Hadley talked near the barn while he worked. When he was done, they shut the horse inside the barn and climbed the steps to Garvey's place. Charlie thought it felt more like a cabin than a house. It was set back in the woods and there hadn't been a lot of emphasis on appearance. It was rustic, designed more for comfort and convenience than looks.

Inside, the interior was lit with low-voltage lights, much like Charlie had seen at Jim's house. One entire wall was filled with radio equipment. Charlie felt a pang of loneliness as it reminded him of

Hugh's place. Since he'd fled the valley, it seemed like he encountered something every day that reminded him of life there. He missed it more than he wanted to admit.

"You ever seen anything like that?" Hadley asked, pointing to the radios.

Charlie wasn't as impressed due to the time he'd spent at Hugh's place. Not seeing any reason to reveal that bit of information, he shook his head. "No, I haven't. I don't know much about radios."

Garvey gestured to the kitchen table. "You guys have a seat. I was just getting ready to cook up some dinner. I've been out collecting mushrooms. Got some Hen of the Woods. You ever had it before?"

"I have." Charlie's dad had been fond of mushrooms. The memory of that only contributed to his feelings of loneliness.

"I dip them in a fresh egg, drag them through some cornmeal, and fry them up in fresh homemade butter. That's good eating."

"Sounds delicious," Hadley said. "Anything you need me to do?"

"Not a damn thing," Garvey said. "Just sit your ass down and stay out of my way because I get serious about my cooking."

As Garvey worked, the kitchen filled with the smell of butter and pepper. While mushrooms sizzled in the pan, he served them a cold tea he made of herbs he found on the mountain. Charlie drank the concoction because he was thirsty enough to drink out of a puddle, but it wasn't like any tea he'd ever had before. It tasted like weeds and grass clippings.

"Garvey used to work for the state police," Hadley said.

Garvey turned from his frying pan to add to the story. "I wasn't a highway trooper. I was on the intelligence end. Radio systems, electronic surveillance, and that kind of thing."

Charlie nodded as if he knew what that meant, though he understood in only the vaguest sense.

Hadley took a sip of his tea, made a nearly imperceptible grimace, then leaned toward Charlie. "The government is trying like hell to get things back on the right track, Charlie, but they've run into a lot of resistance from people like your buddy Jim Powell."

At the mention of Jim Powell's name, Garvey gave Hadley a look.

He turned his attention to Charlie and asked, "You're a friend of Jim Powell's?" The tone of his voice was no longer conversational. The words came out like an accusation.

"He worked with my mom. They got stuck in Richmond together when the shit hit the fan and walked back together with some other people they worked with. She got killed not long after they got home. I didn't have nobody left so his people took me in. I lived with them all winter."

Garvey used a fork to lift some mushrooms out of the frying pan, setting them on a paper plate. "Are you still with them?"

Charlie shook his head. "No sir."

"What happened there?" Garvey asked. "Most people don't take off on their own if they got a good thing going, especially when times are hard."

Charlie looked at the table, tracing a finger along a gouge in the wood. "Too many rules. I guess they're good people, but they insisted on treating me like a kid and I wasn't having it. I finally had enough."

"Good people," Hadley snorted.

Garvey agreed with Hadley's sentiment. "Good people don't do the things Jim Powell has done, Charlie. Good people help their neighbors. They don't work against them. They certainly don't go around destroying power plants. This whole region would be in a different boat entirely right now if Jim Powell had kept to himself and let the government do what they were trying to do."

Hadley leaned over and patted Charlie on the shoulder. "He's right, Charlie. They might have been good to you, but they shoved a pencil in the eye of the rest of this community. A lot of folks died because they didn't get the aid they should have got."

The mention of "aid" made Charlie think of all the MREs he saw piled up back at Hadley's little business in town. Hadley said that food came from his connections, but Charlie didn't see him using it to help feed the community. If he was so concerned about the people of his town, why wasn't he working harder to try and help them? That wasn't a question he could ask right now.

"Were you going to move into the camp when it opened up?" Charlie asked Hadley.

"I'd have had a role in that camp, son. I'd have been helping people get what they needed. That was the plan all along. Local officials were supposed to help administer the aid."

Charlie couldn't see Hadley enjoying all that work, but he could easily imagine him relishing the praise that came with such a role. "What about you, Garvey? Would you have given up this place on the mountain to live in one of those camps?"

"Probably not, Charlie. I have access to all the supplies I need because I still do some work for law enforcement. Right now, law enforcement at the state level is basically an extension of the federal government. We're all working together."

"So if the government said you had to give up your weapons to get electricity restored, would you do that?" Charlie asked. "That's the part Jim has such a problem with."

Hadley and Garvey exchanged a look, but it was Hadley that fielded the question. "Folks with official roles wouldn't have to surrender their weapons, Charlie. I'll have a permit from the government to carry a weapon. Garvey will too. Most folks won't need weapons anymore. They'll be in good hands. They'll be safe."

"I get it," Charlie said, though he didn't get it at all. It sounded like Hadley was saying "you can trust us" when it seemed to be the farthest thing from the truth. Hearing those words from Hadley's mouth made the camps sound even creepier than Jim had ever made them sound.

Hadley started to take another sip of his tea, then thought better of it, placing the cup back on the table. "So, I know we just met for the first time today, Charlie, but the reason I brought you here is because you told me you had a problem with Jim Powell. You understand the problem he's caused for folks, don't you?"

"I do."

"Would you be willing to tell Garvey and me a little more about the situation there in the valley?" Hadley asked.

"I guess so," Charlie said.

Garvey spoke as he carefully turned mushrooms in the pan. "You see, the old way of doing law enforcement fell apart when things collapsed. Not everyone knows this, but the government is trying to get a new system of law enforcement in place now. The Department of Homeland Security and the FBI are working with a private military contractor to build the framework of this system. As they're working to bring this online, they're relying on private citizens within the local communities to keep them informed of hot spots that might need attention."

Charlie perked up. This was exactly what Jim and Hugh had talked about. "You mean like spies or informants?"

"Kind of like that," Garvey replied. "Concerned citizens within your community bring bits of information to Hadley and I relay those concerns up the ladder by radio. The private military contractor partnering with the government is called Catalyst Security. They're still fleshing out the new law enforcement framework they're building, so right now they only have a handful of men in each state. Each contractor is assigned to a pretty large region and they're kind of like U.S. Marshals in the old Western movies. I communicate local concerns to these regional 'marshals' and they deal with those they see as the biggest problem. You understand what I'm saying?"

Charlie turned this over in his head. "I guess you're saying that you want me to give you information about Jim so you can pass it on to this marshal guy for him to deal with?"

Both Hadley and Garvey nodded.

"We've been passing on information about Jim Powell for nearly six months now," Garvey said. "Since the spring, really. Once that bounty was placed on him, our pipeline got jammed up with all kinds of rumors and other unsubstantiated crap. There's been a real shortage of true, actionable intel. That's what we're needing. Some actual eyewitness information would hopefully round out our picture of the guy. Then we might get something done about him."

Charlie's expression hardened. "I can do that. After what happened to my mother, that man owed me a little respect and I never got it. He deserves what he's got coming to him."

Hadley grinned and winked at Garvey. "I knew it! I knew this young man was going to be helpful."

Garvey gave Charlie a broad smile. "You just became what we call an 'asset', Charlie. That means you're like a spy. You share information with us and get rewarded for being part of the network."

"Rewarded?" Charlie asked.

"Yeah, you'll get supplies just like me and Garvey do. Ammo, MREs, survival gear, and even clothing if you need it."

"Are there lots of these 'assets' around town?" Charlie asked.

Hadley affected a wicked grin. "Son, you'd be surprised just how many people we got out there sharing information with us. The lure of a little food or ammo can make a spy out of anyone these days. We've got a little group we call the Community Security Council. Think of it as a neighborhood watch program on steroids."

18

Without fail, the folks from Jim's group attended the market each day. It wasn't always the same group. Debra, Gary, Will, and Sara rotated through the operation of their vendor stall. Randi and Pete did the same with the other. Sometimes only one of them would man the booth. Other days they'd all come. No one was that concerned about it as they became more familiar with the market. Most days the atmosphere was pretty calm.

Though selling was not their primary goal, they were doing a steady business, gradually converting items they didn't need into items more beneficial to them. They even managed to trade firearms for some livestock to introduce new bloodlines into their farm. Pops and Hugh mingled and looked around, but Jim had no intention of returning anytime soon. He'd accomplished what he had set out to do, stirring things up enough that those who shared information would have something to talk about. Now they just had to follow the path of that information and see where it led them.

Just as they'd discussed in the valley, Randi, Debra, and Sara took on the role of speaking to the other vendors about refusing to pay Hadley's fee. They decided it was less threatening for them to approach the other vendors than for any of the men to do it. Though some of the sellers felt pressured to pay the fee, most were in agreement that this was no time for the county to be skimming money off people who were barely scraping by.

Hugh continued to spend some of his time at the market with Ian. It wasn't only about cultivating an informant. Hugh found that he and Ian genuinely shared a lot of interests even beyond stabby pieces of metal. It was through his relationship with Ian that Hugh finally obtained a piece of information that both he and Randi were desperate for.

Hugh was at Ian's booth, watching Ian work with a metal rod he was trying to turn into a spike. He had a piece of sandpaper he'd glued down to a thin steel plate. He shoved the rod down the length of sandpaper, twisting it as he went. Gradually a sharp point was forming on the steel rod.

"I've got a pedal-cranked grinding wheel at home that's faster, but it's too big to haul to the market," Ian said. "I can turn these things out a lot faster at home."

"If it's not too nosy a question, where do you live, Ian? You've never said."

"I rented a little house on one of the backstreets above town. Like most people, I'm no longer paying rent, but I'm still there. I haven't even seen my landlord in months. He could be dead for all I know."

"I've been into that neighborhood a few times with Jim," Hugh said. "I don't know the area really well."

"I live in the same neighborhood as that little twerp, Hadley Wright," Ian said with an eye roll. "We don't live on the same street, but I pass the little bastard nearly every day. He tries to act all nice, but you know it's fake. It's *politician* nice."

"I didn't know where Hadley lived."

"He's there. Kind of behind the library. Back in that part of the neighborhood."

"He married? Kids? I've never seen him with anyone."

"There's a woman lives there with him. She seems to be about his age, but I don't know if it's his wife or not. You don't see her out much and she's not real friendly. I've seen a kid there this week, too. Don't know if he's related. I've seen him here at the market before. Not sure of his name."

Hugh perked up. "A kid?"

"A teenager, I guess. Older teenager."

"Does he have a horse?" Hugh asked.

"Yeah, which is weird because there aren't many in town. Most people are afraid they'll be eaten. You think it could be the kid you've been looking for?"

"It could be, but I wouldn't expect him to be staying with Hadley."

"Which is why I never mentioned it before," Ian said.

Hugh went on to ask more questions about the kid's physical appearance and the more he heard, the more it sounded like Charlie.

"You're welcome to come home with me after the market one day," Ian offered. "I could show you where the house is. I could even put you up for the night if you've got low standards. I'm not the house-keeper I used to be."

"I might take you up on that, Ian. I can't do it tonight because there's some gear I'd like to bring along. Tomorrow might be good."

"Then it's a plan."

Hugh got to his feet. "Well, I'll let you get back to work, my friend. Appreciate the information."

Hugh left Ian to his grinding and wandered toward the pavilion. He joined Randi and Pete at their booth, waiting until they finished negotiating the sale of some .22 rounds. When they were done, Hugh slipped around the booth. Randi and Pete were sitting on the built-in bench and Hugh squatted beside them.

"I might have a lead on Charlie," he whispered.

Randi was desperate for information, having struck out on all fronts. She didn't even have a picture of Charlie and found it painfully difficult to describe the missing boy without one. Everyone she spoke to imagined they'd seen him somewhere and in each case, they turned out to be wrong. There was no shortage of teenage boys running around the community and they all looked pretty much the same at this point. Dark tans and long hair.

Randi latched onto Hugh's shoulder. "Where? What have you heard?"

Hugh held up a calming hand. "Easy now. It's something I've got to follow up on. I can't be certain it's him yet."

"I want in," she hissed. "I'm going with you. I need to talk to him. I can make him come home. He'll listen to me."

Hugh shook his head, realizing a little too late that he probably shouldn't have mentioned this to Randi until he was certain. "You've got to trust me here, Randi. I can't take you yet."

"Why the hell not?"

"I don't want to spook him. I'm going to set up tomorrow night and keep a watch for him. Once I'm sure it's him, I promise I'll take you there to speak with him."

She sucked in a long breath and blew it out her nose. Her frown told the whole story. She wasn't satisfied with Hugh's offer. She was gritting her teeth and ready to pop. "I don't like this one bit. None of you have the relationship with him that I do. I can get to him. He'll talk to me."

"And you'll have that opportunity," Hugh assured her. "I need to make sure it's him first. There might be some complications and this needs to be discreet. We can't just go up and bang on the door. I'll explain it once I know more."

"When are you going?"

"Tomorrow evening," Hugh said. "I'll be out all night and let you know what I find when I see you at the market the next day."

"He might not come back," Pete said. "He knows where we are. He could come back home if he wanted to. He must not want to."

Randi shook her head, refusing to accept that explanation. "He's just confused, Pete. He thinks we're mad at him for not following orders and he's having a hard time. We're his family and he needs to come back to us. It's okay for family to fight, but they need to stick together in the end."

"I don't know," Hugh said. "Sometimes a young man goes through things. He needs to get away from his family and figure out who he is.

That might be what Charlie is dealing with now. It could be years before he's ready to be part of a family again."

That thought hurt Randi and she turned away, watching the crowd. She didn't want Hugh and Pete to see the tears forming in her eyes. She couldn't accept that Charlie was unreachable. She just couldn't.

19

———————

Hugh updated Jim on the information Ian had provided when he got home that night. Whereas Randi struggled with the suggestion that she might not be able to talk Charlie into coming home, Jim struggled with the idea that Charlie would be staying with Hadley Wright.

"How the hell did that even happen?" Jim asked.

Hugh shrugged. "No idea, but I intend to ask that question of Charlie if I get the opportunity to speak with him. The boy needs to choose his friends better."

"Clearly," Jim replied. "I throw down with one guy at the market and Charlie is living with him? That's messed up."

Jim was onboard with the idea of Hugh staying over in town and trying to verify Ian's report. He also agreed that it would probably be best if Randi didn't go with Hugh. "Of course, short of tying her to a tree, there's not much I can do to stop her if she's determined. You know how she is."

"I know," said Hugh. "Will you talk to her? I have Charlie's best interests at heart and I want her to know that."

"I'll talk to her, for what good it will do."

Jim didn't know if she'd talk to him about the matter. As much as she understood why Jim was being hard on Charlie, she wanted to protect him. It was a maternal struggle that she'd been unable to reconcile. Regardless of what Charlie did, her instinct to protect him pushed all reason aside.

The following day, the vendors' group went to the market as they normally did. Randi was preoccupied with the possible sighting of Charlie, but for the most part, it was business as usual. At the end of the day, when the vendors began packing up, Hugh caught up with Randi and Pete as they were leaving. Gary's group had already started back through town, toward the valley.

"I need you to take my horse," Hugh said, handing the reins over to Randi.

She took the reins with a frown. "I will, but I ain't happy about it."

Hugh smiled. "I didn't think you would be. I promise I'll update you as soon as you get here tomorrow. You just have to trust me on this."

"If that's all you can do, then I guess I have to accept it. Don't have to like it, though." Without so much as a good-bye, she mounted her horse and rode off with Hugh's in tow.

Pete had an unhappy expression. "I hope you know I'm going to have a pretty lousy ride back to the valley, Hugh. She's going to cuss and complain the whole time." He climbed onto his horse and reluctantly headed after Randi.

Hugh found Ian packing up his wares for the day. Despite the pack and rifle Hugh carried, he offered to take some of Ian's load, but Ian declined.

"It all fits in the child carrier. I forget it's even there."

The two set off, Ian pushing his bike. They were lost in small talk and Hugh failed to notice what was taking place at the fire station just beyond the farmer's market. Randi had dismounted her horse and was trying to hand the reins over to an extremely frustrated Pete.

Pete was adamant in his protests, but there was no arguing with Randi. She cursed and threatened, refusing to be sent home to worry about Charlie all night.

"But Dad said—" Pete began.

"I quit taking orders from men a long time ago!" Randi snapped. "This girl does what she wants. Any man who can't accept that can kiss my rosy red ass. You make sure and tell your daddy that."

Pete flushed and let out an exasperated breath. If the older and more experienced of their group couldn't stand toe-to-toe in an argument with Randi, Pete had no chance. He surrendered to her fury, mumbling to himself as he snatched the reins from her hand and rode off.

With a grin of satisfaction, Randi slipped on her pack and hustled back to the market, searching for her quarry. Easily spotting Ian's distinctive bike and trailer rig, she followed them at a safe distance.

She'd follow them wherever they were going. If she had to sleep in the bushes, that was fine. She'd done it before. If she had to spend the night in the rain, she could do that too. The one thing she couldn't accept was giving up on Charlie.

Though she and Alice had never spoken of it, Randi had made a promise to her on the day Alice died. She'd agreed to look after Charlie as long as she still drew breath. She fully intended to keep that promise. Neither Hugh, nor Jim Powell, nor Charlie himself would keep her from it.

20

Each day after the market, it usually took Ian around ten minutes to bicycle home. However, this time it took considerably longer since he was walking along with Hugh. It was nearly thirty minutes before the pair reached the quiet street on the hill above town.

"I got recruited to come here and work for that little software company in town. They helped me find this place. It's a quiet neighborhood and I could ride my bike to work. I might have chosen my location differently had I known the apocalypse was imminent. Being in the middle of town isn't ideal for hunting and fishing."

Hugh laughed. "I'm sure most people could say the same about their living situations. We would have all done things a lot differently if we'd known what was coming."

"It was mostly elderly folks here when I moved onto this street. There are a few left, but most moved off or passed away, I guess. I helped bury some of them, then just gave up when the numbers rose. It seemed like all I was doing was digging graves. There are still a few bodies laid out in these houses."

"Not to be indelicate, but have you checked those houses for things you might use? There's no use suffering when there might be gear or supplies around that could help you survive."

Ian didn't meet Hugh's eye. He'd hit on one of the ugly aspects of survival within the town that people didn't like to talk about. "I have checked. Got some camping and gardening gear. Some canned food. Things like that. I tried to be sensitive about it and leave things as I found them. Not everyone is so careful. The kids in town are bad to trash a place if they know it's empty. No respect."

The discussion of kids reminded Hugh of Charlie again. This generation, the kids that grew up in this collapse, were going to be a different breed. It was unavoidable. Their attitudes toward education, employment, and rules would be totally different. It was something no amount of counseling or well-intentioned legislation would change.

Hugh had brought enough food for the two of them. He'd insisted on it despite Ian's claims that he had plenty of food. They cooked on an old cast-iron hibachi grill Ian had found in a neighbor's shed after his own grill rusted out. Hugh fed it twigs and small blocks of hardwood that Ian found in a deceased neighbor's woodworking shop. He heated a pot of water and made a family-sized packet of freeze-dried pasta with meat sauce. When it was done, they ate on the shady back porch, looking out on the overgrown yard and the woods beyond it.

They talked into the evening. Hugh was still guarded in some areas, not talking much about the details of his past. There were only small pockets of his life he felt he could share with people. His high school years and the period immediately afterward were pretty routine. The years between government contracting, when he sat in the United States fighting boredom, were a safe topic. So were the early days of the collapse when he was living at the superstore and working the radios for local law enforcement. The rest of his life was a story that very few knew.

When the lightning bugs came out and bats began dipping from the sky to eat mosquitoes, Hugh felt it was time to get to work. He stood and began pulling the gear he'd need from his pack. He lashed on a pair of night-vision goggles with a skull-crusher head rig, then switched out his fixed-blade knife for one even larger. He'd travel light, paring down the gear he carried until he could move through the darkness as silent as the smell of death.

Ian watched with amusement. "I'm trying not to ask any questions, my friend, but one does have to wonder..."

"About what?"

Ian searched for a way to summarize what he was thinking. "Where you got all this gear. You have to admit it's a notch above that of the casual prepper."

Hugh grinned. "Never considered myself a prepper, and people who know me will tell you I'm not *casual* about anything. I grew up in the country and prepping is just what we called 'getting by.' I've never spent any time preparing for survival situations. I simply assume that every day already is a survival situation."

"Interesting way of looking at things," Ian said. "By the way, I enjoyed our conversation this evening."

"Me too, my friend. Not sure when I'll be back. No need to leave a door open for me. I'll be fine stretching out on your porch here. Just don't step on me if you venture out in the night."

"Whatever suits you, but I'll probably be up. I'm a bit of a night owl. I work by lantern light and grind on stabby things until I feel ready for bed."

"Thanks, Ian. Hopefully, I'll see you later."

Ian raised a hand and waved. "Good luck. I hope you find what you're looking for."

Hugh descended the back stairs and was soon lost in the shadows. As he'd walked into the neighborhood with Ian earlier, they'd worked out a route that would get him back to Hadley Wright's house with less of a chance of being seen. Hugh stuck to the overgrown yards of abandoned houses. He followed fences and tucked himself in against shrubs that would break up his outline.

When he approached cross streets, he took long pauses before moving. He listened for people sitting on porches or strolling in the darkness. He scanned all directions with his night-vision, the grainy green image amplifying even the smallest sources of ambient light.

He only moved when he was confident there was no one out there to see him.

The street Hadley lived on was closer to Main Street and more crowded than Ian's. Not only were there more houses, but more of them appeared occupied. Hugh had no way of knowing if all of these people had lived there before the collapse or not, but there were certainly plenty of them now.

Even among this more populated street, Hadley Wright's house stood out simply for the level of activity taking place there. Hugh approached from the back and saw several horses tied up to the deck railing. Hugh didn't recognize any of them as belonging to Charlie, though it was hard to tell in the darkness. He also noted the horses were saddled, as if they belonged to people who'd just stopped in for a visit.

The downstairs of the house was well-lit, which stood in sharp contrast to most of the other houses on the street. To conserve resources, most people made everyone huddle in a single room at night to share a candle or lantern. Hadley's house was illuminated in several rooms. Somehow he was not experiencing the same supply limitations that his neighbors evidently were.

On the still, muggy night, both the curtains and windows of Hadley's house were open in hopes of catching any breeze that might stir. Through those gaps in the curtains, Hugh caught glimpses of multiple people moving around. He hadn't had any idea of what he'd find at the house. Hadley, and maybe Charlie, but it looked like there might be a half-dozen or more people in there moving around. It was enough to make Hugh wonder what he'd stumbled upon.

Voices on the street caught Hugh's attention and he shrank back into the darkness. Two more folks came into sight. They were walking without lights, guided perhaps by familiarity with where they were going. They climbed the back steps of Hadley's house and entered without knocking.

Intrigued by the unusual goings-on at this house, Hugh crept forward. He moved down a side street, then cut across the paved alley until he was directly behind Hadley's house. He looked for a position that would get him close enough to see into the windows, yet keep him concealed in case more people showed up.

He noticed an old cinderblock garage building at the corner of the property. It was one of those old-style garages built in the 1940s and 1950s with a flat roof and wooden doors that swung on hinges. Hugh wandered in that direction and studied the building through his night-vision. He found two wooden sawhorses sitting outside. The tops were scarred by hundreds of cuts and they seemed of questionable strength, but they were all he found that might give him a boost up to the roof.

Hugh carefully moved one of them closer to the garage, then stepped up onto the sawhorse. It creaked, groaned, and wobbled but didn't break. It got him high enough that he was able to put one foot on the power company's meter base, then use the electrical service weather-head to pull himself up onto the flat roof. He sat there, listening but not moving. He wanted to make sure no one had noticed his movement. When he didn't hear anything concerning, he flipped his night-vision out of the way, then crawled across the roof until he was looking directly at the back of the house.

From this vantage point, he could see into the kitchen, where several people were seated around a long dining table. He spotted Hadley at the head of the table with a bottle of liquor in front of him. Hugh was stunned to see Charlie seated to Hadley's left like a guest of honor. Hugh didn't know any of the folks at the table, but a couple looked familiar. He assumed they must have been people he'd seen at the market since he'd been spending so much time there lately.

A set of heavily tattooed arms moved in and out of his line of sight as the owner of those arms talked animatedly. Hadley emitted the occasional laugh, then poured himself another drink. At times he'd lean across the table and pour drinks for the others who had glasses in front of them. Not everyone was drinking. Some guests were sipping from water bottles.

To Hugh's surprise, there was a glass sitting in front of Charlie. For some reason, Hugh found comfort in the fact that Charlie didn't appear to be hitting it too hard. Each time he raised the glass to his mouth, there appeared to be just as much liquid in it when he put it back on the table. Perhaps he was just trying to act older and harder in front of his new friends.

Hugh shifted to the right, trying to get a better look at the tattooed man through the gap in the curtains. What he saw made him furrow his brow. The man with the tattooed arms wore a black uniform of sorts. Hugh extracted a small pair of binoculars from his pocket and studied the black polo shirt the man wore, trying to make out the logo over the pocket. When he saw it, he shook his head in surprise.

"Oh shit," he mumbled to himself.

It was the Catalyst Security logo. Hugh knew a lot about that logo. He'd worked for Catalyst in the 90s. As a kid growing up in a remote farming community in Southwestern Virginia, he'd longed for adventure. Instead of choosing the military route, he'd joined up with Catalyst and spent over a decade in their employ. He had the opportunity to work on every continent except Antarctica and had seen more adventure than he'd ever expected. He'd stuck around until the company changed hands in the early 2000s.

His personal history with Catalyst wasn't as concerning to him at the moment as the information he'd received from the Mad Mick. According to him, the Department of Homeland Security had awarded Catalyst the primary contract for securing the homeland during this period of reconstruction. It was a team from Catalyst that had recently tried to kill the Mad Mick and blow up his compound. Catalyst also had some role in sending the Mad Mick to kill Jim. With all that in mind, the presence of a Catalyst man in their community was highly concerning, especially if he was allied with Hadley Wright.

Deciding that he had to hear what was being said, Hugh looked for a spot where he could hide within earshot of the window. He spotted a five hundred gallon propane tank positioned near the hedges and decided that might be his best shot. He grabbed his rifle, carefully crawled backward, and dropped from the roof.

As soon as he hit the ground, Hugh flattened himself against the garage to see if his movement had attracted any attention. When he was certain it hadn't, he circled the structure, cut across the yard, and crawled into the gap between the propane tank and the house. As he crept forward, his face brushed through what felt like dozens of spider webs. They clung to his sweaty skin in a way that made them impossible to remove. No amount of brushing or wiping at his skin made the sensation go away.

As if the feeling of the webs wasn't bad enough, he couldn't shake the feeling that spiders were crawling all over his skin. He'd been bitten several times over his life and was fully aware of how unpleasant a spider bite could be. A mild case could mean a swollen, angry, and oozing wound. At the worst, it could mean necrosis and an ugly death.

Hugh had to just suck it down. He couldn't obsessively brush at his skin and clothing in these tight quarters or he'd end up banging the propane tank with his elbow. That would be the same as ringing a gong and announcing his presence.

He tried to put the spiders out of his mind and focus on the conversation taking place inside. He could hear voices but not all of them. Some of the guests spoke louder than others. Hugh sat there for several minutes trying to make sense of what he was hearing, but then decided he needed to get even closer. He crawled the rest of the way through the gap between the tank and house, plowing more webs from his path, emerging directly below the window.

He got to his feet and flattened himself against the house. He was exposed now, no longer hidden behind the propane tank, so he dropped his night-vision back into place to monitor his surroundings. If someone came toward him, hopefully he'd see them before they spotted him. He cocked his head, eventually finding the sweet spot that allowed him to hear what was being said in the kitchen.

"It's incredibly frustrating," said one unknown male. His voice was deep and his pronunciation crisp, as if he prided himself on his elocution. If Hugh had to summarize the speaker in a single word, he'd guess it would be "snooty."

"It's not that unusual. This is not an isolated incident. There are communities all around the country dealing with this exact same thing."

"Is that right?" asked another man. Hugh knew this voice from the argument with Randi at the market. It belonged to Hadley.

"Definitely. Every community has its insurgents to one degree or another. Some are militia, some are gangs of outlaws, some are right-wing or left-wing fringe elements, but everyone has them." Hugh wondered if this voice belonged to the Catalyst contractor since he seemed to be relaying outside information. He spoke with a Southern accent, as if he might be from Georgia or Alabama originally.

"When Charlie and I radioed you from Garvey's house, I mentioned that bounty I'd heard about. Did you look into that?" Hadley asked.

That was interesting information to Hugh. Hadley's people had radio access to outside people. That must be how they were passing on information.

"Yeah, I looked into it," the Catalyst contractor replied. "There are no bounties out there. It's just not how the government is doing things. They have multi-disciplinary strike teams dealing with insurgents."

"What does that mean?" Charlie asked.

"Teams made up of Catalyst contractors and federal agents. No one I spoke with was familiar with this Jim Powell you asked about. He may have been telling the truth when he said this bounty was put out by some rogue actor who had a grudge against him. On the other hand, it could just be compartmentalized information I don't have access to."

Hadley sighed. "Well, that's unfortunate. I was hoping there was a bounty."

"Agreed," the snooty man said. "I was hoping it was still available. Then we could encourage the public to take on the unpleasant task of taking him out."

"They tried," Charlie spoke up.

"No one tried hard enough," said Hadley. "Maybe we should offer our own bounty and see what happens."

There were murmurs of agreement around the room.

"You could," the Catalyst contractor said. "Not sure how it would go over with my command though. We're *discouraged* from murdering people. Contractors like me are supposed to be performing a regional sheriff role, trying to work things out without killing. They don't want us to alienate any locals who might not have the stomach for such a heavy-handed approach."

Hugh crinkled his brow at the use of the word "sheriffs." What the heck did that even mean? Was Catalyst replacing the local police forces decimated by the collapse or had the government instituted some new method of law enforcement?

"I hope this doesn't mean we have to play nice with Mr. Powell," Hadley said. "I'd be so disappointed by that."

"Certainly not," the Catalyst man said. "We can apply pressure. We can bend people, but we're not supposed to break them."

That got a burst of laughter from Hadley. "That's why I wanted you to meet my new friend, Charlie. Like I told you on the radio, he lived with Jim Powell's folk for a while and knows a good deal about how they do things. He says he knows how we can get to him."

Hugh felt sick upon hearing Hadley's words. Surely this was an exaggeration and not something Charlie had volunteered for. Hugh knew the boy's head was twisted around. Charlie was upset that Jim had gotten so angry with him for shooting at the Mad Mick's daughter, but surely he wouldn't turn his back on the people who loved him. Even if he was still angry at Hugh and Jim, what about his feelings for the rest of the people in the valley? Could he offer up Pete and Randi to this man? Nana and Pops? Could he put everyone in danger just because he was reprimanded for going off the rails?

Hugh wanted to believe that Charlie wouldn't. Then Charlie spoke again and his words hit Hugh like a hammer.

"I'll tell you anything you want to know. Those people are nothing to me."

Hugh couldn't believe what he was hearing. He was not often surprised by the actions of others. In general, he had a low opinion of people, which was why he and Jim got along so well. Still, this was a devastating revalation. He was floored.

"Well, Charlie, hopefully it won't come to that," the Catalyst man said. "Perhaps he'll listen to reason and we won't have to hurt him."

"He won't," Charlie said. "Jim Powell does what he wants to and all those people out there in that valley follow him blindly. They're afraid not to."

Hugh shook his head at Charlie's words. Again, they were almost beyond belief. Charlie was totally mischaracterizing the relationship between Jim and his people. Jim had never led through intimidation.

Another man began to speak. Hugh hadn't heard his voice before, but Hadley addressed him as Garvey. Before Garvey finished his sentence, Hugh caught movement from the corner of his eye. Someone was hiding behind the block garage Hugh had been on top of only moments earlier.

Hugh didn't react at first, remaining frozen against the wall of Hadley's house. The longer he stood there, the more afraid he became that this person at the garage might see him in the ambient light spilling from the window. Reluctantly, he sank to the ground and crawled backward through the gap between the house and the propane tank. Once he was through that gap, he turned and crawled from the yard.

Seconds later, he was on the paved street that ran alongside the house. He got to his feet and stalked toward the garage building, making certain to lift his feet high so he didn't scuff any gravel as he walked. At the garage, he peered around the edge of the structure and saw a figure still looking around the opposite corner, toward the house. It was exactly where he'd spotted them earlier.

Hugh was angry that this intruder was causing him to miss whatever was being discussed in the house. He considered retreating into the darkness and returning to Ian's place. After all, he had found what he was looking for. He'd seen Charlie and now understood what he was up to. But whoever this person was behind the garage, they were either watching the house or they'd been watching him. Hugh wanted to know who they were.

Hugh took three rapid steps and clamped a hand around the figure's face. His gloved right hand sealed their mouth, while his left arm locked around their neck and hauled them backward. The person exploded like an angry cat, kicking and trying to fight back. They grabbed at Hugh, trying to elbow him. Fingernails dug into his forearms, but he only increased his pressure, covering their nose now too.

Once Hugh had them behind the garage and out of sight of the house, he dropped to his back, locking his heels around the body. He suspected it was a woman, but a woman could give him away just as easily as a man could. Hugh wasn't going to allow her to give anyone away though. He was locked in and she'd be unconscious shortly.

Once she was out, he'd drag her off into the hedges, then bind and gag her. He'd throw her over his shoulder and find a nice secluded spot where he could ask her some questions. Above all, he wanted to know why she was there and who she was watching. Then, if all went well, he'd let her go.

She continued trying to elbow him, so he brought his own elbows in to restrict her movement. She could still strike at him, but she couldn't build much power. She was speaking beneath his hand, but his grip muffled her words. As he waited for her to lose consciousness, he began to realize that he'd misheard what she was saying. What he'd heard as "help" was actually "Hugh."

She knew his name.

Hugh dropped the thumb that was holding her nose shut. Her ribs expanded as she sucked in a breath.

"Did you just call me Hugh?" he hissed in her ear.

The woman in his grasp struggled to bob her head in confirmation.

"I'm going to uncover your mouth," he whispered. "If you try to scream, I'm going to slit your throat. Are we clear?"

Again, the woman struggled to nod. Hugh loosened his grip on her mouth, just barely. His hand hovered there millimeters from her lips, ready to clamp down again if she was lying.

"Who are you?" he demanded.

"Randi."

Furious, Hugh released her and shoved her off him. With her back to him, he'd been unable to tell who she was when he crept up on her behind the garage. He could have killed her. "What the hell are you doing here?"

"Isn't it obvious?"

Of course it was. She was here to see if the lead about Charlie panned out. She refused to go home and leave this to him. Taking orders from men wasn't her style and he should have expected this.

"Randi, I could have killed you."

"No shit," she hissed.

He got up, then helped her to her feet. "We need to get out of here. They may have heard the scuffle."

Randi turned to him and he caught the full sight of her in his night-vision. Grainy, angry, and furious as a demon. "I'm not going anywhere until I know if Charlie is in there."

Recalling what Charlie had said, Hugh wanted to shield Randi. He didn't want her to know the depth of Charlie's betrayal, understanding just how deeply it would hurt her. He made a snap decision and shook his head. "It wasn't him, Randi. It's some other kid. A nephew or something."

Even with the way that his night-vision distorted her face, Hugh could see the disappointment wash over her. This was not the news she wanted. As much as he hated lying to her, he didn't want to see what the truth would do to her. While he was certain she'd find out eventually, it wasn't going to be tonight.

He threw an arm over her shoulder and corralled her off into the darkness. "Let's get out of here before someone sees us. I have a place we can stay tonight."

21

The next day, Randi, Hugh, and Ian returned to the market together. Just as Ian had said, he'd been awake when Hugh returned to his house the previous night. Ian was glad to let Randi join them, though she wasn't very conversational. Hugh stuck to his story that the kid wasn't Charlie until Randi disappeared outside to visit the bushes before bed. Then Hugh told Ian the truth and said he'd explain the rest of the story at the market.

Even after a night's sleep, Randi was gutted that the lead on Charlie had fallen through. Hugh had already figured out how he was going to handle telling her the truth about Charlie.

He was going to let Jim handle it.

After all, Jim was used to delivering bad news to Randi. Randi was used to going off on Jim. She would scream and curse, then probably hit Jim a few times to get it out of her system. Jim would figure out what to say. Eventually, they'd hug it out and go on with their lives. Yeah, Hugh knew that was the perfect solution to his problem.

When they reached the market, Pete was at the pavilion getting his booth set up for the day.

"I brought your horses," Pete said when Hugh and Randi

approached the booth. "I started not to. I figured you deserved to walk home after ditching me yesterday." He was still pissed.

Randi hugged him. "I appreciate you bringing him."

Pete shrugged. "Gary helped. It's a pain in the butt to lead two horses."

"Thanks, Pete," Hugh said. "I appreciate it."

Randi smiled at Pete when she released him. "I'm sorry for doing that to you yesterday. I'm just worried about Charlie and you know how I am. I get something on my mind and I have to do it."

Pete shook his head. "Well, I'm not worried about Charlie and you shouldn't be either."

Randi looked surprised. "Why not?"

"It's the rest of the world you should be worried about," Pete explained. "Charlie is my friend, but he's got anger issues. Eventually, there'll be a trail of dead bodies leading us right to him."

As much as the comment surprised her, Randi knew there was a degree of truth to it. Charlie was going through the same thing that a lot of abandoned, abused, or neglected children eventually went through in life. Those traumas impacted them. They changed the way they processed feelings and the way they coped with the stressors in their lives.

"Well, just so you know, we didn't find him," Randi said. "The lead turned out to be a mistake. It was a different teenage boy."

Pete didn't look surprised. "I figured. You won't find Charlie until he's ready to be found."

"I'm not sticking around the market today," Hugh told them. "I need to get back to the valley and tell Jim what I heard last night."

"What did you hear?" Pete asked.

"It's a long story, but the short version is that I heard that jerk Randi went off on the other day, Hadley Wright, meeting with some people. They had a lot to say and some of it might be important to us. I'm sure your dad will tell you about it after the market today. Randi, you staying?"

Randi planted herself on the bench behind their table and

yawned widely. "I am. I can't make Pete work by himself after ditching him yesterday."

"That's right," said Pete. "You owe me."

"I'll see you guys this evening then," said Hugh, heading off with long strides.

He stopped by Ian's booth to fill him in on the actual events that took place last night, including an explanation of why he'd lied to Randi. When he was done, he went to pick up his horse. In an unusual demonstration of generosity, the corral tender didn't charge Hugh for the short time he'd kept the horse. Hugh thanked him, mounted up, and headed back to the valley.

As he rode, his mind played through the discussion he'd overheard yesterday at Hadley's place. He couldn't spend much time processing it last night because of running into Randi. He was still angry she'd shown up like that, but he chose not to address it with her. There was no point, really. Randi was predictable and he should have expected it. The fiasco was as much a failure on his part as on hers.

The reason he was upset was that she'd caused him to miss out on the rest of that meeting. Sure, he'd been there long enough to hear damning evidence that Charlie was helping them, but what else had been on the table? Had they developed any plan as to how they were going to deal with Jim? He didn't know because he hadn't been able to listen all the way to the end.

He let it go. There was nothing he could do now other than report back to Jim what he'd learned. If he had the opportunity later, he'd shoot a text message to the Mad Mick through the radio. He could let him know what he'd learned about Catalyst performing some sort of regional law enforcement role and see if he had any additional information about it.

When he reached the valley, Hugh rode straight to Jim's house and found him working in the garden. With so much of the group's effort devoted to the market, that left fewer people to work the garden. Those who weren't at the market or in the various gardens were busy taking care of children or helping preserve food for the coming winter. Jim was already reconsidering his choice to send so many people to the market during harvest time. It had definitely increased the workload of those left behind.

"How's it going?" Hugh called as he rode up.

Jim was picking ears of corn and tossing them into a wheelbarrow. When it was full, he'd deliver it to the porch where Ariel would shuck the corn with a demoralized and disgruntled look on her face. Nana and Ellen would then slice it from the ears and can it.

"I'm rethinking my life decisions. Maybe if I'd paid attention in school and tried to be a better person, I might not be a prisoner to this garden."

Hugh released his horse into the corral by Jim's barn and it went straight for the watering trough. Hugh joined Jim in the garden and helped him with the corn.

"So, how'd it go? Did you find Charlie?"

Hugh let out a long sigh. "Jim, I don't even know where to start. I paid a visit to Hadley's house and Charlie was there, along with several other people. Some were from the community and came on foot. There were two horses tied up in the yard with saddles on them so I think some of the guests rode in. I hate to break the news to you, but you were one of the main topics of conversation."

Jim shook his head in irritation. "Not surprised really. What else would they talk about if not for me?"

"True." Hugh snapped off two ears and tossed them gently into the wheelbarrow. "Just as he said he was going to do, Hadley was trying to confirm with one man whether there was still a bounty on you, or not. He was sad to hear that the situation was exactly as you described to him at the market and that the bounty must have been a rogue action."

Jim frowned. "So, he was discussing this with someone at his house? Who was he talking to that could have confirmed that in any official capacity?"

"There was a guy there from Catalyst Security. I could see the logo on his shirt through the window. You remember our discussions at the Mad Mick's place about Catalyst?"

"I remember."

"Well, I used to work for them back in the 90s. All of those people who launched the attack on the Mad Mick and tried to blow up his compound, except for Browning, had on Catalyst uniforms. Apparently, the company has some sort of role in the national recovery, working under the Department of Homeland Security umbrella."

"The Mad Mick's friend, Ricardo, told us something about that," Jim said.

Hugh nodded. "The guy in the Catalyst uniform at Hadley's house referred to himself a couple of times as something like a regional sheriff."

Jim straightened his stiff back and stared at Hugh. "A sheriff? We already have a sheriff."

Hugh shrugged. "I know that, but this is different. This guy has more of a regional role. He's supposed to help solve problems on the regional level without killing people. He said they have a national-level response team for the hard cases. He did admit that he could apply pressure to people who were becoming a problem."

"Guess that's me again," Jim snarled. "Let them apply pressure. I'll press back."

"And I will gladly help you with that," Hugh said. "There's more though and I'm not even sure how to say it."

"Just spit it out, Hugh. It's not like you to be all evasive."

"Charlie is working with these people. He was at the meeting I was spying on last night."

Jim was in the process of leaning back over to pick more corn when Hugh came out with it. He stopped mid-bend and stared at Hugh in shock. "Excuse me?"

Hugh shrugged. "I heard it myself, Jim. He said he'd tell them anything they wanted to know about us because we were nothing to him."

Jim took that last part personally, his expression flying between anger and hurt, then back to rage. "Why that little..."

"I know. I wanted to climb through the window and wring his little neck. I don't know what's gotten into him."

"We've done nothing but help that kid," Jim said, practically shouting by now. "There's no coming back from this. I don't care what Randi says, I'm fucking done with him."

"Oh yeah, speaking of Randi..."

"Yeah, Pete told me that she took off after you. I guess I'm not surprised. She's kind of a loose cannon herself."

"It's worse than that, Jim. I had no idea she was following me until I saw someone outside of Hadley's house. I didn't know it was her and thought I might have been compromised, so I took her down. It wasn't until I was choking her out that I realized it was Randi. I could have killed her."

Jim frowned. "I'm sorry. I know that had to suck."

"What sucks is that I didn't get to hear the rest of what was said because I had to deal with her. Then I was afraid that we made too much noise out there wrestling in the dark. Once I figured out who she was, we had to take off."

"That's a lost opportunity we might not get back."

"Yeah, tell me about it," Hugh said.

"What did Randi say about Charlie working with those people?"

Hugh grimaced, then grinned sheepishly. "I didn't tell her, Jim. I was afraid she'd flip out and do something stupid. Maybe try to get to him or yell his name, so I lied to her. I told her it was a mistake and that it was a different teenage boy."

Jim looked concerned now. "She's going to find out the truth, Hugh. We can't keep this from her. What are you going to do when she finds out?"

"I was going to let you tell her," Hugh confessed. "She's used to being pissed at you. She's used to you giving her bad news. I thought, why ruin my relationship with her when yours is already fucked?"

Jim cocked an eyebrow at Hugh, uncertain if he followed the logic of that argument.

"I know she's loyal to us, Jim, but her following me into town was almost as bad as what Charlie did. People need to follow orders. They need to do what they're told. I didn't get the intel I was after last night because she interrupted my operation. She could have been killed. Hell, we both could have been killed."

"I get what you're saying, Hugh, but not everyone comes from a world where they follow orders. Randi and Charlie are both hot-headed, though for different reasons. They act out of emotion. Charlie may eventually outgrow that but Randi probably won't. Her...*spontaneity*...has caused problems since the beginning, but we overlook it because she's one of us and she brings other skills to the table. Charlie may be one of us too, but he's crossed a line here that there's no coming back from. Providing information to the enemy is dangerous for all of us. Someone could get killed because of it."

"He knows a lot, Jim. He knows routes into the valley. He knows our capabilities and our patterns. The only advantage we have right now is that we're aware of what he's up to, so we can act accordingly. We can switch things up and break our routines."

"I agree. We could scale back selling at the market and only set up there every other day."

"That would give you more help in the garden."

Jim looked around at long rows of corn. "Tell me about it."

"We should probably amp up our security. This Catalyst guy said he's not out to kill anyone, but it's possible he could pay us a visit. I'd like to see him coming in advance so we can give him a proper welcome."

"I agree," Jim said, knowing exactly what constituted a proper welcome to Hugh. "We could have shooters hidden around the place, ready to react if he became threatening. Maybe we'll meet about that tonight when everyone gets home from the market."

"Sounds like a plan." Hugh straightened. "You ready for me to push this wheelbarrow to the house?"

"I'll go with you. I need a drink of water. If you don't have any objections, I might get you to help Ariel shuck the corn too. She's a little half-hearted about getting the silks off."

"I'd be glad to," Hugh said. He dipped down and grabbed the wheelbarrow by the handles, then headed for the garden gate.

22

Pete and Randi were having a good morning at the market. They'd traded off some baby clothes, some .243 rifle rounds, a knife, a backpack, and two sleeping bags. In exchange for those items, they took in some samples of toothpaste and dental floss from a hygienist, some .22 rounds, tea bags, and a ginseng root the size of Randi's palm. They also got a five-pack of shotgun slugs, two meat rabbits, some cloth diapers, and a gallon baggie of hotel-sized soap bars.

A lot of people had given up on personal hygiene. It was evident in the state of their clothes, the smell of their bodies, and the condition of their skin. They suffered from rashes, lice, and were covered in infected scratches that would leave permanent scars. Folks in the valley still insisted on staying on top of all those things. Neglecting their teeth and cleanliness only increased the chance of infections, disease, and other medical problems. There was no sense in suffering from conditions that were avoidable. Plus, it was generally a lot more pleasant to socialize with people who didn't reek like a carcass.

Just before noon, Randi dug into her pocket and counted the .22 shells she carried for making purchases.

"You going to get you one of those cat kebabs?" Pete teased.

Randi frowned. "No smartass. I'm needing some medicine for my nerves."

"What kind of medicine? We have nearly everything you need back in the valley. Don't waste your shells here."

"It's not *that* kind of medicine. This whole situation with Charlie has me twisted up in knots. I'm going to go down there and buy me a tiny bag of weed from one of those vendors."

Pete's jaw dropped. "You're going to do *what*? Drugs are illegal."

Randi cocked her head at him. "Hell, Pete, murder is illegal and look how your dad rolls. He'd give the grim reaper a run for his money. Nothing is really illegal now. They're selling weed right there in the open and all kinds of people are buying it. I'm about to be one of them. And like I told you, it's for medicinal purposes."

Pete looked doubtful. "I don't know what Dad is going to think about that."

"Jim Powell can kiss my ass," she snapped. "I ain't his to raise. I'm a grown-assed woman and I can do whatever the hell I want to do, whenever the hell I want to do it."

Pete was used to her tone so he didn't take offense. In fact, she'd bawled him out like this just yesterday. He pointed from their pavilion toward the weed vendors down in the parking lot. "Knock yourself out."

She bobbed her head and got to her feet. "I think I will."

When she was nearly out of earshot, he mumbled, "Batty old pothead."

She turned around and put her hands on her hips, glaring at him. "Don't think I can't take you, boy. You keep running that mouth and you'll get your ass spanked in front of all these people."

The vendors within earshot hooted with delight. Some urged her to do it. Pete flushed red and pretended to ignore her, but wisely kept his mouth shut.

"That's what I thought," Randi said, heading off.

Randi hadn't smoked weed in years, but she needed something to help her unwind. She felt miserable, consumed by a range of emotions around Charlie's disappearance. She needed something to numb her. If nothing else, it might help her sleep.

As she was walking down the concrete path toward the parking lot, she spied a crowd in front of Gary's stall. She hoped it was a sign they were doing as well as she was today. Then, as she got closer, she spotted Hadley Wright standing in front of Debra with his floppy, basset hound jowls. She groaned with revulsion. The very sight of him drove her blood pressure up until she could hear her heart pounding in her ears.

As much as she hated to get into another public altercation, Randi had to know what Hadley was doing. Was this another shake-down attempt? Was he back again for the vendor fee he'd promised to collect?

She curled her lip, let out a long breath, and cut through the crowd toward Gary's booth. When she was within earshot, she hung back in the crowd so Hadley wouldn't notice her presence. There was no use injecting herself into the situation if it was avoidable. Considering their history, it would probably only make things worse.

"I've been to most of the booths in this parking lot," Hadley said, speaking loudly enough that all of those gathered around could hear him. It was a favorite technique of politicians, turning every conversation into a performance. "I've been explaining to folks selling goods here today that the Board of Supervisors has arrived at a reasonable fee for vendors using these facilities, as I mentioned before. I told everyone I spoke to that collection of these fees would begin tomorrow. I simply can't put it off any longer. You know what folks told me?"

Debra shrugged in response. Gary, standing at her shoulder, stared at Hadley with a blank expression.

Hadley pointed a finger directly at Debra. "The people I spoke to told me that you and another vendor spoke to everyone here and told them they should stand together against paying a fee. Several of them also went on to say that you had made disparaging comments about my character. As a public figure, I take that very seriously."

"Yeah, that's all true. People are barely scraping by and I can't believe you're here with your hand out. You politicians act like you care about people when you're running for office, but that disappears as soon as you get elected. Then all you think of is lining your own pockets."

"Surely you can't expect to use these facilities for free?" Hadley exclaimed, as if it were the most absurd idea he'd ever heard. "The county owns this facility. They built it."

"With taxpayer dollars," Debra clarified. "The *people* own it. Not you. Not the county. This is a case of the public using a facility their money paid for."

Hadley shook his head. "Now you're just trying to play to the crowd."

"And who would recognize that better than you?" Debra quipped.

Gary held his hands up, trying to intervene and keep this from descending into a shouting match. "Hey, if you want to charge, that's just fine with us. There's no use fighting about it. We already have a backup plan. If you don't want us here, we'll move."

Hadley frowned. This wasn't what he had in mind. He didn't want them moving. He wanted them to stay here so he could tax them. "Excuse me?"

"We have a backup plan," Debra confirmed. "We found a car dealer just outside of town who said we could use his lot for the market if you insisted on charging. He said people could sell there for free. He said he'd love to have us and we could even set up inside when the weather turned cold. What do you have to say to that?" She smiled with satisfaction.

Hadley's face grew beet red with anger. "I guess I shouldn't be surprised that you're trying to sabotage this market."

"If anyone is trying to sabotage the market, it's you," Debra said. "You're trying to steal from people who have nothing. What are you going to do now? Force us to sell here so you can tax us?"

Hadley was done arguing. He turned to the crowd and waved a man forward. He was dressed in black cargo pants and wore a black polo shirt with a logo over the pocket. He was wearing a tactical vest and had a rifle slung over his shoulder, barrel down. His black cap carried the same logo as his shirt.

Debra's ire was raised. She stared this new arrival up and down. "What this, Mr. Wright? He here for intimidation? To threaten us if we don't pay?"

Hadley gestured at the man in black. "This is my friend Isaac. He's the regional sheriff for Homeland Security. He just happened to be here on an unrelated matter, but perhaps it's time I formally introduce you. Especially if you're going to insist on being troublemakers."

The crowd was growing bigger. The more people gathered, the more others flocked to the scene.

"The county already has a sheriff!" someone in the crowd shouted out.

Isaac turned toward the speaker. "This is different. I'm not here to replace your existing sheriff. I work for a security company out of Washington, D.C. and we have a contract with the government to keep the peace in communities around the country. I cover the southwestern Virginia region. My job is to keep an eye out for any insurgent or resistance activity. If I spot something of concern, I report that back to my superiors and they deal with it appropriately."

As the mention of "insurgent activity," Hadley jabbed an accusing finger at Debra and her family.

"So our refusal to be shaken down counts as resistance? You're going to consider us 'insurgents' if we refuse to let you steal from us?" Gary asked, stepping closer to Isaac and Hadley. It took a lot to make Gary mad, but he was there now, face red and eyes hard.

Hadley stepped back, putting Isaac between himself and Gary. Isaac didn't budge. He was a big man, well-trained, and didn't scare easily. He'd been in situations like this all over the world. It was just part of the job.

"Well, we might not consider you 'insurgents' for refusing to pay a county fee, but your role in assisting Jim Powell, a *known* insurgent, speaks for itself," said Isaac. He made his accusation loudly, wanting to make certain that everyone in attendance knew the connection between these vendors and the man responsible for the community losing out on aid.

Isaac's smug proclamation spread like wildfire, the crowd

descending into furious chatter. Gary and Debra looked at each other, both of them angry but also uncertain. They'd been doing pretty well at the market up until this point, but being publicly associated with Jim might put an end to that.

Pushed to the brink, Gary took another step forward. He loomed several inches over Isaac. He raised a finger and jabbed it toward Isaac's face. "We're not paying a fee and that's final. I suggest you get moving and leave us alone. You can take your accusations and your *sheriff* bullshit somewhere else."

Before Gary could react, Isaac swept his left hand and grabbed Gary's finger. He bent it backward, driving Gary to his knees. There was a popping sound and Gary cried out as his finger broke, bent nearly back to his wrist.

With his other hand, Isaac whipped an expanding baton from his belt. He deployed and swung it so quickly that Randi lost track of it. His first blow caught Gary in the forearm, just above his injured hand. Gary screamed as his arm broke. He doubled over, cradling the injured limb, but Isaac wasn't done with him yet. He snapped the baton back over his head and brought it down on the back of Gary's skull, knocking him out.

Eyes blazing, Debra took a step backward and drew her Glock, but Isaac had been expecting that. His baton was already in motion, swinging back-handed, and striking Debra in the hand before she had the weapon fully raised. The handgun fell from her grip as the tiny bones of her hand shattered beneath the tip of the baton. Isaac immediately whipped his bludgeon back again and caught Debra on the temple. She dropped like a puppet with the strings cut. Sara screamed and rushed to her mother's side.

Enraged, Gary's son-in-law Will launched himself over their pile of wares. It was a purely instinctive reaction, but he'd have been better off using his weapon at a distance. He was ill-equipped for the years of combatives training that Isaac brought to the table. Isaac took a stance, then lashed out with a low kick to the side of Will's knee. Will stumbled from the blow and Isaac took full advantage of it. He dropped the steel baton and rushed in. Latching onto Will's head with both hands, he pulled his head forward as he fired a knee upward. Isaac's knee met Will's face with a sickening crunch and a splash of blood.

The scene unfolding before Randi happened so fast she didn't even know how to respond. She'd left her rifle at the booth with Pete, but she drew her handgun and fired a shot into the air. Some in the crowd scattered at the sound, but others stood their ground. Isaac spun on Randi, the fire of combat still raging in his eyes. He was in the zone, ready for the next threat, and Randi was now in his crosshairs.

She wasn't intimidated. She'd faced down many men, both before the collapse and after. She leveled the gun on Isaac's face. "You take one step in my direction and I'll kill you."

"Surely you wouldn't murder a lawman in front of all these people!" Hadley shouted, suddenly emboldened with Gary's family out of the fight.

Randi moved her point of aim slightly, putting Hadley in her sights. "If I have to pull the trigger, I'm not just murdering one man. I'm murdering two. I'll kill the asshole who hurt my friends and the asshole responsible for it."

Before Hadley could respond, Randi was struck by a powerful blow between her shoulder blades. Someone in the crowd had charged her, shoving her off balance. She lost her aim as she shot out both hands, trying to keep from eating pavement. Then Isaac was on her, throwing a powerful downward strike to her head.

Randi lost her grip on her handgun as she hit the pavement. She rolled onto her back, feeling the heat of the asphalt through her clothing. Her vision blurred and the last thing she saw before losing consciousness was Charlie stepping from the crowd with a look of satisfaction on his face. Hadley reached out to pat him on the shoulder, grinning at Randi. Randi met Charlie's eyes and then she faded into darkness, unable to even comprehend that it had been he who had shoved her. He who'd betrayed her.

Pops had been talking to another vendor, not noticing what was taking place until Randi fired a shot. He limped toward the scene and pushed through the crowd just as Randi lost consciousness. Normally a peaceful man, Pops lost his cool at the sight of what had happened to his friends. He bellowed with rage and swung his wooden walking stick, clouting Hadley in the face with it.

Hadley staggered and dropped to his knees, blood running from his hair and streaming down his face. Charlie stepped to the side, fear in his eyes.

Pops glared at Charlie and shouted, "You're with them now? After everything we did for you?"

When Charlie failed to answer, Pops raised his walking stick back over his head, ready to finish off Hadley. He looked like a man splitting firewood and Hadley's head was the log. Pops' face was a grim mask of determination. He'd been pushed too far.

Isaac shouldered his rifle and the red dot of his laser showed up on Pop's chest. "Drop the stick, old timer. Don't make me kill you."

While the crowd had looked on with relative impartiality while Gary's family and Randi were beaten, the sight of an elderly man—a patriarch of their community—being held at gunpoint was too much for them. There was a ripple in the crowd and a chorus of metallic clicks. One by one, dozens of men and women raised their weapons and leveled them on Isaac. The message was clear. They would not tolerate Pops being harmed.

"You people have no idea what you're doing!" Isaac barked. "I am a legal representative of the United States government. I have the authority to deal with threats to the peace."

A large, bearded man with tattoos, rings on every finger, and leather cuffs on his wrists pushed through the crowd, his rifle pointed at Isaac's face. "Looks like you're the biggest threat to the peace around here right now," said Ian.

Isaac glared at Ian. "You got no idea what you're doing, big boy. You need to put that rifle down while I'm in a forgiving mood."

Ian shook his head. "It's my forgiveness you need to be worried about. If you don't lower that rifle and get out of here, you're going to die. We've been pushed about as far as we're going to be pushed."

Isaac didn't immediately lower his weapon, and Ian began counting aloud. "One."

When Ian got to the next number, it was not his voice alone that spoke it. A chorus of united voices rose from the crowd, the volume of their proclamation so powerful that it reverberated deep within the chests of everyone present.

"Two."

Aware now of just how large a force he was facing, Isaac quickly lowered his rifle before they reached the next and final number of the countdown. He let it hang from the sling and raised his hands over his head.

Ian gestured at Hadley. "You best take him with you before I decide to let Mr. Powell finish splitting his melon."

With a scowl, Isaac hooked a hand under Hadley's bicep and tried to haul him to his feet. When Hadley couldn't rise under his own power, Isaac gestured at Charlie to get his other arm. Together, the two of them got Hadley up. He swooned between them, but they steadied him and led him away. The crowd parted to let them through, many rifles still following them.

"Tell Hadley he ain't welcome here anymore," Ian called after them.

Isaac ignored the taunt, but Ian knew this wasn't the last of it. They hadn't seen the last of Hadley Wright. Just as Ian turned his eyes back to Pops, the older man sagged and went down to the ground.

23

Pete and most of the other vendors at the covered pavilion were oblivious to what was taking place in the parking lot below them. It wasn't until Randi fired a shot in the air that everyone lurched to their feet and noticed the crowd gathered in the parking lot. Pete grabbed his rifle, then grabbed Randi's too so no one would steal it while the booth was unmanned. He slung his pack on his back and cautiously made his way down the path to the parking lot.

Pete wasn't alone. Probably half the crowd in the pavilion was heading down the hill to see what was taking place. Along the way, the crowd parted and Pete saw Hadley Wright being led away. He didn't know the large man in the black uniform who was escorting Hadley, but he certainly recognized the younger man hurrying along behind them. It was Charlie.

Pete started to call out to him. The reaction was almost automatic, rising from their close friendship and the adventures they'd shared this past year. Yet something silenced him. Why would Charlie be with those people? Why would he come to the market and not even stop by to say hello or just tell them he was okay?

As Pete stood there watching him, Charlie must have sensed the eyes upon him. His head popped up and he scanned the crowd. When he found Pete, they briefly locked eyes. Pete's eyes asked a lot of questions, but Charlie's held no answers. Then Charlie looked down at the ground and didn't make eye contact again.

Pete began to get a sick feeling that there might be some relationship between Randi going down the hill, the gunshot, and Hadley being led away injured. Had she attacked him? Had she been shot? He took off running, the gear slung on his body bouncing as he headed for the crowd and shoved his way through. Pete's pushing was met with glares and mumbled curses, but it didn't faze him.

"Get out of my *way*."

He was uncertain if it was his upraised rifle or determination that caused the crowd to let him through, but he eventually reached the front. When he did, the scene before him froze him in his tracks. Pops was seated on the ground, holding his chest and trying to catch his breath. Three people were holding onto him, trying to calm him down. One of the men helping him was Ian, Hugh's friend.

Randi was on the ground at Pete's feet and someone was holding a wet compress to her forehead. Her eyes were open, but she kept blinking as if she were dazed and unable to focus. Sara, Gary's daughter was crying hysterically as she moved between her barely-conscious father and mother. Folks were trying to help her, including one who held a grubby rag to Will's shattered nose. Pete winced at that, vividly recalling the sensation of his own broken nose a few short weeks ago.

"Pete!"

Ian's voice snapped Pete to attention. He'd been paralyzed by the sight of what had happened to his people. The big man waved him over.

"Come help your grandfather!"

Pete hurried to Pops and dropped to his knees. "Are you okay?"

Pops gasped, "I'll...be...fine."

Ian put a hand on Pete's shoulder. "We probably need to get your people out of here. You go get your horses and pack your booth up. When you're done, come back here and I'll help you get everyone else packed and loaded. We'll take them to my house because it's closest and I can start treating their injuries. Then you'll need to get home and let your dad know what happened."

"Are they going to be okay?" Pete asked, shooting a worried glance toward Gary and Debra.

Ian shook his head. "I don't know, kid, but help me get your grandfather up and then you get moving."

Pete got to his feet and the two of them helped Pops up. Someone handed Pops his walking stick and Ian helped him over to Randi's side. Pops took a seat beside her on the ground and patted her on the shoulder.

Pete ran for the corral. He paid off the tender and got the two horses that belonged to him and Randi, then led them to his booth. He was glad to see that another vendor had kept an eye on things, so nothing was missing. Pete gathered the tarp that lay beneath their wares, wrapping everything into a hasty bundle and shoving it into an enormous pack. He lashed that pack behind his saddle, then led the horses down to the parking lot.

Randi, Gary, and Debra had regained consciousness and were sitting up, but everyone looked rough. At Ian's direction, Pops held the reins for Pete's horses while Pete ran to the corral to get those belonging to Pops, Gary, and his family. When he returned, Ian and Pete gathered all their wares and loaded them onto the horses. Then began the slow process of trying to get everyone to their feet and on horseback.

"This is what happens if you go around causing trouble," someone in the crowd commented. It was a man who hadn't lifted a finger to help any of the injured.

Pops cut him a hard look. "I was in local politics for over twenty years. Sometimes you have no choice but to tax people to improve life for everyone. There are always people who resent it, but that comes with the territory. There are other times that you don't dare raise taxes because times are too hard and people are too beat down. This is one of those times. You all elected Hadley and you have a right to tell him how you feel. Expressing an opinion is a freedom in this country and you shouldn't get beat down for it."

The man in the crowd grumbled at his scolding and stomped off.

They managed to get everyone on a horse, but Debra could only ride by doubling up with Sara. Debra held her broken hand to her chest and sobbed quietly, clutching onto her daughter with the other. Randi mounted her horse, but cursed and complained to the point that even the most foul-mouthed mothers were covering their children's ears and rushing them off. With his arm likely broken, Gary needed assistance in mounting his horse, but could hold the reins in his good hand once he was in the saddle. Finally, Ian helped Pops mount up and they began the ride through town to his place.

They moaned, grunted, and cried out as they rode, but no one had the stomach for conversation. They followed Ian's bike until he pulled up to his house and hopped off. One by one, Pete and Ian helped everyone dismount and climb the steps to the shady porch. Will tied the horses off to the clothesline.

When Ian had everything under control, he gestured at Pete. Pete scrambled onto his horse and nudged it into a canter. He hurried through town, taking shortcuts in a desperate bid to shave every minute he could off the ride to the valley. Not comfortable with galloping his horse on pavement, he took the river crossing at the back entrance to the valley and kicked his horse into a gallop.

Minutes later, he approached his home from the back, yelling as he rode up to the gate. He hastily fumbled with the chain, rode through, then closed it behind him. By the time he cleared the gate, his entire family was standing on the porch with Hugh, all of them waiting nervously to hear what had him in such a state.

"There was trouble at the market," he gasped. "I didn't see it happen, but Hadley got mad because we told the vendors not to pay his fee. There was some kind of argument, then Hadley brought out this man in a uniform that he said was some kind of sheriff or something."

Hugh and Jim exchanged a glance, both understanding this had to be the Catalyst Security man they'd discussed earlier.

"Pops said the guy in the uniform got in Gary's face and Gary got mad. The guy beat Gary, Debra, and Randi unconscious. Will jumped in and got his nose broken."

"Dammit!" Jim erupted, his face twisting into a mask of rage. He bolted for the front door.

"Then Pops jumped in," Pete added.

Everyone on the porch froze at this piece of information, terrified of what Pete was going to say next. Even Jim stopped in his tracks and turned to face his son.

"Pops cracked Hadley across the head with his walking stick and was going to kill him, but the sheriff guy pulled a gun on him. He might have shot Pops but a bunch of people in the crowd pulled guns and held them on the sheriff guy. Ian made them leave."

"Is Pops okay?" Nana asked, her face clouded with worry.

Pete shrugged. "He fell down after it happened. He must have overdone it, but he was fine when I left."

"Where is everyone now?" Hugh asked.

"Ian's place. Ian said the injured people couldn't ride this far so he'd take them to his place until we could get them bandaged up. He told me to come get you. They need medical supplies."

Jim snapped into action. He pointed at Ellen. "Get the big medical kit and one of the trauma kits. Set them out here on the porch."

"I need to see Pops," Nana said, tears streaming down her face.

Jim shook his head "Not now. You have to stay here until we bring him home."

Nana cried harder and Ariel wrapped herself around her grandmother, giving Jim a mean look.

"Pete," said Jim, "stash the stuff from your booth in the barn and turn your horse out. Get a fresh one. You're going back to town with us."

"You think that's wise?" Ellen asked.

"I might need his help if the others can't take care of themselves," Jim said.

She fell silent, understanding he might be right.

"What can I do?" Hugh asked.

"You're going with me. You can grab the horses while I get the gear together."

Hugh jogged off toward the barn.

"Be careful," Ellen called as Jim ran by her.

Pete shook his head. "I don't think it's Dad you need to be worried about. Hadley Wright is a dead man."

24

———————

After Hugh, Pete, and Jim gathered their gear, it took them nearly an hour to reach Ian's house. Neither Ellen nor Nana were happy about being left behind, but there was no point in dragging everyone into town.

Blinded by anger, only two thoughts blazed clearly within the confines of Jim's brain. He was going to get his people home, then he was going to kill Hadley Wright.

After riding through town, Hugh, Pete, and Jim barreled through the quiet neighborhood to Ian's yard. Jim turned his reins over to Pete, hurriedly untied the med kits, and scrambled up the porch steps. He nodded at Ian as he dropped the gear on the porch. "I can't thank you enough, man. I'm in your debt."

"Not a problem," Ian replied. "Glad to help. I've tried to keep everyone hydrated and comfortable."

Jim rushed to his father's side first and rested a hand on his shoulder. "You okay?"

Pops shrugged in embarrassment. "I just got overheated. I was so mad I was about to split Hadley's head open. I felt a little weak afterward."

"He's been drinking steadily and his pulse is steady," Ian said.

"He's right. He probably got a little too worked up. It took him a while to catch his breath."

While Pete tied off the horses, Hugh grabbed one of the medical kits from the porch and started checking out the others. Debra and Gary were stretched out on chaise lounges with Sara and Will attending to them.

Ian stepped to Hugh's side. "They're both lucid and oriented to time and place. There's a strong possibility of concussion after the blows they took, but I couldn't feel a skull fracture. Doesn't mean there isn't one, though. Her hand is broken and his arm is likely in the same state."

"What's your medical experience, Ian?" Jim asked. "You seem to know what you're talking about."

"I worked as an EMT for several years before I went to college. I've seen a lot of fights and car crashes over the years. A lot of split melons."

"We have a nurse," Jim said, tossing his head toward Randi. She was smoking a hand-rolled cigarette at the far corner of the porch and staring off into the distance. "She's a little contrary, but she's ours and we love her."

Randi frowned. "You're not one to be calling anyone else contrary."

"Are they going to be okay?" Sara asked Hugh. Her voice sounded weak and hoarse from long spells of crying.

Hugh was carefully examining Debra and Gary's wounds. "That's above my pay grade, Sara. With a head injury, only time will tell. We don't have imaging equipment or a doctor."

"You have a nurse," Randi reminded them.

"A nurse who might also have a head injury," Ian clarified.

"I got hit harder than that fighting girls in high school," Randi snarled. "That big meathead didn't hurt me."

"That's because your head is harder than most football helmets," Jim quipped.

Randi pointed her cigarette at him. "I'd laugh if it didn't make my head feel like an evil clown was beating it with a ball-peen hammer."

Hugh and Jim both cocked an eyebrow at her, wondering where that weird analogy had come from.

"Check Will," Sara requested. "He took a knee to the face."

Hugh checked Will's face, gently running a thumb to each side of his nose. "It's broken, but I can set it if you'll let me."

"Will it hurt?" Will asked.

"Like nothing you've ever felt before."

"What happens if you don't set it?" Will asked, not excited at Hugh's description of how much it would hurt.

"Potential sinus problems," Ian interjected. "And it'll be crooked as a dog's hind leg for the rest of your life."

"Then leave it," Will said. "I'll take ugly over more pain."

"As you wish," Hugh said, removing his hands from Will's face.

Sara didn't look as convinced as Will had been, not certain she was ready to settle for an ugly and deformed husband.

"What do you need me to do, Dad?" Pete asked, standing at the top of the steps.

Jim looked around the group. "Can you guys travel?"

While no one was exactly enthusiastic, everyone indicated that they were capable of riding as long as they went slowly. Most agreed that they wanted to be out of this town and back to their safe, familiar valley.

Jim looked pleased with their answer. "Then let's clean and bandage the cuts. Some of these head wounds are going to need butterflies to close them up. We also need to tape Debra's hand and put a sling on it. Same for Gary's arm."

"You should pack Will's nose until it quits bleeding," Ian suggested. "When you get home, apply compresses to your wounds with the coldest water you have access to."

"You have any pain meds with you?" Gary asked Jim. "My arm is killing me. It's throbbing so bad I can feel it with each heartbeat."

Jim shook his head. "Sorry, man. I've got them, but I'm afraid to give you anything until we know if you have a concussion or not. You're not supposed to sleep."

"What difference does it make?" Randi asked, flipping her

cigarette butt out into Ian's yard. "It's not like we can run to the emergency room if you suddenly decide we have concussions. We'll either live or die. Hell, we could all be bleeding from our brains right now. I might have a seizure while we're riding home. Gary or Debra might throw a clot and stroke out in their sleep tonight. I say you should give him a pain pill if he wants it."

She got wide-eyed frowns from nearly everyone for her blunt assessment of their medical conditions. She shrugged and threw her hands open as if to say "Well, you know it's true."

Jim met Ian's eye. "Again, Randi there is what we have for medical. Charming bedside manner, as you can see."

Randi gave him the finger.

Jim ignored her. "Pete, you help Ian and Hugh get these folks ready for travel. Then you guys head back to the valley. I'm going to go pay Hadley a visit before I leave town."

"Alone?" Hugh asked.

"Yes. These guys need your help more than I do. I'd rather you escort everyone safely home. I'll be fine."

"Then that's what I'll do."

Jim got to his feet and approached Ian, sticking out his hand. "As I said, I'm in your debt. If you ever need a place to stay, you're welcome in our community anytime. We could always use another medic."

Ian smiled and patted Jim on the shoulder. "I appreciate the offer. I'm fine where I am for now, but things can change on a dime. It's always good to have options."

Jim approached his dad and patted him on the back. "Thanks for cracking Hadley one. I'm going to go finish the job. Nana is pretty worried, so you better take it easy when you get home."

"You be careful!" Pops warned. "Hadley's a wimp, but that other fellow is no joke. He knows how to fight."

"I'll be careful."

Pete came up and hugged his dad. "Like Pops said, be careful."

Jim gripped his son's shoulder. "You did well today, Pete. I'm proud of you."

"Thanks," Pete said. "But seriously, Dad, be careful."

"I'll do my best, Pete."

Randi joined Jim and Pete, pulling them off to the side while the others were getting bandaged.

"What is it?" Jim asked.

Her voice low, Randi explained, "I had that big bastard with Hadley at gunpoint. It should have been over then, but someone charged me from behind and knocked me down. That's when the guy in black beat the shit out of me."

Jim furrowed his brow. "Did you get a look at who did it?"

"I'm pretty sure it was Charlie."

Pete nodded eagerly. "I saw him too, Dad. He left with Hadley and that other guy."

Jim let out a long breath. "I don't know, Randi. I don't know if we can save him."

Tears in her eyes, Randi shrugged in defeat. "I don't know either, Jim."

25

Jim waited around until his people left Ian's house, headed for the valley, then he followed Hugh's directions to Hadley Wright's house. He thought he knew where it was, having passed it perhaps thousands of times over the years as he traveled through town. Sweat ran down his face and back as his horse clopped along the narrow residential streets. It was late afternoon, the air still and muggy. A miserable heat was trapped over the town like it was stuck beneath a heavy blanket it could not kick free of.

Even this physical discomfort did not distract him from what lay ahead. His nerves were calm, but his mind raced as he checked his weapons and made sure his spare mags were accessible. He wasn't even certain he'd need spare mags, but he had no idea how many men he'd find at Hadley's house. Would Isaac be there? Charlie? And if Charlie was there, what would Jim do if he found himself staring down the barrel of Charlie's rifle?

Through several blocks of tree-lined streets, Jim passed people working in their yards or gardens. Others loafed beneath the overhangs of their porches, hiding from the sun like lizards beneath rotting logs. Some people seemed to recognize him and whisper as he passed. Others shied away simply because of the anger this lone rider projected, a searing rage that only increased the misery of the hot day. Perhaps they understood that the seething hatred he carried must certainly guarantee an unpleasant end for someone, whether it be the man carrying it on his shoulders or the man whom he was carrying it toward.

As he approached Hadley's house, Jim studied each of the windows facing his direction. He looked for any indication of a sentry or waiting gunman, but noticed nothing. He checked the hedges and the corners of the house with the same scrutiny. There were no signs that he was expected.

Jim rode through the high grass of the backyard and tied his horse off to the porch rail. He climbed the steps, making no effort at stealth. With his rifle at his shoulder, he tried the knob and found it locked. Undeterred, Jim knocked in classic Jim Powell fashion, which was to say he knocked with the sole of his boot, applying it heavily beside the antique knob.

The century-old poplar door splintered and split. The rippled glass in the upper half broke into several jagged shards and fell out of the frame, shattering against the porch floor. Jim delivered another kick to clear the doorframe of any lingering remnants, then strode into the kitchen, glass crunching beneath his boots. He paused and listened for any sound in the stuffy, closed-up house. Somewhere in the bowels of plaster and dark wood he heard a lock click shut.

He wound through a hall, past simple wainscoting with precise joinery, past oft-repaired horsehair plaster beginning to separate from the poplar lath to which it had been applied over a century ago. The hallway led to a square nook that held three tall doors with transom windows at the top. The old iron hardware was painted black. One door stood open to an office and another to a guest room. One was closed and Jim decided that must be the master bedroom.

He stepped to the side of the door, outside of the line of fire, grasped the knob in a sweaty hand, turned it, and shoved. The door swung open with a painful creak, like an arthritic and protesting joint, banging softly against the wall behind it. Jim raised his rifle and eased to his right, just enough to peer inside the room.

Despite the heat, Hadley had taken to his bed. He lay beneath an old quilt, a damp towel wrapped around his head like he was a sultan. One of his eyes was black. Pops had done a number on the little tyrant, ringing his bell like it was Sunday and time for church.

Hadley's wife sat in a chair off to the side of the bed. She watched Jim enter the room with a terrifying intensity, like he was a mountain lion creeping into the backyard to devour her poodle. Despite her fear, she did not look surprised. Perhaps she knew this moment was coming. Perhaps she'd expected it for a long time and understood that, had it not been Jim, it would have eventually been someone else.

"You need to go," Jim said, not taking his rifle off Hadley.

"He's hurt," she protested.

"He'll be dead when I'm finished. No need in you sticking around to watch it."

"Why do you have to kill him?"

"'Cause he kept pushing until he pushed too far."

"I don't think he'll keep pushing," she said, staring at her husband laying there, eyes closed. "Not anymore."

Jim snorted. "Then you don't know him as well as I do and I barely know him at all."

Her eyes flashed to Jim's and he saw that he'd touched a nerve. There was a lifetime of truth in those eyes, an admission that Jim was right to an extent that he'd never even understand. This woman didn't know her husband. In all their years of marriage, they'd never progressed past the superficial. She was no stranger to mourning, having mourned her marriage for over thirty years.

She frowned and rose from her chair, then leaned over her husband. She kissed him on the forehead and whispered something that Jim couldn't hear.

Jim kept his rifle on Hadley the entire time, even as his wife brushed by Jim and padded through the house. Even as she left out the front door, pulling it shut behind her.

"I know you're awake," Jim said.

One of Hadley's eyes twitched and Jim spotted movement beneath the quilt, the creeping of Hadley's right hand. Jim dropped his point of aim, the red dot of his optic resting on the lump of fabric that suggested a hand. He pulled the trigger.

The crack of the rifle rang off the plaster walls with a deafening boom. Hadley flinched, yanking his hand from beneath the quilt, a revolver hanging from limp and blood-soaked fingers. The pistol slipped from his hand, slid off the bed, and clattered onto the hardwood floor. Hadley raised his injured hand in front of his face, looking as if he were trying to peer at Jim through the hole the round had made.

"Where are the others?" Jim asked.

"Who?" Hadley croaked. He bunched the quilt around his hand and squeezed it, trying to stem the flow of blood.

"Charlie and whoever that 'sheriff' fellow was that you brought to the market."

"They're...together. We thought it best that Isaac get out of town after what happened today."

"Isaac? He the security contractor?"

Hadley grimaced in pain as he nodded, but Jim couldn't be sure if the grimace was from the head injury or the damaged hand.

"Where'd they go?"

When Hadley didn't respond fast enough to suit him, Jim stalked across the room and drew back his rifle, ready to crack the butt against Hadley's already-throbbing skull.

Hadley shrunk away. "Stop! I'll tell you, dammit."

Jim flipped his rifle back to his shoulder, barrel leveled on Hadley's head, and backed away from him. "Talk."

"They're at a cabin near Hidden Valley Lake. It's on the road going up the mountain. Belongs to an old state trooper named Garvey. He's my connection to Isaac."

"What are they doing with Charlie?"

"I suspect they're grilling him for information...about you."

"Why?" Jim demanded.

Hadley winced, closed his eyes, and rolled his head in pain. "Because, the sooner this county is rid of you and people like you, the sooner things will get back to normal. Besides, that kid came to us.

It's not like we had to convince him to work against you. He was only too glad to do it."

That revelation stung Jim. It was consistent with what Hugh had observed when he was spying on the meeting at Hadley's house. It also matched up with what Randi and Pete had seen at the market. Still, it hurt every time it was thrown in his face.

As if sensing the thoughts running through Jim's head, Hadley grinned through his pain. "It's because that boy knows the truth. He knows we need rid of you. He knows that everything you do turns to shit and everyone who stands by you is going to step in it."

Jim wasn't there to deliver a monologue and he'd already asked Hadley every question that came to mind. He was done here. He backed toward the bedroom door, paused, and pulled the trigger. The 5.56 round punched a hole in Hadley's forehead, spraying his pillow and headboard with gore.

His ears ringing, Jim wove his way out of the house. He paused in the kitchen when he noticed the boxes of government-issue MREs stacked against the wall. He had no doubt they'd come to be in Hadley's possession through some underhanded, conniving scheme. He briefly considered burning the place down, then talked himself out of it.

Jim tromped back through the broken glass and stood on the porch. Several neighbors stood in their yards watching him with morbid curiosity. While no one appeared to be armed, their faces were all clouded with concern. Gunfire in a neighborhood never meant anything good.

Jim mounted his horse and rode across the street to the nearest neighbor. The guy was paralyzed with fear, terrified of Jim yet too scared to run away.

"Hadley's kitchen is full of government MREs," Jim said. "I suspect it's some kind of aid he was supposed to share but kept for himself. There's not enough for the whole town, but there's enough to help some of you. You might grab a few people and get it before someone else does."

"What about Hadley?" he asked.

Jim frowned as if it was the stupidest thing he'd heard all day. "Hadley's dead."

Before he could ask any more questions, Jim headed back through town. He kept his rifle handy and the safety off until he was clear of the place. On the road toward the valley, he stopped to let his horse drink from the creek and thought about what had taken place.

He felt nothing for killing Hadley. Through all of the indecision he'd experienced over the past few months, he'd eventually reached the conclusion that this was where things inevitably had to go. There was no more laying low, no more avoiding conflict to spare his friends and family. The only path forward was directly through the middle of all who were working against him.

Part of him felt like he should be appalled by this realization. Shouldn't he feel guilt and revulsion that he'd decided to kill people because he saw them as a threat to his family? He didn't. The struggles he'd experienced with violence were in the past. There was no use feeling guilt over Hadley because he was only the first of a new surge.

Jim wasn't done yet.

He was just getting started.

26

———————

With the swelling and bruising on Gary's arm, they were all convinced it was broken, but fortunately it wasn't a displaced fracture. Cold compresses, an elastic bandage, and a sling were all they could do for him. Debra ended up with two broken fingers, which they covered with foam-lined aluminum splints and taped securely. Her hand was swollen and too painful for Randi to probe, but everyone was convinced there were broken bones in the hand itself. Without x-rays, diagnosis was sometimes just a matter of consensus and best guesses.

The head injuries were more troubling. It was probable that Gary, Randi, and Debra all had concussions, but there was nothing to be done for them. Most people recovered from concussions, though there was always the possibility of lingering brain injury. If that was the case, it would simply become one more thing they had to live with.

The members of Jim's clan didn't meet that night to discuss what had taken place in town. After the trauma of the day, everyone needed the love and warmth of their family to heal their aches. Jim went to Gary's place to let them know they'd be taking a few days off from the market, then they'd regroup and see how everyone felt about returning.

After he left Gary's house, Jim went to see Randi. For as much as he liked Randi, he dreaded this visit. They had things to talk about and it was sometimes hard to predict how Randi would react. Like himself, she tended to kill the messenger.

He found her sitting on the porch with one of her grandchildren. She had a glass in her hand that held either moonshine or water. Something in her slouch, in the way she was oozing into the porch swing like melting plastic, made him think it was moonshine. Lloyd must have left her with a supply.

Randi scowled as Jim rode up to the porch. "What the hell do you want?"

Jim grinned. "If that's how you talk to your friends, how do you talk to the people you really dislike?"

"About that same way," Randi admitted. "And even after all this time, I'm still not sure we're friends. I need a little more time to think about it."

Jim dismounted and tied his horse off to the porch. "Got a second to talk?"

She rolled her eyes, knowing it couldn't be anything good. "I guess." She patted her grandchild on the knee. "Why don't you go in there and play with your sister for a minute. I need to talk to this mean, nasty man."

The little boy cackled and gave Jim a smirk that clearly came from Randi's genes. He gathered his toys and went inside. When he was gone, Jim took the seat he vacated. Typical of porch swings, the chains creaked in a way that made Jim wonder if it was about to give way and drop him to the ground.

Randi frowned at Jim's proximity, having to straighten her slouch to avoid their sweaty elbows bumping. "I don't recall anyone inviting you to come sit on top of me. There's plenty of perfectly good floor where you could have planted yourself."

"If you can relax and quit being so contrary for a minute, we need to talk."

Randi took a sip from her glass. "Well, talk. I ain't got all damn day."

Jim looked around. "I'm pretty sure you do, but that's beside the point. I wanted to talk about Charlie."

She shook her head bitterly. "He was there, you know. Charlie was at the market when this all happened and he didn't do a damn thing to help us. He had a gun. He could have stopped it, but he didn't. I'm pretty sure it was him who hauled off and shoved me to the ground. I don't know. That changes things. It's hard to feel the same about a boy who can stand there and watch you take a beating like that and not even lift a finger in your defense."

Jim was bobbing his head in agreement. "I don't know how he came to hate us so much, Randi. There were times we had to correct him, just as we'd do with any of our own children, but he couldn't handle it. It had to be something related to losing both his parents. Some kind of post-traumatic stress or something."

Randi took a sip from her glass, the careful, controlled swallow betraying that it indeed held liquor. "You're right. In better times, a little therapy might have helped him get back on the right track. It's hard for him to take any therapeutic direction from us. There's too much connection. Too much history."

"I need to tell you something, Randi. A few days ago, you might have had a hard time believing me, but I think you'll have less trouble now."

She looked concerned. "What is it? Charlie again?"

"Charlie was at Hadley's house when you showed up there the other night."

Her eyes went wide. "When Hugh was spying on them?"

Jim nodded.

"That lying bastard!" she slurred. "That camouflage-wearing, long-haired, skinny, sneaky, gun-toting, horse-riding son-of-a-bitch."

Jim frowned at her. "Are you drunk? I've never known you to be cursing-impaired before, but you were struggling there."

She ignored his comment. "He told me Charlie wasn't in there."

"Don't be too hard on Hugh. He didn't know how to tell you. He was also afraid if he did tell you, you'd go off and start yelling for Charlie."

She shrugged. "I might have done it. I am known for my spontaneous eruptions."

"Nah, you're more like Old Faithful. You're kind of predictable."

"Asshole."

"Hugh thought you'd take it better coming from me since you're used to bad news coming out of my mouth. He wanted to preserve his good relationship with you."

"And since I already hate you, you had nothing to lose. Right?"

Jim smiled. "Exactly."

"So, what was Charlie doing there? Any idea?"

"Hugh says that Charlie agreed to give Hadley and that other man information about us."

"The one who walloped me?"

"Yeah, the guy in the black uniform calling himself a sheriff. He was there too and Charlie said he'd tell them things about the valley. Hugh says Charlie told them he didn't like the way he was being treated here and felt nothing for us anymore."

Randi tightened her mouth and shook her head in disgust. "That little...I'd like to chase him down with a switch and show him what bad treatment really is."

"He's too big for that, Randi. He's nearly as tall as me, but probably weighs eighty pounds less. That still puts him at about twice your height."

Randi fake-laughed. "You're so damn funny, I don't know how you stand yourself."

Jim shrugged. "I'm trying to make light of it, Randi, but there's no way to ease the hurt of what he said. I feel betrayed by him too and I know you have to feel worse. Even though you saw him with Hadley at the market, I needed you to know the rest of it. This may get worse. You need to emotionally prepare yourself for the fact that something bad might happen to Charlie before this is all over with."

Randi stared at Jim in shock. "Don't tell me you're thinking about killing him? He's just a kid!"

"I'd never hunt Charlie down the way I did Hadley. Don't forget, I owe Alice for saving my life. But repaying my debt to her doesn't include getting myself killed. I just want you to understand that if it comes down to him or me, he's the one meeting Jesus."

"I get it," Randi said. "I'm not happy about it, but I'll try not to blame you. Your obligation is to your family. Not Alice. Not Charlie."

"I'm glad you understand, Randi."

"I might understand, but I can't promise I'll react the same way. If it comes down to him or me, I'm not certain I can pull the trigger on a child I fed and helped raise."

Jim knew she was telling the truth. Despite her hard edges, Randi would probably let Charlie kill her before she'd harm him. It wasn't that she hadn't killed a young man before, because she'd had. She'd shot a boy who ambushed their camp on the Appalachian Trail when they were coming home from Richmond. This was different. She knew Charlie and she still loved him, regardless of how he might feel about them.

"Let's just hope it doesn't come to that," Jim said. "Maybe we'll find another way or he'll decide to move on."

"Let's hope."

27

———————

When Jim visited Gary and Randi he mentioned they should keep a watch that night because of all that had happened. He didn't expect trouble. There was no inner voice warning him of an imminent attack. Still, things had gotten ugly at the market. Then there was the little matter of Jim killing Hadley Wright with witnesses.

If Isaac, the man from Catalyst Security, did indeed have any official law enforcement role it was possible they might get a visit from him. Hadley's wife had been there when Jim went into the house. The neighbors had also seen him come out of Hadley's house after the gunshot and he'd not made any attempt to conceal his identity. In fact, he'd admitted to what he'd done. If Isaac wanted to speak to Jim, he knew where to come. He also had Charlie as a guide.

Later that evening, as Jim's family wound down for the night and trailed off to their beds, Jim insisted on taking the first watch. Pete offered, but Jim was too amped up to sleep. He had a lot on his mind and he hadn't had a lot of downtime to process it.

"How about if I come wake you up when I start to get sleepy?" Jim offered.

Pete looked downcast. "I guess that means I can't go back to Lloyd's house yet?"

Pete and Charlie had been staying together in Buddy's old house ever since Jim returned from his road trip with Lloyd. Allowing them that degree of freedom was intended to teach them some responsibility. Jim had hoped it would help settle Charlie some, but it hadn't worked. The boy had still found himself unable to rein in his impulsive behavior.

"Yeah, I'd rather you stay close to home tonight, Pete. That house is too far away from the rest of us."

Pete shrugged. "That's okay, Dad. I'll be fine here for a day or two."

Jim hugged his son, pleased with the mature response. Pete went to the couch, took his boots off, and stretched out fully clothed. Jim kissed Ellen goodnight and began pulling on his gear. He heard a sneaky giggle and caught sight of Ariel running from her bedroom to his. With him keeping watch, she'd decided she would climb into bed with her mother and take his spot. It made him smile that she still wanted to do that because there'd be a day when that was no longer the case.

Once he was outside, Jim stepped away from the house and went to the barn. With this heat, everyone slept with their windows open, and talking just outside the house might wake Nana and Pops, who were already asleep.

At the barn, Jim took a seat on a bucket, found his radio, and keyed the mic. "Jim for Hugh, Jim for Hugh."

Despite various efforts at call signs and communications security, it had all proven too complicated for the residents of the valley. They assumed they were probably the only people in their community still using radios. With the range on the cheap handhelds being so limited, it seemed pointless after a while to take great efforts with being too tactical. Pete had spent some time coming up with a list of call signs for everyone in their group, but no one could ever remember them when they didn't have the list handy. Much to Pete's disappointment, they'd eventually given up on any efforts toward communication security.

"Go for Hugh."

"What you seeing, my friend?"

"All quiet, Jim. I'm up here at Pete and Charlie's house, watching the road from the porch."

"Yeah, I wanted to let you know that Pete would be staying at my house tonight. I might get him to relieve me if I get tired later."

"My plan is to roam the valley. Let me know if you need any help."

"Definitely. I'm going to keep my eyes on the back entrance from the river crossing."

"Copy that. Hugh out."

Jim went to the springhouse and filled a Nalgene water bottle, then dumped in a flavoring packet. The spring water tasted fine on its own, but the flavor packet contained caffeine and a generous amount of sugar. It would help keep him perky as the night dragged on. He screwed the lid back on and shook the bottle as he walked off into the night.

He was familiar enough with the terrain this close to the house that he could navigate by memory, but he switched to night-vision after he crossed through a gate and into the pasture. The last thing he wanted to do was step in a hole or fall over a rock and break a leg. He didn't head for Outpost Pete or the concealed observation post that Hugh had built near the river crossing. Instead, he picked a random spot somewhere between the two.

His logic was if Charlie was guiding a group of men to the valley, he knew about those positions and might suspect that they would be manned, and try to avoid them. Jim wanted to be someplace random that Charlie wouldn't know about. Someplace that they'd never positioned a watch before.

He found an exposed rib of limestone that curved from a hillside and sat on its smooth, inviting surface. It still held the heat of the day and felt pleasant, like a heated car seat. Jim laid back on it, letting the heat seep into the tired muscles of his back. He stared at the stars, spotting a few airplanes and a satellite. They reminded him that there were places in the world where life was still normal and people were going about their lives without a care.

Like many people, Jim had always been appalled when the news would cover some region of the globe that was still in shambles a year after a tornado, a hurricane, a flood, or some other disaster. He found it difficult to imagine that there could be parts of the world suffering such deprivation when his life went on as it always had. He wanted to believe that normality seeped back into disaster zones almost immediately, but the news often revealed that wasn't the case.

Jim understood that phenomena now with a clarity he'd never experienced before. Life was far from normal for everyone he knew and they had no idea how far off life as they'd once known it might be.

He knew there were still people out there living normal lives. They were watching news stories about the United States in the same way that he'd watched stories about Puerto Rico, Haiti, Nepal, India, and a host of other countries who'd experienced disasters. They were probably shaking their heads at the poor people they saw on the screen in the same way he'd once done. Perhaps they even donated to charities that were supposed to be sending aid to America.

He recalled seeing news stories in the past where they interviewed starving people in disaster zones who said they weren't receiving the aid everyone sent because of "politics." Now Jim got it. It was the same thing going on in America. For all of the years he'd been taught about American exceptionalism, there were some areas where that concept didn't hold true. American politics was just as dirty, just as greedy, and just as blind to the needs of their people.

Frustrated at where his mind was going, he decided he needed to walk to distract himself. Being angry in the middle of the night wasn't productive. He got to his feet and walked around for several hours, never venturing far from his own property.

It was a beautiful night and the valley was alive with game. Jim spooked a few deer, walking right up on them in the dark before they flicked their tails and bounded away. He watched a heron noisily fight off a raccoon intent on raiding its nest and devouring its young. He listened as coyotes sang on the hunt. He watched a mother possum wobble by with its offspring strung along behind it.

A little after 2 AM, Jim was at the springhouse for another drink of water when he heard a rhythmic slapping sound in the distance. He set his water bottle on the lip of the concrete trough and stood. He could still hear the sound, but it was difficult to tell anything about it with the spring box constantly burbling into the trough.

Jim had to walk all the way to the pasture fence before he could isolate the sound. Now he heard it clearly and he was certain that he understood what it was. It was the sound of someone running in wet shoes. Jim dropped his night-vision back over his eyes and threw up his rifle. He was still awkward at using both the night-vision and the rifle scope together, so it took him a moment to get both optics aligned on the source of the sound. When he did, he caught sight of Charlie running as hard as he could through the dark field.

"Son of a bitch!" he muttered. He yanked his radio from his belt and keyed the mic. "Jim for Hugh."

"Go for Hugh."

"I've got Charlie in my sights and he's beating feet through the pasture behind my house. He must have come across the river."

"Is he coming for your place?"

"I can't tell yet, Hugh. Could be my place. Could be Randi's."

"What do you need me to do?"

"Pull back to my house and keep an eye on the driveway. I'm going to try and intercept Charlie." When there was no response, Jim hit the mic again. "You get that, Hugh?"

"Acknowledged," Hugh replied.

Jim knew that tone. Hugh had something to say, but understood this wasn't the time to say it. It also wasn't the time for Jim to worry about it. He set an intercept course for Charlie and took off at a trot. For as much as he could, he didn't want to give himself away until he was within reach of Charlie. If the younger boy spotted him and took off into the woods, Jim would never catch him. The kid was quick. But Charlie was running dark and didn't have any night-vision as far as Jim could tell. If anyone had the advantage here, it was Jim.

As Jim closed in, he saw Charlie take the path toward Randi's house. Jim veered in that direction and angled his course to where he'd intercept the boy just as he crossed into Randi's yard. As that moment approached, when collision was imminent, Jim sped up and closed the distance.

By the time Charlie heard Jim's footsteps closing on him, it was too late. Charlie twisted around to look, then cried out in response to the shadowy figure barreling toward him. Jim tossed his rifle to the side and launched himself through the air. Feelings of anger at Charlie, rage at the betrayal, overtook Jim as he landed on the young man and took him to the ground.

Any thoughts of going easy on Charlie dissipated when the boy began to fight like a wildcat. Charlie had lost his rifle when he fell, but tried to elbow Jim in the face, kicking and screaming. One of his blows knocked Jim's night-vision askew and it fell to the ground.

As Jim fought to subdue Charlie, his mind bounced between seeing this boy as a son and knowing that people he cared about could have died because of things Charlie had done. He could have lost Pops, Pete, or any one of them. That was what he had to remember. Charlie wasn't a son. He was a traitor.

Charlie could get every member of Jim's family killed. He'd demonstrated time and time again that he couldn't be trusted. He was constantly going behind their backs to wage war on anyone who pissed him off. How long would it be before one of Charlie's rogue activities got someone in the valley killed? It wasn't even a matter of *if*, it was a matter of *when*. That he would be their downfall was as inevitable as time itself.

Jim managed to turn Charlie face down and wrapped a forearm around his neck, tightening his grip. Charlie screamed and tried to bite at Jim's arm. Jim rolled to his back, taking Charlie with him. The boy bucked and kicked. He raised a leg high in the air and tried to donkey-kick Jim in the groin. Jim threw a leg over his waist. Soon he had both legs locked around Charlie and a vise grip around his neck. Charlie tried in vain to elbow Jim, but the blows did no damage. He was locked up tight.

For as much as Jim hadn't wanted to kill Charlie, this was where they were headed together. It was like drinking a bottle of liquor and claiming you didn't want to get drunk. One thing led to another. One action inevitably led to the next.

Jim knew in his heart that he had no intention of releasing Charlie. There was nothing to discuss and no other chances to give. Charlie had burned every bridge and Jim was done with him. Charlie was a liability. He was the enemy.

Charlie's struggling began to subside and the fists beating against Jim weakened. Jim felt sick. Was this yet another of those bitter pills he had to swallow to keep his family safe?

Was this where Charlie died? How was he going to tell Pete what he'd done? Was he going to tell his family at all? How would he explain it? How could he convince them this had to be done? How would they look at him if they knew?

The shotgun blast off to his side nearly caused Jim to lose control of his bladder. His ears rang and his stomach knotted. He shoved Charlie off him and drew his handgun. Rolling to a prone position, he leveled his handgun on the shooter.

It was Randi, her shotgun pointed in the air. A headlamp strapped to her head shone directly into Jim's eyes. He raised one hand to block the painful beam. He'd been so focused on Charlie he hadn't even seen her approach.

"Let him go, Jim."

"We talked about this, Randi. You knew this could happen."

"It can't happen like this, Jim. I can't stand here and watch you strangle the life out of him right in front of me. You don't want this either."

The sound of footsteps approaching through the high broomsedge hit Jim and Randi at the same time. Both directed their guns into the field. Jim yanked a flashlight from his gear and hit the button on the cap.

Hugh threw his hands up at the sight of weapons pointed in his direction. "It's me! I was looking for you guys and heard the shot. I thought there might be trouble."

Randi lowered her weapon and rushed to Charlie's side. Jim mumbled a curse and sat up in the grass. He got to his feet and found his night-vision, then picked up his rifle. Only when he'd collected his gear did he turn his attention toward the young man.

Charlie coughed and choked as Randi cradled him in her arms. The sight of him being coddled like that only infuriated Jim further. He would never understand Randi. Charlie had let her get beat down yesterday and had not even lifted a finger to help, yet she held him like one of her children. It was too much to bear and Jim couldn't keep silent about it.

"You got a lot of damn nerve, kid. I've got three friends with head injuries and two with broken bones. They might have been beaten to death and my father killed because of you."

"I...I didn't..." Charlie tried to speak but broke into a fit of coughing, his throat raw from Jim's chokehold.

"Don't even try to lie to me," Jim said, disgust in his voice. "Hugh got a tip you were staying with Hadley and he overheard you. He heard what you said about us and how we meant *nothing* to you anymore. He heard you tell Hadley and the others that you'd give them anything they wanted to know about us."

"It's not—"

"Were you going to lead them here, Charlie?" Jim was shouting now, too angry to control himself. "Are they out there now? Were you going to let them kill us? Were you going to help?"

Charlie fell silent, no longer attempting to defend himself. He stubbed up, his mouth twisted in defiance.

In the silence, Randi, the woman who'd vowed so many times that she had no tears left, began to sob. "How could you do this, Charlie? We were all friends with your mother. We promised to love you like one of our own. I would have done *anything* for you, Charlie."

Randi's sobs turned into a wail. It was only then that Jim understood the depth of her pain at the betrayal. Randi had suffered many things in her life, but this was among the most painful. She'd taken Charlie to raise and she'd lost him.

Charlie wrestled his way from her grip and shot to his feet. Jim stepped toward Charlie, fists clenched and heaving with rage. Hugh came closer, ready to intervene, but uncertain exactly what he'd do. He too was very angry with the boy he'd come to call his friend.

Randi drew her knees to her chest and lay her head on them, sobbing. Jim hadn't seen her this despondent in some time. She was broken.

"It's not what you think!" Charlie screamed. His face was blotchy and tears streamed from his eyes. Spittle flew as he spoke.

Jim shook his head in disgust. "So, what is it, Charlie? If we're wrong, then what's the truth? You have some story made up for us? Something that's supposed to make us trust you again? That isn't happening. If we're dead to you, you're dead to us. That's how it works. You're not welcome here anymore."

Then Charlie did something unexpected. He dropped to his knees in front of Jim and looked up at him, all the anger gone from his face. "Jim, I know I fucked up when the Mad Mick was here. I only shot at his daughter because I was trying to protect Pete. I know you told me to stand down, but I couldn't. I thought you were about to let your son get killed. I love you all and I couldn't let that happen."

Seeing that Jim was too angry to respond, Hugh stepped forward. "Charlie, if you can't listen, if you can't take orders, you can't live here. It's that simple. We have to be able to trust you. We have to know that you won't put us in danger by running off half-cocked. You've become a liability."

"I know that," Charlie sobbed. "I know. I'm ready to give up my guns and do anything if you'll let me come back. I'll do whatever you ask me to do."

Jim threw his hands up in the air. "Why the hell would we ever do that? Explain to me how I could ever trust you again. If you have an answer for that, so help me God, you better be giving it to me right now because I'm about to lose my shit."

Charlie reached into the pocket of his dirty checked shirt and removed a thick stack of folded papers sealed in a Ziploc bag. He extended them toward Jim.

"What's that supposed to be?" Jim asked, not taking it.

Charlie snuffled, then wiped his face on the tail of his shirt. "After

I took that shot at the Mad Mick's daughter, I knew I screwed up. I was mad and embarrassed, so I ran off. The longer I stayed gone, the harder it was to come back. I knew you guys were angry with me, so I wanted some way to make it up to you. Some way to show you that I would do anything to stay part of this group."

Hugh crouched beside Charlie. "How? How did you try to make it up?"

"I found the people who didn't like Jim and I offered information to them," Charlie replied. "There's a whole group who keep tabs on anyone speaking out against the government. They call themselves the Community Security Council and Hadley was their leader. They reported what they heard to Hadley and he reported it to a radio man outside of town named Garvey. The radio guy passed it on to that sheriff, Isaac, and then I guess he passed it on up the ladder."

Jim took a deep breath, forced it out, then glared at Charlie. "What's on those papers, kid? You expect me to believe it's going to change what happened? You think it's going to make me forget everything and welcome you back in with open arms?"

Hugh took the baggie. He opened it and unfolded the sheaf of papers. "What is this, Charlie?"

Charlie wiped his nose on the back of his hand. "That's all of them. It's the network you've been trying to uncover. Every name. All the people who are spying on the community. Everyone working with Hadley and Isaac. They all get supplies from the government for providing information on their neighbors. Hadley even ran a whorehouse in town and used that as a way to get information."

Hugh extended the papers to Jim. "You should look at this."

Jim looked from Charlie to Hugh, then took the papers. He was still holding the stack in his hand as he marched off into the darkness, back toward home.

"Jim!" Randi called after him.

Jim ignored her.

Hugh looked at Randi and shook his head. "Give him space. Give him time."

Charlie started crying again and walked on his knees toward Randi. He threw his arms open and wrapped her in a hug.

As Jim walked off through the darkness, he couldn't escape the wails of grief and pain that rose from Charlie and Randi. It was a sound not unlike that of the coyotes who hunted so boldly in this sweltering night.

28

—————

Jim spent the rest of the night sitting on his porch, studying the papers Charlie had given him. He was still there when the sun came up and Ellen joined him on the porch, sliding in beside him on the swing.

"What's that you're reading?" she asked, handing him a cup of tea made from fresh mint they picked along the creek.

Jim let out a tired sigh. "I don't even know where to start."

Uncertain of how to respond to that, Ellen asked him if anything had happened overnight.

Jim folded the papers and replaced them in the baggie, then shoved them in his shirt pocket. "Charlie came back."

Ellen's eyes went wide. "After everything that's happened? You said he'd joined up with those people and was working against us now."

"That's what Hugh heard him say, but Charlie is telling us it was all a ruse. He says he was working undercover to collect information for me."

Ellen shook her head in confusion. "Why would he do that?"

"He said he felt guilty about shooting at the Mad Mick's daughter and he knew he was in trouble. He was trying to make up for it by gathering information he knew we wanted, which was to root out the people working against us in the community."

"That's what's in those papers?"

Jim's expression was somber. "It's Hadley's network of spies. They call themselves the Community Security Council. Apparently, the people on this list are getting aid from the government for working with Homeland Security and this sheriff from Catalyst. There's a whole system for funneling information up the chain of command. It's all here." He tapped the stack of papers.

"What are you going to do about it?"

"I'm going to go to Randi's right now and talk to Charlie again."

Ellen frowned. "Jim, you haven't even been to bed yet. Can't it wait?"

"We didn't leave it in a good spot and I can't sleep with this on my mind. There needs to be some resolution. I either have to make peace with it or send that boy away for the last time." He got up from the swing, stretched, and placed his cup of tea on the rail.

"Are you sure I can't talk you out of this?"

"I'm sure."

Jim went directly to the barn and saddled his horse. It took longer than usual because of his exhaustion. His fingers didn't work like they were supposed to and his brain wasn't firing on all cylinders. He was stupid tired. When he got the horse saddled, he rode to the front porch and collected the gear he'd nearly forgotten.

Strapping it on was nearly as difficult as saddling the horse. Several times he connected the wrong buckles or affixed the Velcro straps to the wrong place. He was ready to give up and kick the thing into the yard when Ellen stepped in and finished the job for him.

"Thanks," he mumbled.

She handed his rifle to him. "Don't do anything you can't live with."

Jim gave a weary shake of his head. "I don't even know what that means anymore. I've come to think that a man can learn to live with just about anything."

Ellen stood on the porch steps in her nightgown, a cup of tea in her hand, and watched him go.

His horse plodded through the field separating his house from Randi's, and Jim was nearly nauseous with exhaustion. He was slightly dizzy and the heat was affecting him worse than usual. The muggy air felt suffocating and sweat poured from him. The sound of high grass brushing against his horse's legs was nearly hypnotizing, nearly enough to make him fall asleep in the saddle.

Jim smelled the bacon even before he reached Randi's house. It was one of the items they'd traded for at the market and each family had a slab of it, wrapped in greasy brown paper. They stored it the old-fashioned way, hanging unrefrigerated in the house.

One of Randi's daughters was feeding a baby on the porch and she called inside as he rode up. Randi appeared on the porch with a dishtowel in her hands and watched Jim approach, staring at him uncertainly.

"Wasn't sure if I needed my shotgun or not," she said. "Maybe you should tell me your business before you get off that horse."

He shielded his eyes against the sun as he spoke. The brilliant morning light was stabbing daggers into his brain. "I'm not here to cause trouble. I'd like to speak to Charlie."

Randi frowned. "I ain't so sure that's a good idea."

"I'm not going to lay a hand on him. I promise. He and I need to talk, though. I need to ask him some questions about those papers he gave me."

"You look like shit. Have you even been to bed?"

"Nope. Can't sleep until this is done."

"You might not be in the best place for being reasonable, Jim. Why don't you get some sleep and come back later."

"It can't wait. He and I need to come to an understanding and it needs to happen now."

"He's still asleep."

"Wake him the fuck up."

"You're a crazy asshole," she mumbled, disappearing back into the house.

Jim sat his horse for a while, wondering if Randi was getting Charlie or if she'd simply gotten tired of speaking with him and gone back to her bacon. He had his answer when Charlie appeared on the porch. In the morning light he looked thinner, younger, than he had last night. Jim saw dark smudges around his neck. He wondered if it was dirt or if it was bruises he'd inflicted when he'd tried to kill the boy a few hours ago. Seeing him in the daylight, it was hard to imagine how much he'd wanted to kill Charlie last night.

"Can we talk?" Jim asked.

"That a question?"

Jim shook his head. "Guess not. We *need* to talk."

Randi watched the exchange through the screen door, uncertain of how she felt about letting the two of them out of her sight.

"How about the shed?" Charlie suggested. "It's out of the sun."

The house Randi had taken in the valley didn't have a proper barn, but it did have an equipment shed cobbled together from round poles and sawmill lumber. The doors didn't close anymore and the whole place was leaning gently to the left. Jim took a seat on a pile of hardened fertilizer bags, leaned back against the board wall, and closed his eyes. Charlie stood in the doorway, uncertain of what to do.

"Did you look through those papers?" Charlie finally asked. His voice held neither eagerness nor dread, just an acceptance of the inevitability that this conversation would determine his future. Depending on the outcome, he might stay or he might be told to pack his belongings and never return again.

Jim opened his eyes and regarded Charlie. "I almost killed you last night, Charlie. Had Randi not intervened, that's probably how it would have ended."

"I know."

Jim's face twisted. "You think I wanted to do that?"

"No."

"I've got a lot of things I have to live with, but I don't want to live with that."

Charlie didn't answer.

"We're not communicating, kid. You're not talking and you're not listening. You're operating like you're all alone here and that can't happen. We keep going down this same road over and over again. You keep going off and doing things without telling anyone. Then you intentionally do things we ask you not to do. That can't continue to happen."

"I know."

Jim flung a tired arm into the air. "You've *always* known it, Charlie, but you still do those things. What options do I have left? Is there anything I can say that makes you understand the magnitude of this problem?"

"I get it now."

Jim gave Charlie a doubtful look. "You've said that before. What the hell is different this time? I hear the words coming out of your mouth, but why am I supposed to be convinced this time? Every other time, it's been a lie."

"I got a good look at what it's like to be out there alone and I didn't like it. There's no place where you can let down your guard and feel safe. There's nobody that cares if you live or die."

"I tried to tell you that before, Charlie."

"I know. Randi did, too. But sometimes I get these things in my head and I can't stop myself."

"So, how are you going to stop yourself next time this happens? That's the problem I have."

Charlie shoved his hands in his pockets and looked around the inside of the shed. He wasn't looking at anything in particular, other than trying to keep from looking at Jim. "Next time, I'm going to remember Randi's face just before Isaac knocked her out. I'm going to remember that look she gave me, like I'd stabbed her in the heart. Since my mom died, nothing has hurt as bad as that look."

"Again, I hear the words but how do I believe them?"

"Let me prove myself to you."

Jim smirked. "How?"

"What are you going to do about the people on that list I gave you?"

"You changing the subject?"

Charlie shook his head. "No sir. I just need to know."

"Why, so you can go tell Sheriff Isaac my plans?"

Charlie winced at the accusation. "No. I just wondered if you intended to kill them. That's what I figured you might do."

"I haven't decided," Jim said.

Charlie met Jim's eye this time. "You ain't being honest with me. You *have* decided. If I'm guessing right, you're planning on killing them."

"What if I am, Charlie? What if I am?" Jim blurted. Exhaustion was making it difficult to keep his emotions in check.

Charlie moved closer to Jim, leaned over, and said quietly, "I want to be part of it. I've had a lot of time to think about this. I know where all those people live because I went to each house with Hadley. You, me, and Hugh. We find the snitches and we kill them."

"There's still people higher up the ladder than this Community Security Council. What about the radio guy you mentioned and this sheriff, Isaac? How are we going to get to them?"

"We start at the top," Charlie said. "Isaac is at Garvey's house right now. He's going to be staying there for a few days. I heard him say so. We can kill Garvey and Isaac, then kill Hadley."

"I've already killed Hadley," Jim spat.

Charlie blinked, unaware of this particular development. "Then we best not waste any time. Once Isaac hears about that, he might pass it on up his chain of command. He hasn't said anything yet because he's afraid he might get in trouble for fighting at the market. Once he talks to his boss, he might get permission to arrest you. We need to hit him before he makes a report."

Jim looked at Charlie, trying to probe the depths of the young man's eyes. In some ways, he was impressed at Charlie's planning and deviousness. In other ways, he was scared that such a young man could be so conniving and dangerous. He had to remind himself that Charlie wasn't born this way. It was the world around him that molded him into this thing he now was. "You can get us to Garvey's place?"

"I've been there a couple of times. I can find it."

Jim got to his feet. "I'm going to bed, Charlie. I haven't slept yet. I want you to meet me at Hugh's house in a couple of hours. We'll come up with a plan." As he passed by Charlie, Jim reached out and rested a hand on the boy's shoulder. "I hope we can work this out. I really do."

"I won't let you down again, Jim. I promise."

"Actions speak louder than words, Charlie. And we keep this plan a secret for now. This is between me, you, and Hugh."

29

Several hours later, after a sweaty nap and a meal, Jim rode up the steep road to Hugh's mobile home. Charlie's horse was tied up to an old clothesline, and Hugh and Charlie were seated at a rickety picnic table in the front yard. Jim tied his horse off and joined them.

"I thought it best we meet up here," Jim said. "Too many ears down at my place."

Hugh was sharpening Charlie's knife on a whetstone, teaching him the finer points of the art. "If you're wanting to keep this meeting secret, I'm assuming it must be about something important."

"You ever watch *The Godfather*?" Jim asked.

Hugh laughed. "Only about three hundred times. One of the best movies ever made."

Charlie wrinkled his brow. "Is that the old movie they used to show on television during the holidays?"

Jim nodded. "It's an amazing movie."

"I watched parts of it," said Charlie.

"There's a scene toward the end of the first movie where Michael Corleone's nephew is getting baptized," Jim said. "Michael is attending the ceremony and accepting the responsibility of being the child's godfather."

Hugh grinned. "Oh, I know it well."

"Since you don't know the movie, Charlie, Michael Corleone is the son of one of the most powerful mafia families in New York. He rose to take active control of the family's crime empire after his brother Sonny was killed and his dad, the old godfather, was semi-retired. One day Vito, the old godfather, falls over in the yard and dies while he's playing with his grandson. Now that Vito is dead, Michael knows that the other crime families will come after him. They all think he's weak and won't be able to run the family, so they want to kill him and take over his enterprises."

"So, what does he do?" Charlie asked.

"While he's at his nephew's baptism, he strikes out against all his enemies. His assassins kill the heads of the other crime families and all of the traitors within their organization who have been working against them. It's an incredible power move that solidifies the family's control over organized crime in the city."

Charlie frowned. "It sounds like a good movie. Now I wish I'd paid attention."

"So, you're considering a move along those lines?" Hugh asked, one eyebrow raised.

"I think so. I always had the gut feeling that I would have to kill the people working against me if I could ever figure out who they were. I knew it would be the only way to stop them. I resisted because there would be no way of hiding a move like that. Now I'm not concerned about hiding it. I'm not going to brag about it, but I won't hide from it either."

"And now you know who the rats are?" Hugh asked, looking up from the oiled blade.

From his pocket, Jim removed the papers Charlie had given him and flattened them out on the table. "If this information is accurate, Charlie has given us a pretty good outline of how things operate. I know who the big players are now."

"That list is accurate," Charlie assured him. "Every night I wrote down the places I went with Hadley and the people he introduced me to. I wrote down the things they said. Hadley liked talking about it. It made him feel important to be part of something like that. He probably bragged a little more than he should have, but I pretended to be impressed, which made him talk even more."

"I could see Hadley spying on his neighbors because it made him feel important," Jim said. "It was probably a more complex decision for some of the others on the list. As you said, they were getting aid through Catalyst Security in exchange for information. That might have swayed some of them. Others were probably working against me out of resentment over the power plant."

Hugh looked wary. "You do know that going on a killing spree isn't going to help with that resentment, right? It might only serve to make you more enemies. People get wound up when their friends and neighbors start disappearing."

Jim looked from Hugh to Charlie. "I don't intend to talk about what I'm going to do and I'll ask the same of you two if you're willing to be a part of it. If you don't want to participate, I understand completely. This is something I have to do."

Hugh's eyes flickered up from the blade and met Jim's. "I'm in."

"Me, too," said Charlie.

Hugh twisted his head to regard Charlie. "You know, second chances are last chances. Are you ready to listen and do what you're told?"

"One hundred percent." Charlie crossed himself. "I swear on my mother's life."

Jim gave Charlie a serious look. "Then I'll give you the opportunity to redeem yourself here, Charlie. But like Hugh said, second chances are last chances."

Charlie bobbed his head. "I understand."

"How are we going to do this?" Hugh asked. "Town is very...*public*."

"We don't do it in front of families," Jim replied. "Hadley's wife knows I killed her husband because I ran her out of the house. I'll try to be more responsible with the rest of them. We might have to conduct surveillance on them and catch them alone somewhere.

Perhaps on a back street at night, or outside of their house. We kill quietly as to not draw the attention of people in town."

Charlie looked at the blade Hugh was sharpening. "With knives?"

"That's risky," Hugh said. "You have to get close and try to ambush them. It's too easy to screw up and get yourself hurt."

"It's a risk we might have to take," said Jim. "The entire town will freak out if we start shooting people every night."

"I might have an option." Hugh got up from the table. He returned in a few minutes with a rolled towel. He unrolled it on the weathered tabletop to reveal the dull gray of a titanium cylinder with threads on one end and a hole in the other.

"Is that what I think it is?" Jim asked.

A slow Cheshire-cat smile spread across Hugh's face. "Indeed it is. A suppressor. A present from the Mad Mick for helping him get his radio antenna back up."

Jim picked it up and examined it, but found no markings. "What caliber?"

"9mm. He also gave me a Glock 19 set up with suppressor-height sights."

Charlie looked incredulous. "He gave you a pistol?"

"The guy probably had two dozen of those Glocks," Hugh said. "And he makes the suppressors. He had dozens of them in several calibers."

"The Mad Mick is a good friend to have," Jim said.

"So, this will allow you to use a gun instead of a knife?" Charlie asked. "I think I like that better."

"Although it's not perfectly silent," said Hugh, "the sound won't carry. It'll make it harder for people to figure out where the shot came from, but at this time of year, with people sleeping with their windows open, it still might be heard."

"So, where do we start?" Charlie asked.

Jim pointed to two names on the list. "We start the way Charlie suggested to me last night. We cut the head off the snake and sever the lines of communication."

"I'm assuming Isaac is the head of the snake?" Charlie said. "And Garvey would be the line of communication?"

"Yes. And you said they're staying together?"

"They were together when I left Garvey's cabin near Hidden Valley Lake. Isaac said he'd be there a few days."

Hugh finished honing the knife and tested the edge by shaving a section of his forearm. Satisfied, he returned the knife to Charlie. "When do we do it?"

Jim looked at his watch. "Now."

30

An hour later, the three were riding from the valley. Each wore a chest rig crusty with dried sweat and laden with the well-worn trappings of violence. They traveled light and spoke little as they headed west, riding past the Wimmers' house, then riding along the valley road to bypass the town. Along the way, they went by the house where Lloyd had grown up, making Jim wonder how his friend was faring at the music camp.

The group had left the valley with little fanfare, not sharing their plans. Jim had simply told Ellen that the time had come and she understood what that meant. They'd discussed it enough that she knew this purge was coming. Jim had made it clear since returning from his trip with Lloyd. The only way they would remain safe in their home was to wipe their enemies from the face of the Earth, and that began today.

If Ellen had doubts or misgivings, she kept them to herself. She didn't want to cloud Jim's head with second-guesses about the actions he might be taking. If he had to fight, she wanted his mind on nothing but prevailing in combat. She didn't want him concerned about her worries and feelings. For as much as she longed for peace, she'd reluctantly come to the same conclusion as he—there was no path forward that didn't track through a badland of blood, murder, and vengeance.

Jim informed Ellen that Hugh and Charlie were going. If she had any reaction to the inclusion of a boy around the age of their son, she kept it to herself. He asked that she not tell Pete. He didn't want his son feeling left out and attempting to follow them, perhaps thinking that Charlie's participation meant he was welcome, too.

They were different boys, with different needs and dispositions. Charlie always struggled to belong. In some way, Jim understood that cementing Charlie's bond to the clan was the only way his struggle would ever be put to rest. It wasn't Jim's need but Charlie's. So, despite the moral quandaries of allowing Charlie to participate in this act of violence, that was where Jim found himself.

On some odd and intuitive level, he knew this might be the thing that set Charlie on the path to healing. For some, growth came from the insights afforded by therapy. For others, it only came from experience. From immersion in seeing, doing, and feeling. Charlie needed to do this to feel like he belonged.

After a few hours of riding, the valley road joined the four-lane highway that ran south toward Wallace County. There were a few houses and businesses along this section of highway, but the riders saw no signs of life. Perhaps the residents of these homes had learned the hard lessons that many others had learned over the past year, discovering that there was no safety in living along a common route of travel. Such visibility only brought loss and inevitable destruction.

Several miles later, the three turned off the highway onto the steep, narrow road that led to Hidden Valley Lake. Perhaps a quarter-mile up the mountain road, they veered off the pavement and onto a forest trail. They found a secluded clearing hidden from the road where they could wait for darkness. They watered their horses in a trickle of mountain spring water and allowed them to graze the lush vegetation.

After hours in the late-day heat, the three rehydrated themselves and ate light meals of protein bars and jerky. Jim was lost in thought, reclining against a rock and staring into the woods. Hugh obsessively double-checked his gear, explaining to an eager Charlie exactly what he was doing and the logic behind it. Charlie soaked it up like a sponge.

As he watched that interaction between Hugh and Charlie, Jim was again struck with the mixed feelings he had about bringing Charlie on this mission. As he'd done before, he pushed them aside. He understood those emotions came from comparing Charlie to his son, but the two were nothing alike. Their experiences had made them different people and that gap between them would only widen as time passed.

Acknowledging that difference made Jim wonder who Pete would have become if he'd never returned from Richmond. Would Pete have become someone who faced violence with such eagerness? Would he salivate as Charlie did for the opportunity to share his pain with others? Would he have taken Ellen and Ariel to go live with the Mad Mick? Fortunately, he would never know the answers to those questions.

"I have a plan," Jim announced.

Those were the first words he'd spoken in a while. Hugh and Charlie stopped their work to look at him.

Jim met Charlie's eye. "This is your chance, Charlie. I hope you're ready."

Charlie nodded without any hesitation. Jim looked for signs of reluctance, of fear, but saw none. Again, all he revealed was that eagerness to share his hurt with others. Jim hoped the boy was as brave as he appeared to be because his plan would depend upon it.

After going over the plan several times, they waited until it was full dark, then mounted their horses and traveled on up the mountain. They navigated by night-vision, pausing at a wide spot in the road approximately a half-mile from the cabin they were looking for.

"We can leave the horses here," said Charlie. "The cabin is just ahead."

They led their horses off-trail and tied them to saplings. Aware that their biggest challenge would be Garvey's dogs, the men wanted to mask their scents enough to confuse the animals. Hugh and Jim sprayed themselves with a product designed to hide hunters from deer, then rubbed their clothing with dirt and pine needles. Charlie took none of these measures. His role didn't require it.

When they were done, Hugh produced a glass jar of beef they'd canned at home. Both of them rubbed some of the cooked meat on their clothing, hoping the scent would appeal to the dogs' appetite more than its protective nature. They pocketed several chunks of the meat to offer to the dogs if they charged. It wasn't foolproof but it was preferable to shooting the animals. That was the last resort.

"There are houses past this point, but they're empty," Charlie said.

"You sure?" Jim asked.

"Garvey said they were. The people who lived in them left for one reason or another. He invited me to move into one of them if I wanted to."

The dense forest was eerie in the glow of their optics. Tall trees were heaped with wild grapevines and kudzu, looming high against the night sky like menacing spirits. Rectangular boulders the size of cars lay jumbled on the steep slope of the mountainside. The group returned to the road and headed toward the cabin, finally spotting the glow of a window in the distance.

"Garvey doesn't stay outside much at night," Charlie said. "He doesn't like the bugs."

"Hugh, I want you to circle around the house and cover the back. Shoot anyone that runs out. Don't let them reach the woods or we'll never find them in this jungle."

"Got it," Hugh said.

Jim looked at Charlie. "You ready?"

Charlie's face was a mask of grim determination.

"Then let's do it," Jim said.

Charlie headed up the road toward the cabin, his rifle slung over his shoulder. Jim let him get ahead, then fell in behind him. Hugh disappeared into the forest like a ghost in fog, taking a circuitous route to the rear of the cabin.

When Charlie reached the end of the driveway, he raised a fist, a prearranged signal that warned Jim to hold back. Charlie whispered a greeting. "Hey, boys. It's Charlie."

Despite the dogs' familiarity with Charlie's scent, they made a fierce show of barking and charged from beneath the porch. They snarled and kicked their feet, throwing divots of soil into the air.

"It's me, boys," Charlie repeated, a little concern in his voice this time. Surely the dogs recognized him. He'd spent enough time with them this past week that they should be familiar with him.

The door to the cabin flew open and the beam of a powerful flashlight cut through the night. "Who's out there?" It was Garvey, shotgun raised to his shoulder, a flashlight taped to the barrel.

"It's Charlie!" He raised his hands slightly to demonstrate he wasn't a threat. The beam of Garvey's light found him and Charlie squinted against it.

"What are you doing out there, Charlie? You alone?"

"Yeah, I'm alone. I need to speak to you. Is Isaac with you?"

"I'm here," Isaac replied, the big man suddenly looming in the door frame, silhouetted against the warm light of the interior.

From his position in the woods, Jim could see a rifle in Isaac's hand.

"Either of you all been into town today?" Charlie asked, stepping closer to the house.

The dogs sniffed at Charlie. They still seemed on edge, as if unconvinced that Charlie was alone. They'd quit barking but circled him nervously, occasionally glancing off into the darkness. Charlie knew they either smelled the other men or the inviting scent of canned meat.

"Your town?" Garvey asked.

"Yeah."

"No," Isaac said. "Garvey and I took the day off and did some fishing up at the lake. I was going to head back into town tomorrow and check in with Hadley."

"We were just frying up some fish," Garvey said. "You're in time for supper, boy."

Charlie didn't react to the invitation to join them for dinner, maintaining a serious expression. "Hadley is dead."

Isaac straightened up in the doorway. "Maybe you should come on in, son, and tell us what happened."

Charlie plodded toward the house, then climbed the steps, and headed for the door.

Garvey patted the young man on the shoulder as he passed by. "I'm sorry to hear that, Charlie. I know Hadley was good to you."

"Like a father," Charlie lied.

Isaac stepped inside and held the door while Charlie and Garvey joined him. Shocked by the revelation Charlie had just provided, Isaac paid no attention to the fact Garvey's dogs were standing anxiously at the end of the driveway, staring off into the darkness. Only after the door was closed did they venture off the property toward the allure of food.

Jim nervously reached into his pocket and pulled out a handful of the greasy beef. It was covered in lint and breaded with dust, but dogs weren't as picky as people. Jim hauled back and tossed the meat in their direction. The dogs stopped, gave it a tentative sniff, then ate it. As they sniffed the ground for more, Jim grinned in the darkness. Predictable.

31

———————

Garvey's cabin was more comfortable inside than most of the homes Charlie had been in recently. The thick forest canopy shaded the cabin and helped keep it cooler. Additionally, the elevation on this high slope of the mountain got a little cooler at night than the lowlands. The windows were open too, the chanting of insects providing an overpowering backdrop to the night. A green Coleman camp stove sat on the kitchen counter and the aroma of fried fish and cornmeal filled the air. Just as he'd always done when he visited Garvey's place, Charlie stood his rifle up by the door and dropped his pack on the floor beside it.

"You walk here?" Garvey asked.

"Yeah, my horse was at Hadley's house and there was a crowd gathered there after they found him dead. They were getting kind of wound up so I kept my distance. I didn't want them to think I had anything to do with it."

"Crowds can be volatile," Garvey agreed.

"Here, have a seat," Isaac said, gesturing toward the couch. "You must be worn out."

"Ain't sure I've ever walked this far." Charlie dropped onto the couch with a satisfied groan. "Feels good to be off my feet."

Garvey was back in the kitchen, poking at a cast-iron frying pan with a steel spatula.

Isaac stowed his rifle nearby and took a seat in the recliner opposite Charlie. "Now, tell me what happened to Hadley."

Charlie sucked in a deep breath and let it out slowly. He lowered his head as if the memory troubled him. He needed to look as if he'd lost someone close to him. With his left hand, he fiddled with the tail of his shirt, trying to look like a kid struggling with his emotions.

"I know it's hard," Isaac said, "but I need to know what happened so I can deal with it. Was it those people from the valley again?"

Charlie kept his eyes lowered. "I think so. That's what the people in town said. There were witnesses."

"I knew it," Garvey piped in. "I told you earlier you should get permission to deal with them, Isaac. This is going to keep happening until we put an end to those people."

Isaac rolled his eyes and sighed. "It isn't that easy, Garvey. Catalyst management doesn't want their sheriffs taking any actions that might turn public sentiment against us. They don't want to get people more riled up than they already are. There's an approval process you have to go through before you take that kind of action. I have to write a report and it has to be reviewed."

Garvey waved the spatula in the air as he spoke. "Sounds like Catalyst is full of shit to me. Nobody else is restrained by rules like that right now. Most people are just doing whatever the hell they want, like this Jim Powell character. You should have started that process already so we could ride over there and put an end to this. We should go ahead and do it and ask for forgiveness later."

Isaac spun his head toward Garvey, frustration on his face. "Listen, Garvey, I'm building my case, so don't tell me how to do my job. I'm not jeopardizing my career over a bunch of hillbillies. Personally, I don't care if they all kill each other."

With all eyes now averted from him, Charlie flipped up the tail of his shirt and drew the 9mm pistol concealed in his waistband. With no hesitation, he pointed it at Isaac's chest and pulled the trigger twice in rapid succession. Isaac jerked and clawed at his chest, eyes wide in horror as he stared at Charlie.

Startled by the explosion of gunfire in the tight confines of the cabin, Garvey spun to see what had happened, spatula still in his hand. He found himself staring down the barrel of Charlie's handgun. Before Garvey could react, Charlie again pulled the trigger twice. The first round smacked Garvey below the left armpit and entered his lung. The second caught him in the left side of his neck. A geyser of blood erupted, spewing in the air like a water fountain.

Garvey dropped the spatula and it clattered off the floor. He swatted at his neck as if he'd been stung by a hornet, then clamped his hand over the red stream gushing from the wound. Charlie raised his point of aim, hoping to erase the wide-eyed and accusatory expression that bore into him. He pulled the trigger again and the headshot dropped Garvey in his tracks.

The front door flew open and Jim rushed into the room, sweeping it with his rifle. Aside from Charlie, the only man still alive was Isaac, arching and gasping in the recliner. Jim put two more rounds in his chest just as Charlie fired on him again with the 9mm. Isaac slumped limp in the chair, eyes open and blood seeping into the faded blue upholstery.

"All clear!" Jim bellowed loud enough for Hugh to hear. He turned his attention to Charlie. "Finger off the trigger, Charlie. It's done. Secure your weapon."

Snapping back to the moment, Charlie cleared his trigger guard and got up from the couch. He slid the 9mm back into the holster concealed inside his waistband.

Hugh stepped in through the front door, rifle at a low ready position.

"We're clear," Jim repeated.

Hugh lowered his rifle. "Charlie, you good?"

Charlie nodded.

"Charlie, get your gear back on," Jim said. "You go get the horses while Hugh and I search the house. Keep an eye out in case the shots drew any attention. If you see anyone headed this way, don't engage them. Just come back here and we'll deal with it as a team."

Charlie didn't say anything.

"Look at me, Charlie," Jim ordered.

Charlie met his eye.

"What do you need to do?" Jim asked.

"Horses. Be careful. Don't engage," Charlie breathed.

Jim smiled. "You got it, buddy. You did good. Now bring those horses back and stand watch on the driveway."

Charlie headed out the door and past the two curious dogs.

Hugh was staring at Garvey's radio equipment with a gleam in his eye and a grin on his face. "Jim, we need these radios. Some of the equipment is a duplicate of what I already have, but it would be phenomenal to have backups. We might even be able to set up a station at Gary's house. He's been wanting to learn the equipment."

"How long to pack it?"

"Depending on how many horses this guy has, I can probably have it broke down and loaded in thirty minutes to an hour. I don't want to damage any of it in transit, so we need to pack it carefully."

"Then get started," Jim said. "I'll help you once I've gone through everything else."

Despite his haste, Hugh couldn't help but examine the papers he found on the radio desk, knowing that any scrap could be something useful. There were frequencies, notes, security codes, and an entire handwritten notebook with even more information. He retrieved a garbage bag from the kitchen and began shoving all the papers into it.

As Jim found more gear they could use, he piled it in the living room. Alongside his pile, Hugh stacked radio equipment wrapped in towels and pillowcases. When he was done searching the house, Jim relieved Charlie in the driveway and had him ready Garvey's horses since he knew his way around the place.

Garvey had three horses and they loaded them down, cramming the gear into every manner of pack, sack, and bag they could find. For each of their own horses, the men strapped on as much additional weight as the horse could bear. When they'd loaded all of the radio equipment, food, gear, weapons, and ammunition they could haul, there was still a sizable pile remaining on the living room floor. Garvey had been well-equipped.

"What do we do with this?" Charlie asked. "It would suck to leave it behind."

"Let's cache it in the woods behind the barn," Jim said. "Wrap it in tarps, garbage bags, whatever we can find. We'll cover it with leaves and horse manure. I suspect no one will go digging in horse shit to see what's under it."

Charlie grimaced. "That's a safe bet."

"When we're done, we need to burn this place to the ground," Hugh said.

Jim nodded.

"Why?" Charlie asked. "This place is kind of cool."

"We need to erase our tracks," Hugh explained. "We burn it to the ground and people can only speculate about what happened here. There won't be any evidence. Then we give it a few days for things to settle down before we come back for our cache."

They shuttled the last of the valuable gear outside and raced to build their cache. When they were done, they used a spading fork to shovel horse manure over the top of it.

"This will work," Charlie said, crinkling his nose. "No one is going to go rooting around in this mess."

When they were done, Hugh and Charlie mounted up and took the horses to the end of the wooded driveway.

Jim dumped the frying pan of fish off the porch and addressed the dogs. "You guys eat up. Then you're going to have to find a new home."

Jim went back inside and scattered a can of Coleman fuel around the living room. When he'd thoroughly saturated the furniture, rugs, and drapes, he stuck a lighter to them. The blue flames spread quickly and Jim sprinted for the driveway, his overloaded web gear rattling as he ran.

He took his reins from Charlie, climbed into the saddle, and they descended the mountain. They rode in single file, each of them towing a packhorse. As much as they could, they stayed to the shoulder of the road, the composting leaves and humus muffling the clatter of hooves.

When they reached the four-lane highway, Jim checked his watch. "We should be home by daylight. That's perfect. You did good back there, Charlie. I'm proud of you."

Charlie turned in the saddle and smiled at Jim, the expression not nearly as endearing in the green glow of the night-vision goggles. "Thank you."

32

The trio rode into their section of the valley as the pre-dawn sky was turning from gray to pink. Long wisps of pearlescent clouds scratched across an infinite expanse of morning. It would have been a beautiful sight for the well-rested, looking forward to a productive day. For this group, weary from their night of violence, it almost seemed a taunt from the universe itself. An accusation that there were still things of beauty in this world that could not be sullied by the ways of men.

Jim saw within it the promise of a hot, humid, and overcast day. That had been the trend as of late. Rain passed them over more often than it paused to share its blessing. Their gardens were browning like the pasture grasses and the harvest was slowing. There were more rocks visible in the river as the water level dropped. Fires were tended with more caution as everyone feared the wrath of an unchecked wildfire in a world with no firefighters. Any runaway blaze would have to burn itself out, just as fires had done for hundreds of millions of years.

Despite the heat, late summer carried the inherent reminder that fall would be upon them soon. It was a reminder that a year had come and gone since the terror attacks. All of their pleas that normality might return to them by this time stood ignored, as if the Creator himself had turned his nose up at them. Barring some miracle, it was likely to be another cold, dark winter of rationed meals and wood heat for some, of deprivation and death for others.

The riders passed the Wimmers' house and saw the family already out working their garden. It was the way of old country people, gardening in the cool of morning at first light. They straightened from their labors as the riders passed their home. They were stark and colorless silhouettes in the early morning, still as scarecrows, with their implements of harvest clutched in cracked and calloused hands.

The Wimmers made no gesture of greeting toward the riders and received none in return. Jim felt nothing for the family anymore beyond a general amusement at the crass, unfiltered old matriarch of the clan. In some ways, she reminded him of what he may one day become if he lived long enough. Some bitter and profane oracle, prophesying in rants and curses, lamenting a time when all things were simpler and—from fruits to friendships—inherently sweeter.

Just beyond the Wimmers' house they turned up the mountain, angling through high pastures to intercept the road to Hugh's place, where it entered the treeline. Like the rest of the group, Jim was so tired that the rocking of the horse nearly lulled him into a trance. He couldn't recall that anyone had spoken a word in the last hour. Even when they reached Hugh's home they still sat on their horses, as if uncertain what to do with themselves.

"Hugh, you want to unload the radio equipment here so you can go through it?" Jim asked, his voice a weak croak from disuse and weariness.

"That'll work. Not sure I can store all of the other gear we brought back. This place doesn't have much storage."

"That's no problem. You take anything off these horses that you want or need and I'll stash the rest at my place."

They all dismounted, stretched, and eased into the process of offloading the radio gear and the few other items that Hugh set aside. When they were done, Jim gathered the reins of the three packhorses and used some rope to tie them in a train. Hugh and Charlie watched, sagged against porch posts like scruffy, dangerous bookends.

"I know we're all tired," Charlie said, "but when do you expect we might be going out again?"

They all knew what he meant by "going out." Charlie wanted to know when they'd be checking the next name off the list.

"Is there anyone in that group that stands out above the others?" Jim asked. "Anyone particularly mouthy or wound up?"

"Damon Sauls," Charlie replied without hesitation. "He always had something to complain about. With Hadley dead, he'd be the one to keep pushing things. I guarantee it."

Jim sighed. "I should have known."

"You know the guy?" Hugh asked.

"He works for the school system. An assistant principal or something. He's a local guy, but speaks with an affected southern accent. I guess he wants people to think he's from somewhere else. He's not, and he gets a little riled up when you ask him about his accent. I've done it a few times just to get under his skin. It's like those people who spend a week in England and come home speaking with an English accent, like it's something totally beyond their control after being there for a week."

"Sounds like an asshole," Hugh said.

"He is," Charlie agreed. "He talks a lot when they have their meetings. I always got the feeling that Hadley was in charge because he was in politics, but Damon was the one really making the decisions. He's always coming up with problems they need to deal with and Jim is at the top of that list."

Jim frowned. "What did I ever do to him?" He meant it as a joke. He was used to not being liked.

"Besides make fun of his accent?" Hugh frowned.

"He thinks you're dangerous," Charlie said. "He said you're a perfect example of a hillbilly who's obsessed with guns. He says you're proof of why they shouldn't be allowed in the hands of regular people."

Jim shook his head in disgust. "Sounds like him."

"You think he'd try to keep this Community Security Council going with Hadley dead?" Hugh asked.

"I'm sure of it," Charlie said. "He didn't seem to have much respect for Hadley and Hadley knew it. He said Damon resented having to go through an uneducated politician like him. Since he knew Damon didn't like him, Hadley enjoyed throwing his weight around. He said it was to put Damon in his place. With Hadley out of the picture now, I wouldn't be surprised to see Damon try to step up and take over."

"He doesn't live far from here," Jim said, rubbing his eyes. "Big subdivision near all those fast food places. I saw him handing out candy when I took the kids trick-or-treating in that neighborhood."

"That's less than an hour's ride," said Hugh.

"That neighborhood has held up better than some," Jim said. "They lost some folks, but I'd say about half the families are still there."

"So, we have to go at dark," Charlie pointed out.

"Definitely. Not a lot of trees to hide our approach, either." Jim yawned, a reminder that he needed to shut up and go home. "I'll be back up here after dinner, then we can go check it out."

With that settled, Jim started down the mountain. Thirty minutes later, he crossed the valley road and let himself through the gate onto his property. As he neared his home, he spotted Pops and Ellen sitting on the front porch. He lifted his hand in a tired wave as he rode past, heading directly for the barn.

He unloaded the horses and stacked the cargo anywhere he could find a spot. He'd sort through it later. The saddles and blankets were stacked on a rickety wooden sawhorse adapted for this purpose. Finally, he led the four horses to the pasture, where he removed each bridle and turned them out. Some shook and rolled in the dust. Others drank from the trough with loud gulps. Jim returned to the barn and hung the bridles on nails, then headed for the house.

He straggled up the porch steps with the last of his energy. Pops and Ellen watched with interest as Jim cleared his rifle, then began stripping off his gear.

"Late night?" Pops asked. He had no clue what Jim had been up to. Pops knew there were a lot of things that went on in the valley he wasn't privy to. Sometimes that riled him up, but other times he understood it was probably best he didn't know. He seemed to understand this was one of those times it was best not to ask too many questions.

Jim shrugged. "Long night."

"Can I fix you anything to eat?" Ellen asked.

"No, thank you," Jim said. "Need sleep more than anything."

"The house is stuffy. You might do better on the back porch," Ellen suggested.

"I'll stow my gear and give that a try."

"I'll warn the kids," Ellen said. "Maybe they can try to keep it quiet."

Jim smiled. "Not likely."

"Everyone okay?" Ellen asked.

Jim understood the nature of her vague question. She didn't want to give too much away to Pops, but she wanted to know if Hugh and Charlie were back home safe too. "Everyone is fine."

That reply appeared to satisfy her. She averted her eyes back to the green mountain ahead of her and took a sip of her mint tea.

33

Later that evening, the sun had just dipped below the horizon when Hugh, Charlie, and Jim dismounted on the knoll across from Damon Sauls' neighborhood. The sky was tinged the color of grapefruit but muted by the summer haze. The subdivision before them had been built in the late 1960s, full of sprawling ranch houses with a few other styles sporadically thrown in.

"It's that brick house." Charlie pointed to one near the front. "I was there with Hadley once to schedule a meeting."

"You know anything about his family situation?" Jim asked. "I can't remember if he was married or not."

"Hadley said he was still single because he thought he was too good for anyone around here. I never saw or heard anyone else at the house when I was there."

"What's the plan?" Hugh asked.

"He knows Charlie," Jim replied. "He might open the door if he knocks."

"He should," Charlie said. "But we'll need to go now. He might not open up after dark. He's kind of skittish."

Jim looked at Hugh. "Why don't you let me borrow that

suppressed 9mm? I'll go with Charlie and hide outside the door. When Damon opens it, I pop him, then go in and put a second round in him."

Hugh shook his head.

Jim looked confused. "You won't let me borrow the pistol? Seriously? They'll hear mine all through town."

"No, it's not that," Hugh replied. "Why don't you let me go with Charlie and you watch the horses?"

Jim frowned. "I don't feel like I should ask you to kill my enemies. It's my problem."

Hugh pointed at Charlie. "You're taking *him.*"

"I'm taking him because Damon probably wouldn't open the door to me. He thinks I'm an asshole."

Hugh raised an eyebrow. "That's a popular opinion. Besides, Damon isn't just *your* enemy. If he's working against you, he's working against all of us."

"Guilt by association?"

Hugh shrugged. "I guess so."

"I don't like it," Jim said.

"Do you have to like it? Is that required?"

"I guess not." Jim stared off at the distant brick house.

"So, Hugh is coming with me?" Charlie confirmed.

"This time," said Jim. "Next one is mine."

Hugh handed his reins over to Jim. "Share the burden, man. That's how this works."

Jim didn't comment, but his frown made it clear how he felt about the subject. As far as he was concerned, this was still his mess to fix. He didn't know if he could ever rid himself of that idea. It all went back to that one weird feeling that Jim had never been able to resolve, which was how did one *take* responsibility for people without *becoming* responsible for them? By helping his friends, he felt like he'd put himself in a role that he wasn't qualified for and couldn't sustain. Sometimes he had to lead them, but he'd never felt like he was a capable leader.

Hugh and Charlie took off through the high grass while Jim tied their horses up in the nearby brush. He extracted a pair of binoculars from a saddlebag and took a seat where he could keep an eye on things.

It took Hugh and Charlie nearly twenty minutes to descend the knoll, cross the road, and head up the opposite hillside. They were intentionally avoiding the main entrance road to the subdivision to minimize how many people saw them, but that meant some bush-whacking. The two had to navigate thorny blackberry bushes, high weeds, and poison ivy. Watching them struggle through it was almost enough to make Jim glad he'd hung back. Almost.

Once they were beyond the brush, Charlie took an established trail through the high grass toward Damon's yard. With no mowing taking place these days, the yards were nearly indistinguishable from the cattle pastures adjoining the neighborhood. Once Hugh and Charlie were in the open, Jim scanned the other houses nearby, watching to see if anyone was paying attention to the strangers walking into their neighborhood. He saw no one outside at all. If anyone was watching, they were doing it from the humid recesses of their powerless homes.

As they closed in on Damon's long, brick ranch house, Hugh diverged from the path while Charlie continued toward the front entrance. Charlie slowed his pace, giving Hugh enough time to flatten himself against the house and take a position alongside the door. Only when Hugh was crouched behind an overgrown Juniper bush did Charlie climb the porch.

He paused at the front door, then raised a fist and knocked. He knocked so hard that Jim could faintly hear it from across the hill. He cringed at the volume of it, wondering why Charlie felt the need to alert the entire neighborhood of his presence.

When there was no answer, Charlie twisted his body toward Hugh and shrugged. Jim scanned the area around the house again, wondering if Damon might be outside. He didn't spot him, but he did see something that made him reach for his radio.

"Jim for Hugh, Jim for Hugh!"

Through his binoculars, Jim saw Hugh fumble with his earpiece before keying the mic on his radio.

"*Go for Hugh,*" came the hushed response.

"You have incoming from the south side of the house. A neighbor must have heard the knocking and she's heading your way. Older female."

"*Roger that.*"

Jim lowered his radio, but kept his binoculars glued to the scene before him. Hugh called a warning to Charlie before ducking deeper into the hedges. No one had any time to coach Charlie on how to act with this unexpected guest, but Jim was truly impressed at the way he so naturally pulled it off. Charlie did not attempt to hide. He acted like he was there on legitimate business. When the woman came around the corner and approached him, he responded with a friendly smile.

The woman didn't appear to be suspicious. Her body language suggested she was relaxed, perhaps even trying to be helpful. When they were done speaking, Charlie descended the porch. He gave the woman a friendly wave as the conversation ended and headed back to her house. Charlie started down the same trail he'd used to approach the house, pretending like he was alone.

"What just happened?" Jim asked into his radio.

"*She heard the knocking,*" Hugh replied. "*She told Charlie that Damon said he was going to a meeting in town.*"

"What did Charlie say?"

"*He did good, Jim. He told her that he was planning on going to that meeting too, but hadn't got word of where they were having it.*"

"Did she know the location?"

"*I don't think so. We'll have to ask Charlie when we regroup.*"

"That lady just went back inside her house, Hugh. The coast is clear for you to get out of there."

"*Copy that. On my way.*"

Hugh extracted himself from the hedges and followed Charlie's lead, walking casually from the yard like he belonged there. Charlie didn't pause to wait for him until he got to the paved road. Once

Hugh caught up with him, the two climbed up the knoll to Jim's position.

It was considerably darker by the time they reached him. Fireflies were a flickering yellow constellation that morphed in the fields surrounding them. Both men were huffing and puffing from the steep climb. They went straight to their horses and retrieved water bottles before joining Jim.

"She didn't know where the meeting was," Charlie said before taking a sip from his bottle.

Jim smiled. "That was impressive, Charlie. You didn't panic. You kept your cool. That was good work." He was tempted to say something about how much better he liked *this* Charlie than the Charlie who never listened, but he didn't want to turn his praise into criticism. He bit his tongue and focused on the positive.

"So, what now?" Hugh asked. "Do we go into town and look for this meeting?"

Jim scrunched his face up as he considered this. "Not sure how we'd cover that much ground. The meeting could be anywhere. And if we start asking around, that might be a little suspicious."

Hugh took a sip of water. "We could ask Ian. Something might have come up at the market. Other people might know where the meeting is being held."

"That might be a good idea," Jim said. "We're nearly to town already and there's no use wasting a trip."

34

———————

Using night-vision, the three rode into the dark town, doing their best to stay to backstreets when they could. Unfortunately, there were no side streets that ran the full length of the small town. At times they had no choice other than to ride directly down Main Street where the sound of their horses attracted attention on the quiet night. They spotted drawn curtains in houses lit by candle or lantern. Other gawkers came into their yards to stare at the riders, grainy sentinels standing in silhouette, offering no greeting or gestures of welcome to these three horsemen of the apocalypse.

When they finally reached Ian's neighborhood, they paused in the street so that Hugh could make the initial contact. All agreed that the appearance of a single stranger at someone's door was generally less threatening than the appearance of several, given the current circumstances. It wasn't like they could just turn on the porch light and see who was out there.

As Hugh dismounted, Jim pointed to the tree canopy behind Ian's house. In their night-vision, it glowed brightly from under-lighting. "He must have a fire."

"There's a fire pit around back. I'll try there first." Hugh set off across the high yard with long strides. Before he even reached the backyard, he was calling out loud to his friend. "Ian!"

He was gone several minutes then reappeared at the side of the house, waving Charlie and Jim forward. The two rode around to the back of the house, where they found Ian standing beside a campfire with a corked wine bottle in his hand. They dismounted, tied off their horses, and shook hands with Ian.

Ian took a seat in an old aluminum lawn chair and pointed the others toward the various upturned logs he used as seating. "I have to admit, you all look a bit intimidating showing up in that night-vision. Even though I know what it is, it has this whole insectile quality that's a little unnerving."

Jim planted himself on a log and removed the optic. "Sorry about that."

Ian leaned forward in his chair and extended the bottle of wine toward Jim. "You want a sip? It's a little something I traded for at the market."

Jim took the bottle, uncorked it, and took a whiff. "What is it?"

"Persimmon wine."

Jim took a tiny drink, cocked his head, and smiled in the firelight. "That's not bad." He made to pass the bottle back, but Ian gestured for him to pass it on around to Hugh.

Hugh also took a sip, then handed it back over to Ian.

"Listen, I don't want to involve you in anything, but I need to ask you a question," Jim said.

Ian took another drink from the bottle, then stood it between his feet. "As far as involving me in anything, I'm already involved at this point, but I know how to keep my nose clean. Don't worry about me. Besides, I trust Hugh enough to know that an enemy of *his* is probably an enemy of *mine*. So, ask your question."

"We're looking for a meeting," said Hugh.

"We were going to pay a visit to one of the town's *prominent citizens*," Jim added sarcastically. "He wasn't home, but his neighbor suggested that he'd gone to a meeting here in town. We were hoping to locate that meeting."

"Ah, yes," Ian said as it dawned on him. "I think I know the meeting to which you're referring. I heard it discussed at the market today."

"What did you hear?" Jim asked. "If you don't mind me asking, that is."

"People in town have been a little up-in-arms over Hadley Wright's death. I'm not sure you guys know that since you've been avoiding the market the last few days." Ian's expression told Jim that he'd heard what happened to Hadley, but there was no judgment in that look.

"We were waiting for the dust to settle before we came back," Jim commented.

Ian chuckled. "I don't expect it will be anytime soon. Some of the more vocal people at the market—all allies of Hadley's, of course—have been talking about something they call the Community Security Council. Apparently, it was an organization Hadley Wright came up with and they're wanting to keep it going in his absence. They're wanting to expand it and bring on some new members."

"I've heard about this Community Security Council," said Jim. "Who's leading the effort to keep it going?"

"A man named Damon Sauls."

Hugh and Jim exchanged a glance. Sauls was just the man they were looking for.

"I'm not from this town, so I don't know the guy personally," Ian said, "but he came by my booth to introduce himself. He was offering himself up as a savior there to help the residents of the community with their problems. He said that even though Hadley's death was tragic, it was time for community leadership to move to the next level."

"I can't wait to see what that means," Jim mumbled.

Ian shrugged. "Sounded to me like this Sauls guy was trashing Hadley without just coming out and saying it. He seemed to think he could do better. The whole time he was talking to me it felt like a visit from someone running for office. He never came out and said that, but that was the vibe I got. Like he was trying to gain community support."

"They say where this meeting was taking place?" Hugh asked.

Ian shook his head. "Sauls mentioned that they had this council but apparently I wasn't 'council material' because I didn't get an invite. Some others at the market did because I overheard them talking about it."

"Is there anyone you can think of that we might ask?" Jim pressed. "Someone who might know where this meeting was being held?"

"Not to go into too much detail," Hugh explained, "but it's really important that we get eyes on this meeting and see who's involved with this Community Security Council. They're up to some shady stuff. I'll fill you in later. We have a list of members but if they're expanding the committee, we need to know who the new people are."

"I'd also like to hear what's being said," Jim added. "Apparently I'm a frequent topic of conversation."

Ian gave a regretful shake of his head. "I wish I could help you guys out, but I don't know who you could ask. I heard people say they were invited, but I don't know any of their names or where they live. As I said, I didn't get an invite to the meeting. Guess it's because I'm an outsider. I didn't grow up in this town."

Jim and Hugh exchanged a disappointed glance, trying to figure out their next move. Maybe this night was a bust. They'd have to go home and try again later.

Silent up until this point, Charlie leaned forward, placing his elbows on his knees. "I might know a place we could ask."

All eyes turned to him with questioning looks.

Charlie shrugged. "Hadley's whorehouse. It's not far from here."

"You think they'd tell us?" Jim asked.

"They might tell me," Charlie replied. "I've been there before."

That comment got more questioning looks and some raised eyebrows.

Charlie grew flustered. "Not for the reason you're thinking! I went there with Hadley one time. They know my face."

"Can't hurt, I guess," Jim said, getting to his feet. "Let's get moving."

35

Jim and Hugh hung back in the dark while Charlie rode into the backyard of the brothel he'd visited a few days earlier with Hadley Wright. He noticed with amusement that the garage door he'd managed to raise still stood open, the galvanized bathtub sitting empty on the concrete floor.

Charlie removed his night-vision and tucked it into a saddlebag before climbing off his horse. He tied the reins to the porch rail and clomped up the steps. He hesitated at the back door, uncertain of whether he should knock or just go in as he had on his previous visit. Realizing that the residents of the house might be armed, he decided knocking was probably a safe choice. He raised a fist and rapped politely on the door.

It was nearly a minute before the curtain was yanked to the side and the beam of a bright flashlight hit Charlie in the face. He squinted and shaded his eyes. A few seconds later the door opened and a woman stood there. She leaned against the doorframe, dressed much like the other women Charlie had seen there before, in a tiny pair of shorts and a mostly ripped t-shirt.

She regarded Charlie with amusement. "What you need, honey?"

"My name is Charlie. I am...*was* a friend of Hadley's. I was here with him the other day."

The woman flashed a friendly smile, her face glowing in the light of the flashlight. "I know who you are."

Charlie looked confused. "How? Did I meet you?"

With a coy look, she pointed at the garage. "Yeah, I was taking a bath."

Charlie blushed. "Sorry. Didn't remember your face."

"Oh, you didn't? Where were you looking?"

Charlie grew flustered, feeling his tongue knot inside his mouth. "Uh, I'm kind of in a hurry. Sorry to bother you but I had a question. I was supposed to go to a meeting tonight, but no one told me where it was. You don't know the meeting I'm talking about, do you?"

She checked her watch. "I know what meeting you're talking about but, honey, you're already late. That meeting started about twenty minutes ago."

"So, you *do* know what meeting I'm talking about? Damon Sauls invited me."

She smiled. "I was invited too but I don't want any part of it. Now that I'm shed of Hadley, the last thing I need is to get hooked up with someone like Sauls. I'm going to run this place myself. I learned a few things over the last year. Me and these other girls don't need to be giving Hadley half the take. He didn't do nothing but hang around and make us fawn over him. I'm glad the little troll is dead."

"Did they tell you where the meeting was going to be held?"

"At the shell building," she replied.

"The old Shell gas station?"

She rolled her eyes. "No. That empty building in the industrial park near the superstore. They call it that because it's just a metal shell."

"Oh. Thank you. Guess I better be going."

She pursed her lips. "You sure you want to do that? You seem like a nice kid. I'm not sure there's any reason for you to get involved in a mess like that Community Security Council. Ain't nothing but a bunch of snooty assholes who think they're entitled to run things around here."

With a sheepish grin, Charlie said, "It's something I got to do."

"Well, come on back when you got more time," she said with a wink. "You're about that age where a girl like me could teach you a few things."

"Uh, ain't sure I got the money for that," he lied.

She reached out and stroked his face. "First time is on the house."

"Gotta go!" He turned and hopped down the steps, nearly springing into the saddle. "You have a good night," he called as he rode off.

In a few minutes, Charlie was reunited with Hugh and Jim. When he got his night-vision back on, the first thing he noticed was their broad grins. They'd clearly gotten a lot of enjoyment from what had transpired on the back porch of the whorehouse.

"You sure you ain't a regular?" Hugh asked. "That girl seemed mighty taken with you."

"Go ahead," Charlie snapped. "Get it out of your system."

"You find out anything?" Jim asked.

"Meeting started twenty minutes ago at the shell building. I thought she meant the Shell gas station, but she said it was an empty building in the industrial park," Charlie said.

"It is," said Jim. "The county built an empty building in the industrial park to attract a tenant. It's just a metal shell and they finish it out for whoever decides to move into it. That would be the place they're talking about."

"Where is it?" Hugh asked.

"The side road by the superstore," Jim said. "The building is hard to see from town because of the way it sits."

"Oh, I noticed that building from the roof of the superstore when I was living there," said Hugh. "I didn't know what it was. It's isolated, so we should be able to approach it easily."

"And then what?" Charlie asked. "What are we going to do when we get there? This isn't just Damon Sauls we're dealing with now. It's a lot of people."

"We can't decide that yet, Charlie. We need to hear what's being said first," Jim replied.

"I'm sorry."

"No need to apologize. Just remember that patience tends to be more valuable than haste. Most actions you'll take in life will benefit from a little more thought rather than less thought."

"We better get moving," Hugh urged.

The three headed across town at a trot. They took the back street that passed the farmers' market and brought them out on Main Street. From there, it was another mile to their destination.

"You know, I like that Ian hasn't immediately latched on when I've offered him help," Jim mused. "Most people these days latch onto you instantly, desperate for whatever you might be able to do for them. He's thoughtful about it. I don't think he'll call on us until he has a genuine need."

"I agree," Hugh replied. "I think there'll be a day when he becomes part of our clan, but I'm not sure if he'd ever move into the valley. As you've said before, that might not even be the best place for him. He may be of more use in town. I feel like he's one of us, though."

"How could he be one of us and not live there?" Charlie was frowning beneath his night-vision. "I don't get it."

"There's family you're born into, Charlie, and family you choose," said Hugh. "Regardless of how you come into a family, you become one of them and a space is made for you. If you screw up and burn the bridge with your family, that space they made for you is still there. Your absence is felt. That doesn't always mean your family will want you back. Sometimes they have to accept that life is better without you than with you. It's a bitter pill to swallow, but it happens all the time."

"Is that why you guys kept looking for me after I left?"

"It was," Jim said. "That bridge between us may have been on fire, but we managed to put it out."

"I'm glad you did."

Jim smiled. "I'm glad we did. too."

36

Charlie, Hugh, and Jim left the paved street and entered the industrial park, cutting through a field that circled behind the vacant shell building. They tied their horses off in the trees and descended on foot toward the rear of the building. As handy as horses were, they weren't made for stealth and could give you away at the most inopportune moments.

The trio stayed in the high grass and brush for as long as they could, but the building was surrounded by a wide gravel lot that offered no concealed approaches. After a hasty conference, they decided the best plan was to split up. With multiple people listening at different locations, they'd have a better chance to pick up what was being said inside. Especially since the interior of the building was so large.

No doors had yet been installed in the shell building, so some wall sections were left open for the future construction of loading docks or office additions. Inside, the floor was gravel and someone had built a large bonfire from pallets that illuminated the interior. Shadows flickered on the high walls as the flames danced.

Charlie was sent to the left, the west side of the building. Hugh went east. Jim was going to take the back of the building, which faced to the south. The group meeting inside was positioned roughly in the center of the building, so none of Jim's group would be any closer than the others. They determined that if the meeting broke up or one of them was detected, they'd retreat into the high grass and head for their horses. With the advantage provided by their night-vision goggles, it wasn't likely that anyone would be able to pursue them into the darkness.

Approaching from the rear, Jim left the safety of the high grass and slid down an eroding embankment of red dirt. He paused at the bottom to make sure he hadn't been spotted, then kept moving toward the building. He placed each foot carefully to reduce the crunch of gravel. To the benefit of Jim and his team, the building was filled with the sound of the crackling fire and loud conversation. Hopefully, that would help mask any sounds made by their approach.

When Jim reached the building, he took cover to the side of a wide opening and flattened himself against the metal siding. He folded his night-vision out of the way since the light put off by the fire was too bright for his optic to be helpful. He peered around the corner and the first thing he noticed was the number of people in attendance. He counted eighteen in total. That was a pretty good turnout for a nighttime meeting under the current circumstances. Some of the people stood, while others were seated in camping chairs.

Even without a podium, it didn't take long to see who was in charge of the meeting. The man they were looking for, Damon Sauls, was clearly serving as the facilitator. He acknowledged each speaker and attempted to maintain order when several people started talking at once. The conversation was pretty animated, with lots of raised voices and people trying to drown each other out.

Sauls raised his hands to soothe the flaring tempers, but no one was in a mood to be soothed. They appeared to be arguing over the leadership of the Community Security Council, the organization Hadley had been running until his unfortunate demise. The very organization responsible for passing on intelligence about Jim Powell and any other people they didn't feel were good neighbors.

"I believe I should be the new head of the Community Security Council," Sauls argued, "because I've had a close relationship with Hadley Wright for the past year. We spent a lot of time together before he was killed and it gave me a good understanding of the kind of issues we face as a community. Not to brag, but I've also been privy to some of the behind-the-scenes plans that are in the works."

Sauls' entire speech was delivered in his affected deep-South accent. Whether it was the content of what he said or the accent with which he delivered it, his monologue was met with skeptical stares from most of the audience.

"Well, if simply knowing Hadley Wright for any length of time makes a man qualified for the job, then I'm probably the most qualified of all of us," said a white-haired man in overalls. "We played together as kids."

The rumbles of disagreement showed that no one bought that argument any more than they'd bought Sauls'.

"You mentioned being privy to behind-the-scenes plans. What kind of plans are you talking about?" a woman asked.

Jim recognized her as being a local businesswoman named Tina Curtis. She was a successful realtor who also owned a small restaurant on Main Street. Jim never had any interaction with the realtor, so he had no reason to dislike her.

Well, he had *one* reason. Her name was among those listed in the papers Charlie had provided. She was part of the intelligence network wanting Jim dead.

"Whatever those security plans are, I hope they address the Jim Powell situation," she continued.

In the darkness outside the building, Jim rolled his eyes and felt his blood pressure climb. She'd just confirmed the one reason he didn't like her. And now Jim wasn't just a person, he was a "situation."

Sauls gestured at her with an open hand, acknowledging her comments, the kind of practiced gesture seen in political debates. "I know how you feel, Tina. I understand your frustration. We don't have power and the aid we expected hasn't come. You can't trust your neighbors anymore. To top it off, a pillar of this community, a man of public service and selfless dedication to the county, was murdered in his home by a common outlaw. We all know who did it, yet the killer is still walking around free when, by all rights, he should be swinging from the gallows."

Bile rose in Jim's throat. He didn't know if his nausea came from the characterization of Hadley Wright as a selfless public servant or from the fact that Sauls felt Jim should be hung for killing him. His sick feeling didn't get any better when nearly every voice around that fire joined in to agree that something must be done about him.

"Yeah, I'd like to know what we're going to do about this," another man chimed in. "All I hear is a lot of talk and nothing ever changes. I know Jim Powell may be the worst of these outlaws, but he ain't the only one running around here with a chip on his shoulder. There's more people think like him out there than you'd believe. They're all over the community, running around complaining about the government and saying they won't comply with any *unconstitutional* demands."

Jim recognized the speaker as a local lawyer named Morgan Gibson. He'd seen the guy's face plastered on billboards along the highway. He had a cheesy smile beneath a 1970s-style mustache. Every billboard asked, "Have you been injured in an accident?" His name was also among those on Charlie's list.

A tall man, his red hair going to white, nodded in agreement. He wore dirty khaki pants and a grubby polo shirt. "There's isolated pockets of that stuff going on all around the county. One day those outlaws are going to figure out they're not alone and they're going to join forces. When they do, we're going to have a full-blown insurgency on our hands. We won't ever get the juice back on."

"You're right, sir," Sauls said sympathetically. "Jim Powell may be the most visible of these anarchists but he's not alone in his beliefs. I've seen it with my own eyes. These people may be in the shadows now, but there's no guarantee they'll stay there. One day they might rise up and present a threat to us all."

"They already present a threat to us all. And you still haven't answered my question about what *specific* security measures are underway that we don't know about," the realtor insisted. "Unless you just pulled that statement out of your ass."

Sauls shot her a sour look. "I didn't make that up. I just need to be careful about what I say. The information I received was privileged and not intended for general public circulation."

The realtor gave a slow shake of her head. "Bullshit."

Sauls looked offended. "It's not bullshit! I'm just not sure how to answer your question without violating the promise I made to use discretion. Many of you met Isaac, the regional sheriff that the Department of Homeland Security put in place. I'm trying to make contact with him now since we no longer have Hadley as our intermediary. If he gives his blessing, I'll gladly tell you everything I know."

"How exactly are you going to make contact with Isaac?" Morgan asked. "Do you have some means of communicating with him or do you simply mean that you *want* to reach out to him once you come up with a means to do so? There's a vast difference between having a desire and having the capability to carry it out. Are you guys in radio contact?"

Sauls looked uncomfortable with the question, but saw no way to avoid answering it. "No, Morgan, I don't have any established channel of communication with Isaac, DHS, or anyone else. All I meant is that I know Hadley had some means of getting in touch with Isaac and I'm working with my associates to figure out how he was doing it. There's a gap in our information that we haven't figured out yet."

"So, you're still not going to answer my question?" Tina, the realtor persisted.

The lawyer exchanged a look with the realtor. "He doesn't know a damn thing, Tina. He's just trying to bluff his way into Hadley's seat."

Sauls was squirming. They were right. He'd only made the public announcement that he had privileged information because he thought that might make him the obvious choice to lead the new and improved Community Security Council they were forming. In truth, he had nothing. Hadley hadn't shared any confidential information with him. Sauls figured he could bluff them, but he'd underestimated their doggedness. He needed to come up with something else if he wanted them to give him the Council chair.

Sauls let out a long breath. "Before I speak to that, tonight was primarily intended to be an informational meeting. When Hadley realized we could no longer depend on the government or local law enforcement to attend to our needs, he formed this organization to take the reins of our own safety and security. He did an excellent job, but the need is perhaps greater than even he understood."

"Amen," grumbled the man in overalls.

"Like me, some of you were part of Hadley's Community Security Council, but some of you are new faces. My fellow Council members and I invited you here because we need to grow and expand our reach. We need to take more definitive and bolder action than we've taken in the past."

"Amen," Tina said. "Finally, you've said something I agree with."

Sauls flashed her a patronizing smile, then searched the faces gathered around the fire. "I guess the basic question I have for you tonight is how many of you are committed to being a part of something like this?"

He let his words settle in before continuing. "Now, I understand that some of you might have come to this meeting tonight out of curiosity, but I need to gauge your level of dedication before we go any further. If there's anyone present who *isn't* interested in being part of what we're talking about, I'd recommend you take your leave now and go on home. If you stay, I'll take your presence as a sign of your commitment. And just so you know, the things we'll discuss beyond this point will require that you take a vow of secrecy. You're not going to be able to talk about them with anyone. Not your friends. Not your family."

When he was done speaking, Sauls folded his hands together over his middle and looked around the circle. A man and his wife looked at each other, shrugged, and stood. They folded their chairs, slung them over their shoulders, and ambled toward an exit without a word.

Another man, wearing shorts, flip flops, and a tank-top stood and folded his chair, too. "Eh, it was a long shot, but I thought there might be refreshments. Guess I was wrong."

Sauls shrugged. "Anyone else?"

Several more stood and wandered off toward the exit, speaking amongst themselves as they went. One admitted he'd only come because he was bored. Another complained that the community had enough government already and the last thing they needed was another committee. The final man to straggle out the door told them he'd only come because he was looking for a way to meet women.

Sauls waited patiently as all who chose to pass on the invitation filed out of the building and disappeared into the night.

37

───────

There were only six attendees and Sauls remaining. Besides the realtor and lawyer who'd spoken earlier, there was a doctor, a man from the state highway department, and two others who Jim didn't know. Some of these were on Charlie's list while others were not.

Tina gestured toward the exit with an open hand. "Well, the gawkers are gone, so I guess we know who's serious. Perhaps we can speak more frankly now?"

Sauls gave the impression of listening, while ignoring her words. Jim had sat through enough meetings in his career to know the look.

"Exactly my thoughts, Tina. I was just concerned about some of the specific actions we might discuss reaching the wrong ears. We don't need people gossiping about our plans. I'm sure you all understand the risk of that. We've done a good job of keeping the work of the Council quiet and we need to keep it that way."

"We could end up like Hadley," said the doctor. "Shot to death in our bed."

Sauls acknowledged him like a student giving the correct response in class. "Exactly, Dr. Jones. No one wants Jim Powell showing up at their house in a black robe carrying a scythe." Sauls chuckled as he said it, but soon realized he was the only one laughing.

"I, for one, see nothing funny about any of this," the attorney said. "We've allowed that ruffian to overshadow this good town long enough. His actions at the power plant have led to an untold number of deaths in this community. But even if you don't count deaths due to a lack of electricity, Powell and his band of heathens have killed plenty of folks with their own hands. Now I'll admit that some of the people they have killed up to this point might have had it coming. They might have provoked him or been in the process of committing crimes when they were killed, but we're never going to get back to normal if we don't rid our community of people like him. He's holding the rest of us back."

"Are you suggesting banishment or something?" asked one of the people Jim didn't know. He was an older man, thin, with white hair.

The attorney smirked. "In a fashion. Albeit banishment of a more permanent and bloody type."

"Excuse me?" Sauls asked. "I'm not following you."

"You all know I'm an attorney," Morgan said. "I've had the often unpleasant task of representing a good many unsavory characters over the years. Drug addicts, murderers, and other bottom-feeders. Some of them owe me a great deal because I kept them on this side of the bars when, by all rights, their asses should have been locked up."

"What are you saying?" Tina asked.

"I'm saying that I have former clients who would kill Jim Powell and his gang, thereby ridding us of the most pronounced blight upon our community."

"There seems to be a consensus that Jim Powell is not the only insurgent out there spreading unrest," said Sauls. "If we kill him, can we stop there? Someone else will just pick up the torch. We should keep stomping until all the ants are dead."

The lawyer threw his hands up, indicating the solution was obvious. "Then we keep at it until we're done." He looked around the room, satisfied with himself. "Am I wrong?"

"Not that I'm agreeing with you, but what would these bottom-feeders of yours require in payment for such a task?" Tina asked. "What is this going to cost us?"

"Their preferred currency is pain medication and I just so happen to have a bottle of Percocet left over from a shoulder surgery I had two years ago. That would be sufficient payment to get the ball rolling."

Tina held up a hand. "But we all know how druggies are, right? We can't pay them until after the work is done. Otherwise, they'll get high and we'll never see them again."

"I agree, and I think they'll accept whatever terms we offer to them." The lawyer looked at Sauls. "What do you think of this? Too bold for your blood?" There was a challenge in the lawyer's comment, an accusation that Sauls might be too soft for the hard decisions that lay ahead of this Community Security Council.

Sauls understood the challenge being put to him and wasn't about to give Morgan the satisfaction of not being up for it. "That's an excellent idea. I'm fully supportive of you pursuing it. For my part, I intend to keep trying to contact Isaac."

"You really think that's wise?" Tina asked. "I'm sure you remember what he said to us at Hadley's house. He isn't supposed to act without approval from above. Perhaps we should wait until Morgan's people kill Jim Powell before we let Isaac in on what we're doing. Sometimes it's better to ask forgiveness than permission."

"I don't have to mention our project, but I still think I should reach out to him if I can," Sauls replied. "Someone needs to tell him what happened to Hadley. I didn't want to mention this in front of the larger group, but we all know that Hadley was our connection to the supplies the Council members have been getting under the table."

"*I* haven't been getting any supplies," the highway department man said, anger in his voice. "What's this all about?"

Sauls held up a reassuring hand. "Don't be angry, Eddie. There's been some aid coming in but in extremely small quantities. Not enough to hand out to everyone in the community. Isaac works for a company called Catalyst Security. As part of his job, he funneled those supplies from the government to Hadley. Hadley gave them out to the people he felt were contributing to the community, most of whom are on this Council."

"I still don't think that's right," Eddie complained.

"Listen, as part of being on the Community Security Council, you'll receive regular aid deliveries as long as you can be quiet about it. If you don't think it's right, I guess we could give them to someone else. Is that what you want us to do?"

Eddie's face clouded with concern. "No need to do that. I need supplies as much as anyone."

Sauls smiled. "I thought you'd see it that way. And for those of you who have already been getting deliveries, we need to get the gravy train reestablished before our pantries are empty."

"And you think you should be Isaac's new point of contact since Hadley is dead?" the doctor confirmed.

Sauls nodded eagerly. "Of course. If it's agreed that I'm to be the chair of the Community Security Council, that would be part of my role. My argument is that I'm the best person for the job."

"Of course you are," the attorney mocked, cocking an eyebrow at the doctor.

"How about we base it on merit?" Tina suggested. "We give the position to the person who earns it."

Sauls looked worried. "Earns it *how*?"

The realtor opened her arms in a gesture that revealed the answer should be obvious. "Through deeds, of course. One of you wants to reach out to Isaac and get the aid coming in. The other promises he can rid us of Jim Powell. I say the first to deliver on their promise should be in charge of the Security Council."

There were murmurs of agreement around the fire. Sauls and the attorney stared at each other. The attorney wore a confident smirk while Sauls glared angrily. He'd anticipated a much easier route to victory.

"I hardly think our proposals are equal," the attorney said. "He's suggesting that he can get those VIP aid packages restored, while I might have to kill a half-dozen people."

"It's not like you're killing them yourself," Sauls scoffed. "You're hiring it out. Anyone can hire people to perform tasks for them. That's not a sign of accomplishment."

"I don't know about that," said Tina. "Some might argue that the ability to put the right man on the job is a better management skill than anything you might accomplish yourself. It shows an acceptance of your limitations and the ability to delegate."

Seeing where this was going, Sauls knew he had no choice but to accept the challenge as it had been presented. His mouth was tight and his forehead creased. He struggled to control the anger that seethed inside him. "Fine then. We'll do it. If everyone is in agreement, let's see a show of hands. I don't want anyone coming forward later and saying they weren't on board with it."

Tina raised her voice. "Let's see a show of hands. Is everyone in agreement that we give the leadership position in the Community Security Council to the person who secures the VIP aid shipments or permanently rids the community of Jim Powell?"

All hands but one were raised into the air. Those casting their votes looked around at each other, all eyes falling on the one dissenting vote.

"You've got to be kidding," Sauls said, disgust in his voice.

Jim tried to make out the one man who hadn't raised his hand, but he didn't look familiar. The lone dissenter stood. Even in this time of poor grooming and general filth, the man was dressed neatly and had his long hair slicked back. He must have been in his seventies.

Tina looked at him with disgust, shaking her head.

The lawyer stared at him with equal disdain. "Seriously, Reverend Cox?"

The old man cleared his throat. "I'm a practical man and I'm here because I seriously care about the wellbeing of this community. I want everyone to be safe, healthy, and happy again. I understand that violence is part of our lives now. I've been forced to resort to violence myself. However, I cannot condone the use of murder to rid our community of a murderer."

Sauls shook his head as he spoke. "You sat right there through this entire meeting. You even stayed after we gave everyone the opportunity to leave if they didn't want to be here. Now, after you've heard the details of our plans, you're wanting out? I'm not sure how I feel about that."

Reverend Cox cast Sauls a pitying look. "Are you going to kill me too, young man? Are you so ashamed of your plans that you have to kill me to keep them secret? You probably should be ashamed. If you start killing people who don't agree with you, where's it going to end? This isn't what I signed up for."

"I'm not ashamed and I'm not angry," Sauls said. "I'm just *disappointed*."

Reverend Cox chuckled. "It's been sixty years since anyone used that line on me. It didn't work then and it certainly isn't going to work now."

"Well, I'm angry," the lawyer said, pulling out a handgun and leveling it on the Reverend. "And I want you to swear *on God* that you'll keep your mouth shut. If you can't swear on it, I'll pull the trigger and silence you myself."

Reverend Cox shook his head. "I don't bow to threats, Mr. Gibson. You don't scare me."

Outside of the shell building, Jim watched with a growing rage. Except for this one man, everyone around that fire had agreed to his murder. The only man to vote against it was now in danger of dying himself.

Jim understood that this was the very heart of the group working against him. It certainly wasn't all of them. There were likely dozens of others out there who grumbled and cursed him, people who didn't care if he lived or died. This had to be the core. This was the cabal of conspirators. These were the people willing to go beyond talk and take action against him. It was this chain of information, passing through Hadley to Isaac and on up the ladder, that led to the Mad Mick being sent to kill him.

Not only did they want to kill *him*, but they now wanted to take out everyone in the community who thought like him. Living in such isolation, Jim hadn't even realized there were others out there who felt like he did, but apparently there were. He was going to have to get out more.

He decided he couldn't let them kill this minister. It wasn't out of any sense of religious obligation, but because Jim was struck by an idea and he needed him alive. He keyed his microphone. He didn't care if his team heard him or not. They'd figure out soon enough what was going on.

"I'm going in," he whispered.

Jim rolled around the corner and into the vast open expanse of the building. In the flickering firelight, no one even noticed him. He put the red dot of his optic on the lawyer first. The man still had his handgun pointed at the minister, screaming at him, but Jim couldn't hear the words. Nothing reached his ears but the pounding of his own heart. His entire world was a fluid montage of purely visual input.

He squeezed off a round. The sound was deafening as it bounced off the hard surfaces of the building. Sauls had the fastest reflexes of the group, sprinting toward an exit before the lawyer's body had even hit the ground. He didn't make it. Charlie stepped through the door and opened fire on him, putting three rounds in Sauls before he toppled onto his face.

Tina got to her feet, drew a revolver from the pocket of her vest, and fired a round at Jim. He was still forty feet away and closing. She hadn't even aimed and her round went wide, not even close enough to cause Jim to alter his course.

She tried to take better aim for her follow-up shot, placing a second hand on the butt of the pistol, but Jim gave her no time to pull the trigger. When his red dot passed onto her body, he pulled the trigger twice in rapid succession. Two rounds caught her in the chest and she heaved backward.

The doctor ran full-tilt toward the nearest exit with Eddie from the highway department hot on his heels. Hugh stepped into their path, rifle raised. The doctor dove to the ground, aimed his pistol, and fired at Hugh. Hugh dodged back out the door, one round ricocheting off a structural steel beam.

Popping back to his feet, the doctor altered his course and ran for a different exit. Hugh tucked his head back inside and found Eddie closing on him, charging like a rogue elephant. Hugh snapped off a round and Eddie stumbled. A second round dropped him and Eddie fell dead at Hugh's feet.

With his rifle still up, Hugh spun in search of the doctor. He found him face down in the gravel, Charlie standing over him. Lost in his own battle, Hugh hadn't even heard their gunfire. He turned back toward the fire and caught Jim in a showdown with the last of the Council who'd voted to kill him.

After Jim had shot the realtor, the only men remaining by the fire were Reverend Cox and another who hadn't spoken. Despite his silence, it was the hand he raised in approval of Jim's murder that stuck in Jim's mind. Seeing he couldn't outrun Jim, he threw an arm around Reverend Cox's neck. He held a knife to the old man's throat and began dragging him backward.

At around eight yards distance, the nameless man grimaced over Cox's shoulder, staring at Jim with rage-filled eyes. Jim didn't even second-guess his ability to make the shot. He fired without warning, aiming for the bridge of the man's nose. His head snapped backward and he released Reverend Cox. The old man cried out as his attacker fell dead, startled by the gunshot in such close proximity.

Jim stood over Reverend Cox. The old man blinked, then wiped at his bloody cheek with his forearm. Jim tugged a bandana from his pocket and handed it to Cox.

Cox sat up and dabbed at his bloody cheek. "If I had to guess, I'd say you're Jim Powell."

"We clear?" Jim called out.

"Clear!" Hugh replied.

Then Charlie, "Clear."

"Check all those bodies! Make sure they're dead and take their weapons!" He returned his attention to the reverend. "Yeah, I'm Jim Powell."

The reverend looked around and shook his head regretfully. "That's a lot of killing. I have to say that I've never seen anything like it in my life and I hope not to again. I'm tempted to ask you if that was necessary, but that's not up to me to judge."

"I consider it self-defense. These people wanted me dead. I've put up with attacks on me and my family for months and I'm tired of it. I swore an oath to make this stop." He raised the barrel of his rifle and gestured at the dead bodies around them. "This is how it stops."

"And me? Why am I still alive?" Reverend Cox asked.

"Because I need someone to tell the truth about what happened here and you were the one man who spoke out against killing me. Once people from town find these bodies, it's going to be the same as when they found Hadley. People are going to be calling for my head on a stick. Then I'll have to kill more people."

"You seem to enjoy killing," the reverend observed.

Jim shook his head somberly. "I don't enjoy it, Reverend. I just want to be left alone. I'd be satisfied to never have to pick up a gun again. I'm tired of the fighting. I'm tired of the worry."

"Then why do it?"

"Because I've tried everything else. I tried ignoring them. I tried running away. Nothing worked. People kept coming for me." Jim spoke more fervently as the memory of everything his family and friends had gone through rushed over him like water spilling through a dam. "I eventually figured out that the only way my family would ever be safe was if I killed the people wanting to kill me. While I'm not proud of it, I'm not ashamed of it either. This is what the world has made us. Sometimes the world doesn't grant you the kindness of a privileged and sheltered life. Sometimes it throws you into a pit like a game rooster and you have to claw your way to the top."

"I'm sorry that's what you see in the world, Mr. Powell." The reverend's words weren't an accusation, but seemed to hold genuine sympathy.

There was a lot more Jim could say, but it was beginning to feel like he was trying to justify his actions and he was done with that. They needed to get moving. He helped Reverend Cox to his feet. "Can you be at the market tomorrow?"

The reverend looked concerned at the question but answered it. "I go to the market most days just to sit a spell and visit with folks."

"I need you to be there around eleven tomorrow. I'm going to address the crowd and I'm going to ask you to repeat what you heard tonight."

The reverend shrugged. "I have no problem with the truth, Mr. Powell. If you're not ashamed to speak of the things you did, then I certainly have nothing to be concerned about. My conscience is clear."

Jim didn't know how to respond to that. "Do you need one of the weapons we're taking off these people?"

The reverend shook his head and reached for his back pocket. He extracted a little .380 automatic and showed it to Jim. "I'll be fine."

38

____

After the reverend left the building, Jim had second thoughts about leaving the bodies behind. There was something about the sight of the dead that hardened people's resolve for vengeance. Even the most hateful and despised could become martyrs when crowds gazed upon their dead bodies and felt they had not received the respect due to them.

"Charlie, could you go get the horses? Hugh and I are going to get rid of these bodies."

Hugh raised an eyebrow. "Don't tell me we're digging graves, Jim. We've got five bodies."

"No graves. There's a manhole out back that's part of the stormwater system. Even if people figure out where we put them, I doubt anyone is going in after them."

Charlie lowered his night-vision and jogged off into the high grass. Hugh and Jim looped a length of paracord through the recessed lifting point on the manhole cover, then dragged it off to the side. They worked together to drag each body to the hole and drop it in. They left their lights off, relying only on the ambient glow of the dying bonfire. Neither had any desire to closely examine their handiwork.

By the time Charlie returned, they were finished and had put the manhole cover back in place. They'd all worked up a sweat, but the night brought no relief. It was still hot, humid, and sticky. They rode out by night-vision, sticking to the fields behind the industrial park. They passed by the superstore, but saw no fires burning around it. Perhaps those living there had doused them after hearing the nearby gunshots.

At Jim's suggestion, they stopped at the river crossing. Jim didn't know what he was trying to wash off, but he soon stripped naked and sat down in the cool river water. Perhaps it was the sweat or the scent of death that he imagined clung to him. Perhaps it was rage and hatred that he tried to wash away, the invisible, psychic remnants of months of indecision and simmering unrest. He lost himself in the coolness of the water and the burbling, almost musical sound it made as it rolled over the rocks.

He wasn't certain how long he sat there. He recalled Charlie and Hugh speaking between themselves as they washed off, but they left him alone to his thoughts. A pebble splashing in front of him caught his attention and brought him back.

"You numb yet?" Charlie asked.

Jim stood and found that he was indeed numb from the cool water, his skin nearly as deadened as his soul. Still, he felt clean for the first time in a long time. He waded from the water and stood there dripping in the moonlight before deciding to use his shirt as a towel. The shirt was damp from sweat, but it was better than nothing and soon he was dressed in his same old sweat-dampened clothes.

"How long was I in there?" Jim asked.

"I don't know," Charlie mumbled. "I fell asleep."

"A couple of cigarettes' worth," Hugh added.

They rode home to the valley. A mile or so before Jim's house, Hugh and Charlie pulled off to head up the mountain. Jim reminded them that they would be going to the market tomorrow and to be at his place early.

No one was excited about doing anything early, especially considering the late hour. Jim had no idea what time it was but it felt late.

He rode onto his farm and went straight for the barn. He unsaddled his horse and turned it out for the night.

He hadn't felt tired all evening, but his legs suddenly felt heavy as he trudged toward the house. At the porch, it took all of his energy and concentration to climb the steps. He regarded the locked front door, then turned his attention to the inviting porch swing with its soft cushions and pillows.

"Maybe just for a minute," he mumbled, heading for the porch swing.

39

Jim awoke to the unpleasant sensation of being stared at. He jerked awake, throwing a hand up to shield his eyes from the head-splitting rays of sunlight. When they adjusted enough that he could peer from beneath his hand, he found Ellen and Pops standing over him with steaming mugs of mint tea in their hands. Jim could smell the bold aroma even though his wiring was scrambled from exhaustion.

"You've been here all night, I assume?" Ellen asked.

Jim nodded warily. There was something in her tone...

"You could have at least come in and let me know that you were alive," Ellen snapped. "I was probably still awake worrying about you when you decided to sack out on the swing."

"I just stopped to take off my boots," Jim mumbled. "Rest my eyes. Tired."

"I'm tired, too. I barely slept for fear that you might be out there dead somewhere."

Jim fought to sit up, which was never easy on a porch swing. Every time he pressed against it, the thing moved in the opposite direction.

"Do you need help?" Pops asked.

Jim frowned. "No, I don't need help." Finally, he righted himself. He leaned back, eyes squinted, trying to find the impetus to stand.

Ellen wasn't done with him. "You're in our seat."

Jim groaned, latched onto one of the chains supporting the swing, and pulled himself to his feet. He took a few stiff steps, then leaned his head against a porch post, eyes closed. "I think I'm going to bed. Need more sleep."

Ellen and Pops settled into the porch swing, their morning ritual as of late. Jim heard them sipping from their mugs.

"Not so fast," Ellen said, placing her mug on the porch rail. "How did last night go?"

Jim turned toward them and leaned his back against the porch rail. He crossed his arms over his chest. "Everyone came home."

She seemed satisfied with his response. "That's good. And did you accomplish what you set out to do?"

Jim considered his words for a long while before responding. "I think everything changes from this point forward, Ellen. We've known for a long time that there were people in the town actively plotting against us. When the Mad Mick was here, he had detailed information about us and our people that could only have come from local sources. We found quite a few of those local sources last night."

She raised an eyebrow. "And?"

"I believe I've broken the chain of information."

She met his eye. "Part of me feels like I should be appalled at what you're saying, Jim, but I'm not. It's hard to have sympathy for people who supported attacks against our family and friends. They wanted us dead. The fact I'm okay with this just reminds me of how much I've changed."

"This period of time will change the landscape of communities for decades," Pops said. "My dad was born thirty-five years after the end of the civil war, but it still affected people throughout his lifetime. Some families hated each other for decisions made during the war. For betrayals, for alliances, for deserting. This will be the same way. People will remember the things that happened. Relationships between people will be redrawn because of it."

As he often did, Jim felt like the words were an accusation against him. He was often on the defensive about his actions, even when people were simply speaking in generalities. Jim had enough self-awareness to understand that his reaction was rooted in guilt, but that didn't prevent the sting of their words. "I did what had to be done."

"I'm not saying that what you did was wrong, Jim, but we need to remember that your actions will impact your children and their children. It's inevitable. William Faulkner wrote that the past is never dead. It's not even past. He was right. That's how life is in the South. The dead are always here with us and their actions continue to shape us."

Jim understood the reference, but preferred not to think of the dead being here with him. He'd put so many people in the ground over the past year that he didn't relish the thought of them following him along like some decomposing conga line. They'd all be waiting for the moment he made a fatal mistake so they could watch him die, just as he'd watched them die.

Jim shook the thought from his head. "I'm going to the market today and I'm going to address the crowd. There was one man last night who spoke out against their actions. I spared his life because I want him to tell the town what happened."

Ellen gave him a wary look. "What can he possibly tell them that's not going to reinforce their opinion of you as an outlaw?"

Pops looked concerned too. "You'll be lucky if they don't lynch you."

"It was a minister. Reverend Cox. He's going to tell them that Hadley was funneling aid to people he felt were important enough to receive it. That's why everyone always kissed his ass and went along with him. The meeting last night was about expanding their Community Security Council so they could maintain the policy of trading information for aid. Reverend Cox is also going to tell them that I wasn't the only person this committee wanted to see dead. I may have been the first name on the list, but I wasn't the last. They were going to go after everyone in the community who was speaking out against government overreach."

"Wait, there are more people out there like you?" Pops' expression revealed his concern at this new information.

Jim grinned. "I know, right? Can you believe it? There are quite a few of us. I had no idea. I thought our little valley was an isolated pocket of resistance, but it's not."

"That's disturbing," said Pops.

"That's *encouraging*," Ellen corrected. "We need to find more of these people and start networking. The problem we've had ever since the power plant incident was that people were networking *against* us. If we can form our own alliance with groups who think as we do, there's a lot of strength in that. It will be harder to take us out."

Jim yawned. "Which was the whole point of going to the market. We just haven't been there long enough to meet people who think as we do." At least that was what he tried to say. Some of it came out as gibberish.

"You'll have to repeat that," Ellen said.

Jim waved her off. "Wasn't important. Need sleep."

Ellen looked at her watch. "You might be able to get an hour, but that's about it. Sleep any longer and you'll miss the market."

Jim opened the screen door. "Then please wake me in an hour."

40

———————

By the time Jim woke from his nap, word that he was going to address the farmer's market had spread through his clan. When he staggered out onto the front porch pulling on his gear, again confronting the blinding sunlight of morning, there was an entourage waiting on him.

Jim fumbled to pull on a pair of sunglasses, nearly jabbing himself in the eye. "What the hell is this?"

"We're all going with you," Ellen said, sweeping her arm around the yard to indicate who "we" was.

There was Gary and Debra, Randi stood alongside Ellen, and Pete was geared up for town. They all had packs, guns, and bottles of water.

Jim clipped his radio onto his chest rig. "We're just waiting for Hugh and Charlie then."

The mention of Charlie's name got some strange looks. Randi and Ellen knew Charlie was back among them, and Pops might also have heard Jim talking to Ellen about it, but none of the others did. Jim had intentionally kept that information low-key in case Charlie's story about collecting information on Jim's enemies turned out to be a lie.

That was why Jim had insisted Charlie stay with Hugh instead of down in the valley where he'd be seen. If Charlie had been lying about his time with Hadley, Jim would have cut him loose and not mentioned anything about it. He was certain now that it hadn't been a lie. So far everything Charlie told him had turned out to be true.

Since they couldn't leave until Hugh and Charlie arrived, Jim went into the story of what happened to Charlie after he fled the valley. He felt it was important to tell everyone about Charlie going undercover with Hadley Wright because people needed to trust him. They had to understand that Charlie hadn't joined the other side for any purpose other than collecting information. Jim hadn't believed Charlie's story when the kid first spilled it, but he was now fully convinced.

"And you're certain about this?" Gary asked. "He's not playing double agent, is he? Collecting information for the other side?"

Jim shook his head. "I'm pretty certain he's being straight with us. The last few nights we've been running all night, mopping up. Everything he told us has panned out."

"Mopping up?" Gary asked, his tone implying he wasn't sure if he wanted to ask what that meant or not.

Jim chose not to go into the whole Michael Corleone/Godfather analogy. That was a little much for this early in the morning. "Hugh, Charlie, and I have been taking out the other side. All the people who've been working against us for the last few months. Charlie's been helping. He's been true to his word. I'd stake my life on it."

"You weren't that sure about him a week ago," Debra pointed out. "I can't believe you're taking him at his word. He stood by while we were nearly beaten to death."

"I'm not taking him at his word, Debra. I was so mad at the boy I nearly killed him when I caught him in the valley. I might have if Randi hadn't pulled me off."

Randi nodded, looking around the group.

"And he changed your mind?" Debra persisted.

"We've been running ops every night and he's been in there with us. It was him who killed Isaac." Jim saw no reason to include the little detail that it was probably him that fired the fatal shot. He'd give Charlie credit for that one. The boy had earned it.

That caught Gary's attention. "The butthead who broke my arm?"

Jim smiled at Gary's attempt at harsh language. "Yeah, same guy." He summarized the story and had just about wrapped it up when Hugh and Charlie came riding onto the farm.

If Charlie was apprehensive about how the clan might react to his presence, those concerns were allayed when he was greeted with eagerness. Pete called to his old friend, riding out to meet him. Gary waved with his good arm, anxious to thank the boy for killing the man who'd injured him and his wife.

As usual, it was Jim who broke up the joyful proceedings and hugs. "We need to get on with it. I need to get to town or there won't be any show for y'all to watch."

"Does this mean Charlie and I can move back into Buddy and Lloyd's house?" Pete asked, overjoyed to have his friend back.

"If your mother is fine with it."

When Ellen gave her consent, Pete cheered at their victory. Charlie met Jim's eye with a look of gratitude. Even while Jim acknowledged Charlie's look, he was struck by how much older Charlie appeared now. He'd been through a lot since his mother returned from Richmond, but the experiences of the last few weeks had matured him more than anything he'd undergone up to this point. Killing had a way of doing that to a person.

Jim had felt no guilt at letting Charlie participate in the purge of their enemies. Of everything Jim's family and friends had done for Charlie, it was that one allowance that may have settled his soul the most. The boy had been granted the opportunity to prove his loyalty and he'd been allowed to participate as an adult. Those had been the two goals that seemed most significant to him and he'd finally attained them. He was as settled and at peace now as Jim had ever seen him.

"Should we break the group up like we usually do?" Gary asked when they reached town. "Ride into the market a few at a time?"

Jim removed his hat and used it to fan his overheated head. "No. We're going in as a group today."

"Show of strength?" Gary asked.

"Show of defiance," Jim corrected.

Jim led the way as they rode through town. Before long, they passed the abandoned fast-food restaurant and plodded down the entrance road to the farmer's market. At first, people noticed them for the size of their party. There weren't many groups of that size, with that many horses, showing up in town. Then as people among the crowd began to recognize the riders, they elbowed their friends and more turned to watch them. Silence spread through the crowd like an unpleasant odor.

The reaction to all this attention provoked mixed feelings among Jim's group. Gary was nervous, concerned that his injured arm might impair his ability to run his weapon if things went ballistic. Hugh was icy calm, always ready to explode into violence if the situation demanded it. Pete and Ellen were nervous, moving closer to Jim and tightening up their group. Randi edged closer to Charlie for the same reason, but Charlie appeared unmoved by all the attention. After what he'd been through, being gawked at by strangers was pretty far down on the list of things that bothered him.

By nature, Jim was a hermit. He didn't like crowds, didn't like attention, and most days just plain didn't like people. He didn't succumb to any of those emotions at the moment. This was a moment he'd been waiting on for some time and he let that anticipation fuel him. Rather than growing anxious, he was amped up. He had a lot to say and these people were going to hear it all, whether they liked it or not.

Jim's mental state reminded him of stories he'd heard working at the mental health agency. People with bipolar disorder described the things they did in their manic phases as almost being beyond their control. It was like a part of them was just sitting back and watching the show while their mania played out on a real-world stage. Jim almost felt like that now, like he had no control over the things he was about to do. Some part of him that he didn't know very well was in control of his body and he was going to roll with it.

He understood that the speech he was about to give would be what people talked about when they went home tonight. For the next few days, it would replace talk of the weather as the subject of casual conversation exchanged between two people meeting on the street or between neighbors lingering in the yard.

He reined his horse to a stop and dismounted, handing the reins off to Pete. "I'm doing this, guys. It's time. Enjoy the show."

"Good luck, Dad," Pete said, his face tight with anxiety.

Jim patted him on the leg. "I'll be fine. Don't you worry about a thing."

He glanced at Ellen, and his wife wore an expression he'd never seen before. She just shook her head, uncertain of what to even say or do under this circumstance. "I got nothing."

Jim smiled. "Love you, too."

He slung his rifle over his back, adopting a less-threatening carry position. He had initially planned to speak from the stage near the pavilion, a spot where the county sometimes hosted bands or events. That stage was at the far side of the market, and there were a lot of people between him and the stage. However, when he spotted a disabled RV in the parking lot with a ladder leading up to the roof, he decided that was an even better option so he headed for it instead.

He latched onto the narrow chrome ladder and began climbing, every eye in the parking lot glued to him. The Winnebago rocked slightly as he hauled himself upward. When he reached the top, he carefully climbed onto the roof. The metal panels popped under his feet with each step and the midday sun reflected back up at him with the intensity of a cutting torch. He could feel the heat through the soles of his boots.

He stared off at the crowd. Even those who'd missed the arrival of his group had now been alerted to his presence. Haggling customers abandoned their negotiations and stared at him expectantly. Vendors wandered out from beneath the shade of their tents. They knew that whatever they'd been engaged in was less interesting than what was about to happen here and they didn't want to miss it.

In the distance, Jim saw vendors and customers streaming from the pavilion and making their way down to the parking lot. Someone up there must have announced that something was about to happen in the parking lot. When Jim looked at the crowd, the faces staring up at him contained the full gamut of expressions. There was everything from curiosity to hate to amusement.

Uncertain of what possessed him to do so, Jim raised both arms in the air and held them there until the murmur of the crowd settled. He lowered his hands and spoke in a deep voice. "Good evening, ladies and gentlemen. My name is Johnny Cash."

There was not a single laugh across the expanse of humanity.

41

Jim cracked an awkward smile that no one returned, not even his mortified friends and family. "Actually, for those of you who haven't had the pleasure, my name is Jim Powell."

While the crowd showed no love for his Johnny Cash joke, the announcement of his real name provoked an immediate reaction. There were boos, jeers, and catcalls. There were hurled insults and some cursed Jim Powell's family all the way back to Noah's ark.

While Jim wasn't bothered by that negative reaction, he did experience a sudden twinge of vulnerability when he realized just how clear a target he was presenting at that moment for anyone who might want to put a bullet in him. There were probably over five hundred people gathered in the parking lot and if any one of them pulled a gun, he probably wouldn't see it until it was too late.

Jim couldn't let himself go down that rabbit hole. He had a message to deliver. He raised his hands to quell the uproar. "Yeah, I know. I'm the devil and you hate me. I get it. I have a few things to say to you, though, and you're going to want to hear them. Before we get started, is Reverend Cox out there?"

The name rippled through the crowd and heads swiveled in search of him. Some were repeating Jim's question to those who hadn't heard him, while others were trying to figure out who Reverend Cox was. After Jim repeated the question, someone in the crowd called out. Jim saw hands raised. The crowd was parting so the diminutive old man could make his way forward. When he stopped in front of the RV, Jim waved him up.

After a moment's uncertainty, Reverend Cox began climbing the narrow ladder. People on the ground helped steady him. When he got high enough, Jim hooked a hand beneath the Reverend's bicep and helped him onto the roof.

The reverend looked uncomfortable but Jim couldn't immediately narrow down which of the elements was causing it. Was it the heat? The height? The hostile crowd?

Reverend Cox drew a clean white handkerchief from his pocket and mopped at his damp face. "Hot up here, isn't it?"

Jim patted the reverend on the back. "Thanks for showing up."

The old man gave a deferential shrug. "I wasn't sure I had a choice. I saw what you're capable of."

Jim ignored the remark and held a hand up to silence the crowd. "I need to address some things that have been going on in this community for several months now. To be blunt, I'm tired of all the bullshit going on behind my back." Jim glanced at Reverend Cox apologetically. "Sorry, I can be *colorful*."

The reverend ignored the comment, laced his fingers together, and waited patiently for whatever Jim had dragged him up here for. He was stoic as a pallbearer.

Jim returned his attention to the crowd. "I know that most of you probably didn't have an opinion on Jim Powell one way or the other until last winter. I grew up here, but I kept to myself and minded my own business. I worked and raised my kids. Most days I stayed out of town because I preferred the peace and quiet of living in the country. But as some of you have heard, six months ago I *might* have assisted with destroying the power plant at Artrip."

That comment struck a nerve. Months of frustration spilled over and people began shouting and shaking their fists. More curses and threats were hurled at Jim. Murmurs of dissent rippled through the crowd.

Jim held up his hands, urging silence so he could speak. "I know a lot you don't agree with what I did and I don't expect I'll be able to change your minds on that. I'm not sure how much you people know about what was going on behind the scenes, but I felt the price of getting electricity back was too damn high."

"That's easy for you to say!" a man shouted, jabbing a finger at Jim. "My mother died because we didn't have power. That's on you!"

"I know a lot of you feel that same way," Jim continued. "But the power generated by that plant wasn't going to your homes. It was destined for Washington, D.C. and Northern Virginia. The only power this region was going to get was for the comfort camp they were building on the fairgrounds. The town and your homes might still have been years away from getting power."

"You don't know that!" the man barked.

"I *do* know that," Jim snapped. "Men from the power company—local men—tried to divert power to town once the Artrip plant was online. Some of you may have seen your lights flicker on as power was restored. Then our government sent in United Nations soldiers to kill those linemen for their efforts and our lights went back off. You talk to their families and they'll back me up on that."

Jim could tell from the crowd's reaction that most of them had not heard this story. "The government also tried to kill me. One of the men injured when the power plant was destroyed put a bounty on my head. I'm sure a lot of you saw the flyers he dropped over the area."

Hundreds of heads nodded in acknowledgment.

"Those flyers put my family in danger. People tried to kill us and most of them died for their trouble. But in case any of you are still thinking about that reward, you can forget it. The man who dropped those flyers is dead and there's no one left to pay the bounty."

Jim saw a lot of disappointed faces at that revelation. There were probably people in that crowd plotting against him at that very moment. The idea that they wouldn't get paid for their efforts took the wind out of their sails. They had to wonder if it was worth the risk to try and kill Jim when all they'd get was a pat on the back from their neighbors.

"Recently there was another man sent to kill me, but instead he came with a warning. He told me he was acting on information that came out of this community. He said there was a network of spies in this town collecting information on those they didn't agree with. And it wasn't just me they collected information on. It could have been any of you out there who ever complained about the government or said you weren't giving up your guns. It could be any one of you who said you wouldn't take orders from United Nations troops."

"That sounds like a conspiracy theory!" a man in the front of the crowd shot back.

"You're partly right," Jim replied. "It *was* a conspiracy, but not just a theory. There was a group of your neighbors meeting in secret at Hadley Wright's house. They passed on information about things they heard in the community and they were rewarded for it."

"Is that why you killed him?" a red-haired woman spat. "He was a good man. I knew him."

"He was an asshole," Jim fired back. "And that's part of why I killed him. The other part was that he was responsible for my friends and family being attacked here at the market. The man who was with Hadley that day, Isaac, was the person to whom they were passing information. He was a contractor who worked for the government."

The red-haired woman looked skeptical, her arms crossed and her hip cocked out defiantly. "Why would Hadley do that? If he was passing on information, it was just to keep the rest of us safe from people like you. That flyer said you were a terrorist or something."

Jim ignored the terrorist comment, though it irritated him. "Hadley was ratting on people because Isaac was paying him in food and other supplies. All of the people who were part of his little group —all of the people he felt were *deserving*—were getting food. But they weren't getting food for helping their friends and neighbors, they were getting it because they were rats. They were spying on you and selling the information to Isaac."

"Why should we believe you?" a short man with glasses and a comb-over asked.

"If you don't believe me, would you believe Reverend Cox? He's a well-respected man in this community."

"Unlike you!" the red-haired woman spat.

Jim opened his hands and gave her a wry smile. It was a gesture that said, "yeah, tell me something I don't know." He ushered the reverend forward, cautioning him against getting too close to the edge of the roof.

Despite the reverend's small stature, he had a powerful voice. He'd likely developed it from years of speaking from pulpits without fancy microphones and sound systems. His was not a multimedia megachurch, but a simple country church with hard pews, no air conditioning, and no fancy stained glass windows.

"First off, I am not a friend of Mr. Jim Powell." The reverend gestured toward Jim with an open palm. "I don't claim to know what's in his heart and I'm certainly not here to tell you what a good person he is. I've seen him kill people with my own eyes, but I have to admit that the people he killed were not very good people either."

A murmur spread through the crowd as people began to wonder who else Jim Powell might have killed.

Jim raised a hand and stepped forward, standing alongside the reverend. "The group of people spying on you was looking to expand their role in the community after Hadley's death. This group Hadley started was called the Community Security Council and they had a meeting last night. There were a lot of people there. Some of you in this crowd might even have been there for the first part of that meeting. Quite a few people left when the organizer of the meeting, Damon Sauls, asked how many were truly committed to their mission. Those who stayed behind, about a half-dozen folks, went on to discuss in detail how they were going to hire men to kill me and my family. Once we were dead, those same men were going to be sent out into the community to kill others who didn't agree with their new Community Security Council. The killers were going to be criminals recruited by a local attorney and he was going to pay them with pain medication. Am I telling the truth?" Jim looked at the reverend expectantly.

Cox spoke so that all could hear. "It's true."

That affirmation spread through the crowd. Heads turned and people whispered.

Jim kept on. "Others in the group were going to contact Isaac and get the secret aid shipments restored. This Community Security Council would then be getting those same food shipments that Hadley was getting, which they intended to keep for themselves." Jim pointed to the crowd. "So, if any of you still think Hadley Wright was a good man, you're mistaken. Maybe I did keep you from getting a comfort aid camp, but Hadley and his associates were guilty of taking food to spy on their neighbors. Did they ever offer to share with any of you?"

No one in the crowd spoke up.

Jim took that as a no. "That's what I thought." He stepped back and yielded the floor to Reverend Cox.

"I ain't saying that what Mr. Powell did was right," the reverend said, "but those folks in that meeting turned on me last night. When I wouldn't go along with their plans to kill folks in this community, one of them pulled a gun on me. He suggested that I should be killed so they could keep their secret. They didn't want you folks to know about their plans."

"Then how come you ain't dead?" a voice in the crowd hooted.

Reverend Cox shot Jim an uncomfortable look. "Reckon it's because Mr. Powell and his folks busted in about that time and killed everyone else."

Jim had expected an outburst at that revelation, but there was none. Perhaps the crowd had heard so many stories about Jim killing people that they no longer had any effect.

Feeling he needed to address the statement the reverend had just made, Jim scanned the faces looking at him. "We killed a group of people who had just agreed to have my family murdered. Once they were done with us, they were going to start killing anyone else in the community they didn't agree with. What would you folks have done?"

Jim's voice grew louder, angrier. "How many of you would have let those people go when you knew what they had in mind? When you *knew* your family might die as a result?"

Faces turned away from him uncomfortably. They looked anywhere but at him. Jim knew they were thinking about what he said. What *would* they have done?

"Despite what you might have heard about me," Jim went on, "I don't like violence. Like many of you, I'm a family man and there's *nothing* I wouldn't do to keep my family safe. Think about your own lives. Think about the actions you've taken in the last year to keep your family safe. Are there things you hope no one ever finds out? Are there things you've done that you'll never talk about? You don't have to answer me because I *know* the answer. Some of you have stolen. You've killed. You've sold your bodies and done things you never, ever thought you'd do. But you did those things because you had to and that's what I did. I'm not apologizing for it. Those people who died last night deserved it. If I had to do it all over, I'd shoot them again."

"My brother was at that meeting and he didn't come home last night," an older woman said. "Does this mean he's not coming home?"

"I don't know who your brother was," Jim said. "But if he was there at the end of that meeting, he's dead and gone."

Reverend Cox gave the woman a remorseful look and nodded. The woman buried her face in her hands and began sobbing.

Jim could feel sweat running down his back. He was baking on this roof and the discomfort only served to forge his anger. He jabbed a finger in the direction of the audience. "Most of you out there are dirty and living in squalor. You stink like rotting corpses and you're one microbe away from some illness that could sweep through this town and kill half of you."

That statement got their attention. Whether it was his words or the vehemence with which he delivered them, they were listening to him.

"You people are wasting your energy being pissed off at me. Your time would be better spent trying to do something about your own situation. Quit waiting on the damn government to come in here and rescue your stinking asses. They're not coming. I've prepared for events like this my entire adult life and there are dozens of things you could be doing *right now* to improve your circumstances. You have everything you need but the motivation. The best thing that each of you could do is to get your heads out of your asses and get to work saving yourselves."

Jim huffed out a breath and started toward the ladder, then thought of something else. He stormed back to the edge of the roof.

"One more thing and I need you *all* to hear this. I am done avoiding you people and staying out of this town. My friends and family are going to be selling at this market. We're going to come into town when we want and try to live our lives the best we can, same as you all are trying to do."

He let his gaze moved around the crowd, meeting eyes with his unflinching rage.

"I don't care how you feel about that. I don't care if you like me or not. But I suggest you keep your feelings to yourself from this point forward. As you've already heard, I'm willing to kill anyone who works against me or tries to harm my family. If you have any doubt about my sincerity, fuck around and find out."

Jim faced the reverend. "Let's get off here. It's too damn hot."

"Not nearly as hot as where you're going," Reverend Cox mumbled, heading for the ladder.

42

The crowd parted when Jim hit the pavement and headed for his friends and family. All eyes were on him, but no one addressed him. Although he met their eyes, he couldn't read what he saw there. He'd halfway anticipated that he might have to fight his way back to his horse, then out of town, but that wasn't the case. Perhaps the heat had sucked the venom from the crowd, much as it was doing with him.

When he broke free of the assembly, no one followed him and he didn't look back. He plastered on a grin as he reached his people and took his reins from Pete. "So, what did you guys think?" When no one immediately replied, he scanned their faces, looking for answers. "Well?"

"That was a strong closing," Ellen said. "Perhaps a little bold."

"Eloquent," Hugh said, unable to control his grin. "Pure poetry."

"I'd describe it as charming," Debra added.

"Randi?" Jim prompted.

She shook her head. "I got nothing, dude."

Jim frowned. It wasn't often he left Randi speechless. "What did you think, Gary?"

Gary looked around nervously. "I think we should go while we still can."

Jim mounted up and took a hard hit from his water bottle. "It was hot up there."

"Not nearly as hot as where you're going," Pete said in a deep voice.

Ellen swatted at Pete while Randi cracked up.

"So what next?" asked Hugh.

Jim pulled his hat off and let the heat escape from the top of his head. "I'm going to jump in the creek and cool off."

"Actually," Hugh said with a wry smile, "I was referring to the bigger picture. You uncovered the core group of people trying to take you out, though I suspect they still have allies out there."

Jim dumped some of his water bottle over his head. He imagined he heard the water boiling away to steam, like quenching a piece of red hot steel in a bucket of water. "We need to maintain a presence here so we can monitor things. We don't want anyone trying to keep that Community Security Council going."

"Well, you have a place to start," Charlie reminded him. "There are more names in those papers I gave you. People who weren't at that meeting last night. Those are the ones you need to watch."

"For now I'm just going to assume I can't trust anyone until they prove otherwise," Jim said. "I also think I'll put out the word that I know who the remaining Council members are and they should leave town because I'm coming for them."

"I expect they'll take that warning very seriously," said Gary.

"So, we're returning to the market?" Ellen asked.

"If everyone is up for it," Jim said. "You might even give it a try yourself, Ellen. It may do you good to see some new faces."

She looked unsure about that. "Yeah, we'll see how it goes."

"Sounds good to me," Randi said. "I miss it a little bit. Not the drama but meeting new people and bartering."

"She likes the haggling," Pete said. "You should see her in action."

Jim replaced his hat on his dripping head and tucked his water bottle back in the saddlebag. "I guess I shouldn't be surprised that someone who enjoys arguing so much would be good at bartering."

"I'm ready to come back," Debra said. "I miss it too. It was a break from the routine."

Gary raised his broken arm. "Maybe one of the other girls can come with you since I'm laid up. I can stay home and watch the kids."

"I might come spend the day at the market, too," Jim said. "Might be able to get a handle on how people feel about what I said today. If nothing else, my presence might force any remaining idiots to show themselves."

His words hung in the air and no one commented. Everyone looked away, conveniently finding something else to pay attention to.

Finally, Hugh broke the ice, pretending to write in an imaginary notebook. "Note to self. Bring extra ammo."

Only Jim and Randi laughed.

They rode in silence until they reached the river crossing. Jim stopped and dismounted. The rest of the group stayed on their horses, watching with amusement while Jim emptied his pockets into his saddlebags. He waded in, then pitched forward, totally submerging himself in the lazy river. When he stood back up, water poured from his clothes, hair, and beard.

He opened his arms, questioning his audience. "What is this? You guys too mature to play in the creek?"

Charlie and Pete glanced at each other, then promptly hopped off their horses and waded in. One by one, the rest of the group joined them, everyone splashing around until they were thoroughly soaked. The water cooled their bodies, but also soothed their overworked minds. For a moment, everyone was able to put aside the constant worry that nagged at them like a pain that never subsided.

When they were done, they all staggered up the slippery bank and mounted their horses. They rode on toward the valley, feeling as if the river had washed years off their lives and flushed worries from their souls. Peace was always a transient state in their world, never lasting as long as they'd like. They were learning to latch onto those moments when they came across them. One never knew when or even if there would be another opportunity.

43

———————

The next day Jim's people returned to the market with their biggest presence yet. While Gary stayed home, Debra returned with Will and Sara. They also brought Charlotte, another daughter who'd yet to participate in the farmer's market. As they'd done before, Randi operated a second booth, manning it with Pete and Charlie.

Hugh, Pops, and Jim were attending but wouldn't be running a booth. Hugh would float around in an intelligence-gathering and security role. Pops, the big socializer of the group, would be gathering information. Jim's main role was to not get himself or any of his people killed.

While the two parties running booths were setting up for the day, Hugh, Jim, and Pops corralled their horses. Pops chose to wander off toward the pavilion, anxious to find shelter from the sun already beating down on them. Jim and Hugh went off in search of Ian.

The burly man was sewing leather sheaths from old belts when Hugh and Jim arrived at his booth. He grinned when he spotted them. "Howdy, gents. Who's that you have with you, Hugh? Is that Tony Robbins, the motivational speaker?"

Hugh laughed. "Not quite."

Ian cocked an eyebrow. "Are you sure about that? Can't recall the last time I saw anyone move a crowd like he does."

"I'm not sure Tony Robbins ever gave a speech entitled 'Fuck Around and Find Out'," Jim mused.

"His loss," said Ian. "That speech of yours was a masterful work of public persuasion."

"You really think so?" Jim asked.

Ian shook his head. "Not really, mate. I was waiting for the crowd to drag you off there and run you up the flagpole."

Jim looked disappointed. "Oh well, I had to give it a shot."

Ian snickered. "I'm joking with you, man. You had some balls to get up there. And for what it's worth, you might have changed some opinions."

Jim shrugged. "Yeah, we'll see about that. I'm not getting my hopes up."

"Anyway, Jim had something he wanted to bring you," Hugh said, changing the subject.

"I do," Jim said, pulling an old backpack off his shoulder. "I wanted to present you with a little gift for the way you've helped us recently."

"That's not necessary, Jim."

"I know it's not, but I wanted you to know that your efforts were appreciated."

Ian got to his feet to take it, the unexpected heft of it making his eyes go wide. "Damn, what's in there?"

"An AR-15 with four mags and a couple of hundred rounds of ammo," Jim said, keeping his voice low.

Ian let out a whistle. "That's a generous gift in these times, my friend. You sure you can spare it?"

Jim and Hugh nodded in tandem.

"We're good," Jim said. "We can spare it."

Hugh flashed a wicked grin. "Besides, the guy who dropped it won't be needing it."

"It's much appreciated," Ian said. "I thank you kindly."

"I had to break it down to get it in the pack," Jim added. "If you don't know how to reassemble it, Hugh can show you."

"I'd appreciate that, Hugh. Building one of these rifles has been on my to-do list, but I never got around to it."

"Well, I'm heading to the pavilion," Jim said. "I'm going to show my face up there and see how it goes."

Ian stuck out his hand and shook with Jim. "I appreciate the gift. Glad I could help."

"I'm going to stick around and talk with Ian," Hugh said. "If showing your face doesn't go so well, Jim, I'm only a radio call away." He had an amused grin on his face, expecting that Jim would be calling for him before the morning was over.

Jim returned the grin with a slightly more sarcastic version and moved off through the growing crowd. He was wearing reflective sunglasses that intentionally hid the movement of his eyes. As he walked, he scanned the people around him and noticed several staring at him. That in itself wasn't a surprise considering he'd made something of a spectacle of himself yesterday with his public speech. Perhaps it wasn't on the level of a presidential address or, as Ian had suggested, on par with Tony Robbins, but Jim had no regrets. He'd said what he needed to say.

He wound his way up the sidewalk to the pavilion, greeting the folks he passed. Some spoke, but others gawped and stared when they figured out who he was. Conditions under the metal roof of the pavilion were immediately more comfortable. There was still a persistent late summer humidity, but the roof spared them from the direct rays of the sun. A gentle breeze wafted through the structure.

Before wandering around to see what was for sale, Jim visited the booth Randi, Pete, and Charlie were manning. They were still unloading their packs and spreading their wares on the tables built into each stall. Pete was helping Charlie, explaining how they'd been doing things and what kind of prices they'd been getting.

"Hey boys," Jim said, wandering up to the booth.

"Oh Lord," Randi groaned, rolling her eyes at Jim's appearance. "Look what the cat dragged in."

Jim winked at her. "You saw me just a few minutes ago and you're missing me already? How sweet."

Randi pretended to stick a finger down her throat and gag. Pete and Charlie cackled.

"Well, if you're going to stick around, you can at least get out of the way of the customers," Randi scolded, waving an arm at Jim.

He stepped to the side and made way for an older couple interested in looking at the items on their table. While they did, Jim slipped around the table and took a seat inside the vendor stall.

Randi narrowed her eyes at him. "No one invited you back here."

Jim ignored her, focusing instead on the couple looking at the items on the table. He didn't recognize them, but knew lots of people like them. A little over a year ago, they would have seen retirement-age couples like this at antique fairs, craft shows, and farmer's markets. He'd probably have been wearing a checked button-down shirt, shorts, and white tennis shoes. She'd have been wearing a long sundress, a floppy hat, and sandals. They'd both have been clean, neat, and well-groomed.

Now they carried the odor of the unwashed like much of the crowd around them. Their sweaty skin was smudged with dirt. Both had oily hair in no apparent style. Their clothes were ringed with salt stains from dried sweat. They had sunken, sad eyes that didn't appear desperate, but revealed a persistent state of longing. They were depressed, miserable, and almost seemed as if they invited the mercy that death would bring.

When the man sensed Jim's gaze and met his eye, Jim looked away uncomfortably. It was then that he noticed the dozen or so men heading directly for him. As casually as he could, Jim keyed the mic on his radio. "Jim for Hugh. Jim for Hugh. Randi's booth. I've got visitors."

Jim didn't even wait for a response. He nudged Pete with his toe. When his son looked at him curiously, Jim tipped his head toward the approaching men. "I think these men wish to speak with me. You tell Charlie and Randi. Stay back and be alert. Got it?"

Pete agreed, panic surging in his eyes.

"It'll be fine, Pete. Don't worry. Stay cool."

Besides the pack Jim had given Ian, he also carried his backpack with his personal gear. It lay on the bench beside him. As casually as he could, he unholstered his pistol and covered it with the backpack. It reminded him of the cantina scene in *Star Wars* when Han Solo blasted Greedo through the table. Jim stood ready to shoot through his backpack if things got ugly.

Sensing the approach of the group of men and not wanting to be caught in the middle of something, the older couple shopping at Randi's table hastily moved on.

"There you go," Randi mumbled. "Driving off my customers, just like I knew you would."

The spokesman for the group of men stopped directly in front of Jim. "We need to talk."

44

Jim stared at the men across the table from him. The situation drew the attention of other vendors who stopped what they were doing to watch and whisper. Jim saw a few faces he recognized among the group of men. Although he didn't know any of them well, he had crossed paths with some of them over the years. Two were the dads of kids the same age as his children. Another worked at an auto parts store. Yet another had briefly been a coworker years ago.

Jim noted that none of them were brandishing weapons, though some had rifles slung over their shoulders or sidearms on their hips. That was normal considering the world they lived in, but the men were definitely giving off a tense vibe.

"What's this about?" Jim asked.

The spokesman for the group held up both his hands. "We just want to talk, man."

"First, who am I talking to?"

The man shot out a hand. "My name is Cook, but folks call me Cookie. I work at the building supply."

Then it dawned on Jim that was where he'd seen the man before. He stood, letting the pack fall to the side, and exposing the gun he'd concealed in his lap. Cookie's eyes dropped to the weapon and he gulped hard, unaware he'd had a gun trained on him. Jim switched the handgun to his left hand and stuck out his right to shake Cookie's.

Cookie grinned nervously. "Hopefully, you aren't going to need that thing. I'm not here to cause trouble. I just want to talk."

Jim shifted the pistol back to his right hand and holstered it. "Well, you can understand how a man in my position needs to be a little cautious. Sometimes I rub people the wrong way."

"'Cause he's an asshole," Randi piped in.

Jim scowled at her before turning his gaze back to Cookie. "So, what can I do for you?"

Cookie gestured at the men behind him. "My buddies and I were talking about the little speech you made down there in the parking lot yesterday."

Jim smiled. "Yeah, I'm sure you weren't the only ones talking about that."

Cookie returned the smile. "No, definitely not. It was quite the topic of conversation around here yesterday."

Jim had already asked Cookie several times what this was about and hadn't got a direct answer yet. The guy was friendly enough, but Jim was about to get seriously *unfriendly* if they didn't get to the heart of things. Cookie's nervousness was putting him on edge.

Cookie shifted uncomfortably. "Some of what you said yesterday sunk in with us. You said there were dozens of things we could be doing to improve our circumstances."

Jim nodded curtly. "There are."

Cookie threw a thumb back over his shoulder, gesturing at the men backing him up. "We have the manpower to do the work, but we don't know what the hell you were talking about up there. What kind of things could we be doing? We're willing to do them if someone could tell us what to do. We don't know where to start."

"Jim, if you're going to give another speech, could you do it somewhere else?" Randi griped, making a shooing gesture at him. "I'm trying to do business here and you're *not* helping."

Jim rolled his eyes. "Okay." Before stepping out of the booth, he patted Pete on the shoulder. "We're good, Pete. You stay here with Randi and Charlie."

"Hugh has your back," Pete replied.

Jim looked and saw Hugh hanging back. He appeared casual, smoking a hand-rolled cigarette, but he had his rifle positioned where he could quickly swing it to bear if needed. Jim gave him an appreciative smile.

Jim led the group of men outside of the pavilion and they found a spot near a retaining wall that was out of the flow of traffic. When all the men had gathered around, Jim hoisted himself onto the low wall and took a seat.

"I see a lot of problems here and one of the big ones is that no one is working together. Everyone is taking a lick at trying to improve their situation, but you guys could do so much more if you tried working together. I don't know how many people you have left in this town, but you might have a thousand people trying to keep five hundred homes running. Before winter gets here, people need to find houses that are set up for heating with wood and begin getting them ready. It may be that several families have to move in together to make it work, but it will work out better for everyone if they do. Food goes farther if meals are cooked together and you won't need nearly as much wood if you're trying to heat fewer houses."

Cookie looked uncertain. "I'm not sure if everyone will go for that."

Jim shrugged. "They may not, but a lot will when you explain the logic. They'll quickly see how much better it works for them. You might also consider setting up a few shelter homes for the elderly. Get woodstoves moved in, get wood stocked, and set up a way they can cook."

"We could use parts of the elementary school," one of the men suggested.

"Exactly." Jim touched his nose. "And no offense, but most people in this town are looking pretty nasty. Get some of those water tanks from the farm supply, paint them black, and move them into a position where they'll collect rainwater off some of these big buildings in town. The sun will heat the water and you might be able to plumb in a couple of outdoor showers that folks can use. You can even get those big rolls of black plastic water pipe from the building supply and plumb those into the gutters. Leave them coiled up. Those black coils will absorb sunlight and heat the water sitting inside them. Seriously, if you guys don't get more sanitary you're going to start passing diseases around."

"We've seen some of that already," another of the men said.

"Which gets us to sanitation," Jim said. "You need to make sure people are drinking clean water that's been treated or filtered. What's the septic situation?"

Cookie curled his nose. "People kept using their bathrooms until the water ran out, then a lot of them continued to use the toilets even after they wouldn't flush. Then they started using the toilets in empty houses. When those toilets filled up they started using bathtubs and other rooms of the house. It's disgusting really."

"People are also using their backyards and even their neighbors' yards," a man said. "You have to step carefully."

Jim shook his head. "People have to start burying their waste. I know most people aren't going to have the time or energy to build outhouses, but you can improvise. Have people dig holes in their backyards. Screen the hole off from view with a tarp or sheets if it's in a public area. You can make a toilet seat by cutting a hole in an old chair or cutting the bottom out of a camping chair. After people use it, have them throw a scoop of dirt in over the waste. For inside toilets, they can use five-gallon buckets with a little water in them. They can dump the buckets in a hole outside the next day."

"That's all easy enough," said Cookie. "Those are things we can do."

"You also have to remind people to quit using their yards," Jim said. "Waste is going to be tracked into people's homes. Kids are going to step in it barefoot. It's a recipe for disaster."

"What about food?" Cookie asked. "Anything we should be doing there?"

"What's the gardening situation in town?"

The group of men looked around at each other and shrugged.

"People are trying to grow gardens, but no one is having a lot of luck," Cookie replied. "People are stealing from each other at night and animals are getting into it. The trash everywhere draws varmints and they've trashed some of the gardens."

Jim looked disgusted. "You could have done this if you'd worked together. You have to centralize all this because of being in town. You could have used all the fenced athletic fields as gardens and stuck guards on them at night, but it's too late now."

Now Cookie was the one looking disgusted. "I wish someone had thought of that."

"That's why you have to work together," Jim said. "The only people in this town who have been working together are the ones who are working *against* everyone else. You all need to take control back from the politicians and put people in charge who actually have practical ideas."

"Anything else we can do since it's too late to garden?" a man asked.

"Ask around about cattle," Jim suggested. "I've seen cattle that are probably up for grabs now because the people who owned them have died. You could turn those cows loose on those same fenced athletic fields. Like with the gardens, they'll need a guard on them. It might be too tempting a sight for hungry people. Then you find someone who knows how to butcher them and you hand out beef to the community when you slaughter one."

There were enthusiastic grins at that suggestion, everyone liking the idea of fresh beef.

"You can also put the cows to work for you," Jim said. "It'll take some work on your part to come up with harnesses, but you can use cows to help haul in logs for firewood. People used to do that in the pioneer days when they couldn't afford a mule."

Jim started to rattle off another suggestion but Cookie held up a hand to stop him.

"I appreciate this, man, but you've given us plenty work on. These are all good ideas and we can get to work on them immediately. Not sure there's room for anything else on our list since it might take us a while to get people organized."

Jim shrugged. "Sometimes you have to be blunt and tell them that if they don't work, they don't eat. Of course, you have to make exceptions for the elderly and disabled. It's just a matter of putting the right people on the right job. People who can't carry firewood might still be able to can food."

Cookie stuck out a hand and Jim shook with him.

"I appreciate this, Jim. I wish we'd had the opportunity to have this talk back in the spring. It would have been really helpful."

"Look, I know you said you don't have room for any more ideas, but let me throw out one more thing you need to be doing now. Talk to people and figure out where all the fruit and nut-bearing trees are. The woods are full of hickory nuts and walnuts. There are Chinese chestnut trees, and there are apple trees all over the place. This is all stuff that could be stored and preserved for winter. Slice the apples and dry them on strings or old window screens. Collecting them is a good job for kids. Give everyone a bucket and make them fill it up."

"We'll get on it," Cookie assured him.

To Jim's surprise, the rest of the men in the group took the time to shake hands and introduce themselves before heading off. Pleased with himself, Jim returned to the pavilion where he found Randi, Pete, Charlie, Hugh, and Pops all waiting to hear what had transpired.

"I'll have you know that some people appreciate me for my wealth of knowledge," he grumbled.

Randi let out a long breath. "I'm surprised you even managed to get that big head of yours beneath this shelter. If it gets any bigger, you'll have to stand outside."

"Duly noted," Jim said.

"So, they just wanted information?" Pops asked.

"I was ragging on the townspeople in my speech yesterday about being so nasty and not doing anything to improve their situation. Apparently, some of them took my comments to heart. That's all they wanted. They wanted me to tell them some specific things they could be doing to improve their situation. I probably gave them more than they bargained for."

"As is often the case," Randi quipped, throwing Jim a fake smile.

"Well, hopefully they'll take it to heart," Pops said. "I've been disappointed by the state of things. I hate to think what life would have been like if Nana and I had chosen to stay in town."

"At some point, I'd have come into town and dragged you back to the valley," Jim said. "There's no way I'd leave you two in this situation if I had a choice."

Pops got to his feet. "Well, the smell of those kebabs down there is about to drive me nuts. I'm going to have to go sample a few of them. Pete? Charlie? You guys want to come with me?"

Pete joined his grandfather. "Sure, I'm always up for a cat kebab."

"Me too," Charlie gushed.

"They're not cat!" Pops said. Then raising an eyebrow at Jim, he added, "At least I hope not."

45

After Randi continued to complain that Jim was driving away her customers, he got up and moved around the market. He hung out at Gary's booth for a while, spent some time talking to Ian, and talked with some other vendors he hadn't spoken to before who were surprisingly friendly.

Certainly, his address to the crowd the previous day had not converted everyone. There were plenty of spiteful looks and hard stares. There were blatantly challenging looks that bordered on outright aggression, but Jim let them pass. He'd said all he was going to say on the matter yesterday and he'd made it clear there would be a price to pay if anyone came after him. There shouldn't be anyone at the market who didn't know that Jim Powell was willing to pull the trigger if it came to it.

The men who'd approached him with Cookie weren't the only ones who'd paid attention to his words yesterday. Several of the vendors put specific questions to him about projects they were interested in. One was looking for a way to power lights in his home. Another was looking for ideas on putting together a greenhouse that he could use to grow food over the coming winter.

Jim had suggestions for both of them. As he talked, others gathered and listened to what he had to say. Even those who might not like him understood they could benefit from his knowledge and Jim didn't mind sharing with them. A childhood spent reading post-apocalyptic books had morphed into an adulthood where he was obsessed with preparedness and survival. While his body of knowledge might not be anything spectacular among the prepper community, it was informative and potentially life-changing to those who hadn't been exposed to the resources Jim had.

The morning passed quickly and before he knew it, vendors were packing up. Jim made himself useful, helping both Randi and Gary's family close up shop for the day. When they were done, Jim and Hugh went to retrieve their horses from the corral. As Jim fished the agreed-upon payment from his pocket, Hatfield stuck his hands in his pockets.

"Your money is no good here anymore, Mr. Powell."

At first Jim was offended, taking the comment to mean that Hatfield was no longer interested in caring for his horse while he was at the market. He must have seen Jim's temper flaring.

"No, I mean I'm not charging you to leave your horse with me. Everyone is talking about the suggestions you've made for how we can improve things. You didn't have to do that after the way some people in this town have treated you. I'm not sure I'd have been that nice about it."

"I haven't always been nice about it either," Jim admitted. "Several people had to die to get us to this point."

Through a dramatic cough, Hugh barked, "More than several."

Hatfield smiled. "Either way, I appreciate what you're doing and I know I'm not the only one. People like Hadley Wright and the other community leaders always acted like they were trying to get things done, but we know now they were just concerned for themselves. That's not entirely surprising, but it's disappointing."

"That's why they kept pointing the finger at me," Jim said. "It was always a diversion. Give the people an enemy. Keep them looking in the other direction."

Hatfield fetched the two horses from the corral and handed the reins over to the two waiting men. Hugh went to hand over his payment and Hatfield turned him down, too.

"That's okay. If you're with Mr. Powell, I won't charge you either."

Hugh tucked the round of ammunition he was going to use as payment into the bib pocket of Hatfield's overalls. "I appreciate the thought but I can afford it and I don't like owing people."

Hatfield grinned. "Suit yourself, buddy. You going to be here tomorrow, Mr. Powell?"

"Call me Jim. And yes, I'm going to be here as far as I know."

"Good. I have some questions for you about running water into my house. Thought you might be able to help me."

Jim smiled. "I'd be glad to share what I know."

"Then I'll see you tomorrow, Jim."

46

Evenings in the valley were more relaxed than they had been in some time. The garden had produced nearly everything they were going to get from it. There were some tomatoes still showing up, though the bulk of the crop had already been harvested and canned. They'd left some peppers on the plants to age to a sweet red, and had begun to plant the fall crops that wouldn't produce their bounty for a few months yet. With the harvest mostly completed, canning was done and everyone was happy about that. The neat rows of jars stored in the basement were satisfying, but a lot of work had gone into producing them.

Randi and Hugh had managed to produce a small crop of tobacco that was now curing in an old shed on a neighbor's property. Besides cigarettes, the two were also interested in seeing if they could produce some hand-rolled cigars. Though their primary motivation for growing tobacco had been their own desire to smoke it, they both anticipated a lot of interest at the market when they began to put it up for sale.

A few days after Jim's speech at the market, he hosted a harvest party for his clan. They gathered at his home and ate together in the backyard, enjoying dishes prepared from the crops they'd grown that summer. They roasted a lamb and grilled fish that Pete and Charlie had caught in a local pond. They had jalapeno poppers wrapped in bacon and stuffed with cheese they'd traded for at the market. They had chicken tenders and French fries for the children. The dinner was a huge hit.

As the evening wound down, Jim couldn't help but notice the sun was setting earlier. It triggered something innate in him, some biological drive that made him think of all the work that remained to be done before winter. He pushed it from his head and built a bonfire while the kids tried to convince Pops to tell them a story. Pops folded like a wet noodle, quickly agreeing to their request.

"I have to go to the potty first," one of the kids said.

"I'll take you to the outhouse," Randi said. "Anyone else?"

A half-dozen kids shot to their feet.

"Well, come on," she said, waving them along. The kids all followed her around the house like ducklings behind a mother duck.

Pops got up and revisited the plastic table that held the food. "I might need one more dessert if I'm going to have to tell a story. I'll need my energy."

As everyone resumed their conversations, waiting for the kids to return, they were startled by an unexpected sound. All heads spun as the source of the noise strolled around the far corner of the house. It was a grizzled man with a banjo hanging around his neck. Surprise turned to recognition.

"Lloyd!" several voices said at once.

Jim was too shocked to move. "I'll be damned."

"Any food left?" Lloyd asked Pops.

Pops winked. "None at all."

Jim got up from his seat and strode over to hug his old friend.

"More importantly, is there any of my liquor left?" Lloyd whispered when Jim got closer.

Jim grinned. "The blackberry is running low. Randi has been hitting it hard, so I don't know what her supply is like. But come on over, grab a plate."

Lloyd scowled. "You're just saying that so I'll quit playing the banjo."

"Not entirely but that is a pleasant side-effect."

Lloyd kept the banjo on but went to the plastic folding table and started filling a plate.

"The lamb," Pops said, his mouth full of a cookie. "The lamb is amazing."

"I'll take your word for it," Lloyd replied, filling his plate.

Everyone was bombarding Lloyd with questions about his trip and why he'd come back. He was doing his best to answer them when everyone suddenly fell silent. Lloyd and Jim turned around to see what was happening and found that Randi had returned with the children. They were all hurrying back to the fireside, but Randi remained standing at the other corner of the house, staring at Lloyd in shock.

"Uh oh," Jim muttered.

Randi stalked directly to Lloyd and carefully extracted his plate from his hands. She shoved it at Jim, who reluctantly took it. Both men were confused, but not prepared to argue with Randi at the moment.

Lloyd gave Randi his warmest smile and a little wave with his fingers. "Hey."

The smile didn't last long. Before anyone could move to stop her, Randi slapped Lloyd so hard that the crack of her hand resounded through the quiet evening like the snapping of a branch. Lloyd raised a hand to touch his pink cheek, wincing.

Randi jabbed a finger into his chest. "That's for not coming home with Jim."

Lloyd took an involuntary step back, shoved by her hard jab. Then, to everyone's surprise, Randi launched herself at Lloyd, wrapping her arms around his neck. Lloyd managed to get out a shrill scream before Randi planted her lips on his in a long kiss. His scream died as the kiss lingered, then Randi released him and shoved him away.

"That's because I'm glad to see you." Randi turned on her heel and returned to her grandchildren.

"What the hell just happened?" Lloyd asked.

Jim shrugged and handed Lloyd's plate back to him. "You're lucky I didn't slap you, too. The rest of us have had to put up with her all summer and it has not been easy."

Jim and his old friend went to the fire circle and took a seat on a bench.

Pete pointed at Lloyd's cheek and grinned. "Nice handprint."

"I see you inherited your father's sparkling wit," Lloyd replied.

"So, what happened?" Jim asked. "I wasn't sure if we'd see you back here again. I thought you were determined to stay at that camp and play music."

Lloyd used his fingers to shove a clump of barbecued lamb into his mouth. As he chewed, he replied, "I loved teaching at that camp. However, I've learned that one of the things I liked about it was that I got to go home when I was done. I'm not cut out for being a daycare worker and staying with kids all day, every day. It was hard on my nerves."

"You missed the drinking, didn't you?" Randi asked dryly.

"That too," Lloyd admitted. "But I also had a powerful insight one day."

Randi and Jim looked at each other skeptically.

"No, I really did," Lloyd persisted.

"What was it?" Pete pressed.

"I realized that I *need* to play music for an audience. It's what I was born to do. There are other ways to do it though. I don't need to live there with those kids all day long like I'm stuck in some lunatic asylum. No offense to you kids."

All of the children were glaring at Lloyd, brows furrowed and bottom lips stuck out. They'd clearly taken offense.

"So, if teaching at the camp isn't your future, what do you intend to do?" Jim asked.

"I'm opening a roadhouse," Lloyd announced proudly. "I'll play music there every night. I'm also going to make and sell liquor."

Everyone in the group fell silent as they turned this over.

"You know," said Hugh, "that's not a bad idea."

"I agree," said Jim. "It would be a great place for gathering information. Alcohol loosens lips."

"It's perfect!" Randi said. "I could work there as a bartender."

"Any thoughts about where you're going to open this roadhouse?" Jim asked.

Lloyd shrugged. "My parents' house is sitting empty. It was the first place that came to mind."

Jim shook his head. "Too far outside town. Since people can't drive, you need someplace they can walk. Someplace closer to town."

"I know the perfect spot," Charlie said. Everyone looked at him expectantly, which suddenly made him nervous.

Hugh plastered a grin across his face.

"Where?" Jim asked. "What am I missing?"

"He's talking about the house that Hadley ran in town. With the girls," Hugh said. "That what you're thinking, Charlie?"

"Yes," Charlie said.

"No!" Ellen spat.

"Makes sense," Pops agreed.

"Hell no!" Randi chimed in.

Jim cocked his head. "I think that's a solid plan."

Nana frowned. "That's just wrong."

"Cool!" said Pete.

"Not cool!" Debra argued.

"Wait, wait, wait!" Lloyd said. "I have no idea what's going on here."

Jim leaned over and whispered in Lloyd's ear, "There's a brothel in town."

Lloyd smiled ear to ear. "Excellent idea." Then he noticed Randi's death stare.

"You want a handprint on the other cheek too?" she asked.

He dropped the smile. "Thank you, everyone, for your suggestions. I'll take them all into consideration. For right now, I'm just going to enjoy this meal and be glad I was able to make it back to you safely."

"You all ready for your campfire story?" asked Pops.

When the kids all shouted out that they were, Pops launched into one he knew they all liked. Lloyd emptied his plate and refilled it again. Instead of returning to the fire, he and Jim slipped around to the front porch. While Lloyd sat on the porch steps and ate by the glow of his headlamp, Jim went to the storage building and retrieved a mason jar of clear moonshine.

He unscrewed the lid and held the jar aloft. "A toast to coming home." He took a sip from the jar and passed it to his old friend.

"To coming home," Lloyd said, taking a long hit from the jar. Having fallen out of practice at sipping the hard liquor, Lloyd coughed and choked for a few minutes before he was able to croak a few words. "Smooth."

A few minutes and several sips of moonshine later, Lloyd finished his plate and set it aside. Now he could fully devote his attention to the jar he and Jim were passing back and forth.

"Things any safer around here?" Lloyd asked.

"Getting that way."

Lloyd chuckled. "Why? You kill everyone in the whole town?"

"No, just the ones who were a threat."

Lloyd didn't want to ask what that translated to in terms of people.

"But it's working," Jim insisted. "I think the tide is turning."

"What's that mean?" Lloyd asked, taking two sips from the jar this time before passing it back to Jim.

"We're gaining a foothold in town. People are getting used to seeing us at the market. They're learning the truth about a lot of things that have been going on both in town and at the government level. I think we're all going to be safer now. This is the beginning of a new phase. I'm sure of it."

"Then I'm glad I got back in time to enjoy it."

In the distance, the moon peeked over the backbone of Clinch Mountain. Jim took another sip from the jar and marveled at the world around him. It was a near-perfect evening. The weather was beautiful, they'd eaten well, his clan was back together, and things felt more right than they had in a long time.

Jim patted his friend on the back. "Come on, Lloyd. We better get around back before Randi comes looking for you. You don't want it to come to blows again. All that liquor will only dull your self-defense skills."

Lloyd staggered to his feet. "Hell, I'm practically a ninja. Next time, I'll backflip out of the way. She'll be standing there scratching her head and wondering what the hell happened to me."

"I'm sure," Jim cracked.

As they walked back around the house, Lloyd began plucking a tune. The kids cheered and began dancing around the fire. Jim smiled at the magic of it. It was going to be a long night and they'd appreciate every minute of it.

The End

ABOUT THE AUTHOR

Franklin Horton lives and writes in the mountains of Southwestern Virginia. He received an English degree from Virginia Commonwealth University and has written over thirty novels. He lives a hermit's life on a remote mountaintop along the Clinch Mountain chain, splitting his day between writing and tinkering in his shop like one of his characters.

You can follow him on his website at franklinhorton.com.

While you're there please sign up for his mailing list for updates, event schedule, book recommendations, and discounts. He's also active on social media so follow him on Facebook or Instagram to keep up with the latest releases.

www.ingramcontent.com/pod-product-compliance
Lightning Source LLC
Chambersburg PA
CBHW071406300726
48976CB00006B/2000